The Dust Will Never Settle

An alumnus of La Martiniere College, Lucknow, the National Defence Academy, Pune, and the Indian Military Academy, Dehradun, Mukul Deva was commissioned in December 1981 into the Sikh Light Infantry of the Indian Army. He took early retirement from the army after fifteen years of service, including a decade of combat operations in India and overseas. Now settled in Singapore, he is an entrepreneur, motivational speaker and Executive, Business and Creativity Coach. Mukul is also a mentor on the UNITAR Afghanistan Fellowship. He is the author of:

Time After Time…It All Happened
S.T.R.I.P.T.E.A.S.E: The Art of Corporate Warfare
M.O.D.E.L.: The Return of the Employee

The *Lashkar* Series
Lashkar (soon to be a major motion picture)
Salim Must Die
Blowback
Tanzeem

For more about him, please visit his website:
www.mukuldeva.com

Praise for Mukul Deva

'The God of all things... it is tough describing Mukul Deva.'

– *Business World*

'Deva has a Nostradamus touch.'

– *The Statesman*

'India's literary storm trooper.'

– *Business Standard*

'You can smell the gunpowder. Such is the power of the words of Mukul Deva... India's first military action thriller writer.'

– *The Hindu*

'India's only military thriller writer.'

– *The Week*

'Here comes India's Clancy or Ludlum or Forsyth.'

– *Outlook*

'Mukul Deva wears the crown of India's premier military thriller writer with great skill and panache.'

– *www.indepepal.com*

'India finally has a writer of international caliber in the genre of military fiction.'

– *First City*

'Deva is a quintessential literary storm trooper... his books are fast-paced thrillers that have broken new ground.'

– *Yuva*

Praise for the *Lashkar* Series

'Exciting... with some action, some introspection, some retrospection... A racy read.'

– *The Times of India*

'An edge-of-the-seat-thriller… His insightful writing is lucid... Deva can play political commentator and soothsayer of national defence and novelist… a heady cocktail of chill and thrill.'

– *The Hindustan Times*

'Fast and furious... the action is non-stop, more sophisticated and terrifyingly real… moves seamlessly across a dozen time zones… thoroughly entertaining and extremely well-researched.'

– *Business Standard*

'Deva is an equal with the likes of Robert Ludlum and Sidney Sheldon… a tight plot bound together by intricate but brilliant narration leaves the reader in awe… Deva's biggest strength is the smoothness of his prose, crisp and fast moving, and you never get distracted from the story.'

– *The Deccan Herald*

'Full of excitement and suspense... the emotive quality in Deva's writing is powerful and the logic crisply military… a surprisingly touching statement from a man who has lived by the gun.'

– *Express Buzz*

'The ease with which Deva combines well-known facts with popular fiction makes for a fantastic read... his writing style is top-notch... the story is tight and gripping.'

– *First City*

'A riveting read... unnervingly prophetic... heartbreaking... a must read... he paints the picture of geo-politics and terrorism with fantastic clarity.'

– *The Hindu*

'Simply superb... the descriptions are vivid, the plot racy and the detail very convincingly developed.'

– *Mid Day*

'Taut and gripping... technical knowledge and research are remarkable, as is the plotting and the premise. Great read for the fans of Tom Clancy.'

– *Delhi Times*

The Dust Will Never Settle

MUKUL DEVA

HarperCollins *Publishers* India

First published in India by
HarperCollins *Publishers* in 2012

Building 10, Tower A, 4th Floor, DLF Cyber City, Phase II,
Gurugram Haryana – 122002, India
www.harpercollins.co.in

2 4 6 8 10 9 7 5 3

P-ISBN: 978-93-5029-331-7
E-ISBN: 978-93-5029-944-9

Typeset in 10.5/13 Adobe Jenson Pro
Jojy Philip New Delhi 110 015

Printed and bound at
MicroPrints India, New Delhi

This book is dedicated to those millions of people the world over, whose lives have been disrupted by the senseless violence that mankind is so fond of inflicting on itself.

Author's Note

This book is a work of fiction although some of the events mentioned here may have actually taken place.

All the characters, countries, places and organizations described or mentioned in this book are fictitious or have been fictitiously used and any resemblance to any place, organization, country or person, living or dead, is absolutely unintentional.

In several cases, artistic license has been taken with the places mentioned in the book, distances between places and the general topography.

In order to prevent an actual attack being carried out on any monument or building, the location and layout of all monuments and hotels mentioned in this book have been suitably altered. Similarly the security arrangements of all places have been fictitiously described.

The technical details of the various weapon systems, the specifications and methodologies of bomb making and weaponry, as well as the tactics and security procedures employed by any police, military, intelligence organization, and/or militant organization, as also all criminal, forensic and investigative procedures, have been deliberately kept slightly vague, inaccurate and/or incomplete, once again to prevent any misuse, accidental or otherwise.

There is no slur or malice intended against any religion, race, caste, creed, nation, organization or people.

Preface

Of all the books I have written, this is the one that gave rise to many conflicts within me. With every page I wrote or person I interviewed, I felt a strange, almost irresistible, emotional connection developing between the characters in the book and me.

I must also confess that with the success of the *Lashkar* series, I await reader and media response to this book with some anxiety. This pressure has also been instrumental in ensuring I've put my heart and soul into this book, so that it lives up to, if not surpasses, the praise received by the previous ones.

While researching and writing this story it became clear to me that race, region and religion notwithstanding, the human race has displayed an amazing and inexplicable proclivity for violence. This is despite the fact that we facetiously call ourselves an *intelligent* life form. Any species that is willing to kill so easily can scarcely be considered intelligent by any yardstick.

We, as individuals, teach our children the virtues of caring and sharing, yet as nations and religious groups show so little tolerance for others. That is why guns continue to roar, bombs go off everyday and the dust never settles.

Mukul Deva

'Negotiate as if there was no war
and fight as if there was no negotiation.'

– Menachem Begin

Day One

She blinked as she emerged from the aircraft into the bright Sri Lankan sunlight. Though it was still early in the day, the light was harsh. As were the thoughts clashing in her head. Lowering her wrap-around shades over her big, almond-shaped eyes, she paused at the top of the stairs and surveyed Colombo's Bandaranaike Airport.

Stark brown fields with intermittent patches of green stretched beyond the barbed-wire fence ringing the runway. Scattered along the fencing were security posts with tall, searchlight-mounted sentry towers, grim reminders of the insurgency that had torn apart the island state.

Barring the odd airport vehicle and the luggage trolleys snaking around, the runway was devoid of life. An air of despondency hung over it. She shivered, trying to shake it off.

As she descended towards the bus waiting to take passengers to the squat yellow terminal, she saw a

Finnair jetliner swoop down like a hawk, its blue and white logo sparkling in the sun. She heard a distant thud, followed by the smoky blistering of rubber as the jet's wheels made contact with the tarmac. The roar of engines faded as it vanished down the runway.

It was a short walk to the bus, but she could already feel sweat in her armpits. After the London chill, the heat annoyed her, causing her to hurry into the air-conditioned comfort of the bus. It did not take long for the bus to fill up. Soon they were on their way. Almost everyone was switching on mobiles, several were already in animated conversation. The young girl standing beside her had tuned out the world with her iPod and was swaying to a silent beat.

With practised eyes, she scanned her surroundings. She had done this many times during the flight, but conditioned by her training, she did it again. Her danger antennae remained quiet. Nothing seemed out of sync. Yet.

Those who did not know her would have assumed she was just another thirty-something attempting to mask her femininity, although the shapeless, almost masculine clothing did little to conceal her breasts and voluptuous figure.

The baggy black jeans and equally loose, full-sleeved blue cotton shirt would let her swing into action if the need arose. She never wore skirts or dresses on the job; they were not practical, and did not quite suit the male-dominant world she worked in. Besides, skirts and dresses were not designed to carry the armoury of an MI6 agent, which comprised a cell phone, a BlackBerry, a weapon, spare magazines and, very often, a secure digital radio. Nor could they conceal her backup, the .22 pistol in her ankle holster.

Today, of course, she was weaponless. Also missing was the protective, standard issue Kevlar vest. She felt naked, the feeling intensified by her hyped up state. She tucked away a strand that had come loose from her neatly pinned-back hair. Black patent leather loafers completed her attire. The one-inch heels and rubber soles ensured she could move swiftly and soundlessly. She wore virtually no make-up. She always dressed down on a job.

As the bus screeched to a halt outside the terminal, she jumped out and headed for the immigration counters. She carried herself with the ease of a professional soldier. And she knew she looked good. The number of heads that turned as she walked past confirmed this.

While waiting in line at immigration, she ran through her operational checklist. She could not afford any mistakes. Time was short and there was a great deal to be done.

Nothing in her demeanour gave away the turmoil in her mind. No one who observed her could imagine the immensity of the mission she was on. Not that she was dismayed by the obstacles that lay in her path – far from it. Though she did wish she'd been able to run a detailed background check on her targets and adversaries before leaving London. But time had been short. Despite that, she felt ready and committed.

'Never forget your purpose in life. You're our weapon of vengeance,' her mother Rehana's words echoed in her head. 'Never forget the blood your family has shed. Never forget what we have suffered, are continuing to suffer. No matter what, you must not let our sacrifice go to waste.'

For a moment, the memory of her mother made her falter. The sight of her shattered, decimated body ripped at her heart. But it was a fleeting lapse.

All these years she had prayed for the day she would finally strike down those who had inflicted misery on her people. And now the day of reckoning was almost at hand. Ten days more and she would demolish the Israeli–Palestinian Peace Summit.

Ruby Gill strode forward. Eager. Focused. Nothing would stop her. She knew.

Ravinder Singh Gill, the tall, lean Inspector General of Police and head of the Indian Anti-Terrorist Task Force, was on his way to his third-floor office at the Delhi Police Headquarters. Conscious he needed the exercise, Ravinder went past the elevators and took the stairs.

Though well past fifty, the years had been kind on him. With a neatly tied turban, flecks of grey dotting his moustache and beard, he cut a dashing figure in black pants, a sky-blue shirt and patent leather shoes. A Mont Blanc pen peeped out of his breast pocket. Black cufflinks embossed with the family's double-headed lion crest completed his attire. The lion had one paw raised, ready to strike. It resonated with his mood.

His day had begun with the never-ending mother–daughter discussion about marriage. It was all they talked about ever since Jasmine's twenty-second birthday. It took only minutes for the discussion to degenerate into an acrimonious harangue. Today had been no exception. Ravinder was in a sour mood when he left the breakfast table and headed here.

He sensed that the day was not going to get better when he came out and saw the driver changing a tyre on his Scorpio SUV.

'Sorry, sir,' the man called out when he saw Ravinder emerge. 'There must have been nails on the road near the metro construction site. Both front tyres are punctured.'

'How long will it take?'

'About half an hour, sir.'

'Damn! I am in a rush!'

'Why don't you use our car?' Ravinder's wife Simran called from the door. 'I will send the Scorpio when it is fixed.'

'I guess I will,' Ravinder replied, looking at the black BMW 750 Li parked in the porch. Jagjit Singh, the family driver, in his bright red turban and pristine white uniform complete with the family crest, was polishing it. Simran loved these royal trappings and ensured they were displayed wherever possible. Ravinder, however, preferred to downplay his wealth and royal background, which was not easy when he was being driven around in a spanking new Beamer. He got into the car and they took off.

As he entered his office, Ravinder dragged his fingers back along his temples, trying to push away a budding headache. The phone rang and he reached for it, relieved to have something intrude on his dark mood.

'Gill?' The Indian Home Minister Raj Thakur's nasal, raspy tone was unmistakable. It felt jarring, which Ravinder thought wryly, went well with the man's personality. Though this assignment was new to him – the previous ATTF Chief's heart had suddenly given up on him – Ravinder had already had some disturbing meetings with the minister. Raj Thakur was not an easy man to like, nor an easy boss.

Though clueless about security, Raj Thakur had a know-all's self-confidence which, coupled with his belligerence and an eagerness to interfere in operational matters, could be dangerous. In their brief association, Thakur had already countermanded several orders given by Ravinder, mostly without bothering to inform him. Consequently, Ravinder now felt he was walking on eggshells, always peering over his shoulder, wondering what would hit him next.

Still not fully settled into his new role, and with his responsibility for the security of the Israeli-Palestinian Peace Summit and the Delhi Commonwealth Games weighing on him, Ravinder wished he had a more reasonable boss. And he was not the only one. Even the Prime Minister was said to be concerned, but was forced to give Thakur the Home portfolio to keep his majority in Parliament intact.

So be it. Ravinder consoled himself. As a professional cop, what choice did he have but to go with whatever the dice threw up? With only ten days left for the Peace Summit *and* the Commonwealth Games to kick off, he had more concrete issues to deal with.

'Good morning, sir.'

'I want you to come to my office, Gill. Immediately. I now have all the updates for the Peace Summit.'

'Right, sir.' Ravinder, with a mountain of urgent tasks to attend to, wished he could tell him to fuck off. 'I will be there,' he checked his watch; it was a good one-hour drive to South Block, where the minister's office was, 'by eleven.'

'Do that,' Thakur commanded brusquely, 'And bring Mohite with you.'

As Ravinder replaced the phone, with a cursory knock, Deputy Inspector General of Police Govind

Mohite walked in. Though not tall, Mohite had a well-muscled body. He was impeccably dressed in dark khaki trousers, a matching earth-coloured cotton shirt and brown suede shoes.

'You have a long life, Govind. I was about to call you. The home minister wants us right away.'

'I know, sir. He called me half an hour ago.' Mohite gave a wide grin.

'But I just got off the phone with him.' The words were out before Ravinder could rein them in. He felt like kicking himself.

'Oh, you know how Thakur sahib is...' Mohite pronounced the 'sahib' with an elongated double-a sound, the way Maharashtrians tend to. 'He likes to sound me out about everything. You see, we became close when he was in the Maharashtra cabinet and I was in the Mumbai Special Crimes Unit.'

Ravinder heard him ramble on about what a great chap Thakur was, something Mohite was prone to doing. He wondered if Mohite knew what the meeting was about and contemplated asking him, but shelved the thought. It would give out the wrong signal. Ravinder was aware that Mohite was gunning for his job and he needed to watch his back, considering Mohite's chumminess with the minister. There had been rumours that the two had been in cahoots in several questionable deaths of members of a particular crime mob. It had raised a lot of media speculation, including insinuations that the murders had been carried out at the behest of another mob boss in Dubai and that large sums of money had exchanged hands. Ravinder shrugged. Whatever the connection, he knew it would be nasty. Since his predecessor had checked out without a formal and detailed handover, Ravinder also knew he needed both his primary lieutenants, of whom Mohite was one, till he had settled in properly.

'You are travelling in style today,' Mohite remarked when he saw the Beamer. 'Might as well come with you,' Without waiting for a reply, he told his driver to follow and hopped into the back seat of Ravinder's car.

'Why bring your car if you're coming in mine?' Ravinder asked. 'Why not save some gas?'

'Oh, just in case we need to come back separately afterwards.' Mohite waved airily. 'Thakur sahib might ask me to stay on. He likes to consult me on many things.'

'Right.' Ravinder kept the sarcasm out of his voice. Not that it mattered; Mohite was oblivious.

Tuning out Mohite's non-stop banter, Ravinder's thoughts returned to the meeting. The sudden summons had caught him unawares. He felt worried.

When Ruby emerged from immigration, her accomplice was waiting near the baggage carousel.

Over six feet tall, the over-sized Mark Leahy occupied an unfair amount of space. Also in jeans and a cotton shirt, his sand-coloured hair was closely cropped and his skin was leathery from having spent most of his life outdoors.

They had travelled on the same flight, but unlike Ruby, he looked rested and refreshed. Not surprising, since he was unaffected by her emotional state.

Good! Ruby smiled. *At least one of us is cool.* She sure as hell was not.

'Feeling distraught is normal when one has been subjected to severe trauma,' the agency shrink had told her when she had returned to London after Rehana's funeral. Ruby's erratic behaviour had prompted her boss to send her for therapy post-haste. 'There is not much you can do about it. Just be aware that your mind may wander and try to control it. Everyone has a different way of processing grief. This is your way.'

Bloody stupid way. Ruby's smile faded into a frown. But she had to cope. And live with it. *Try* to live with it. Especially since she had thrown away the medication as soon as she left the shrink's office. Having her mind stuck on a Prozac-shelf was not for Ruby. She now hauled herself back and concentrated on Mark.

Looking at him made her feel better. She had thought of him the minute she decided to take on this mission, which was as soon as Yusuf uncle had come to know about the Peace Summit. So much had transpired since. She smiled as she remembered her conversation with Mark only yesterday.

'Hey! How are you?' He had sounded so pleased.

'I am very well, thank you. How are things with you?'

'Same old, same old. There doesn't seem to be much happening. Certainly not the right kind of stuff... stuff that interests me *and* pays the rent. So am catching up on life, tending to the garden and painting the fences... y'know...' he said in his thick Irish accent.

Mark had quit the service a few weeks ago and was now freelancing.

'That can get kind of boring.'

'Tell me about it.'

'Well, I may have something for you.'

'You? Nah. The government doesn't pay enough.' She'd expected that. 'Besides, haven't you heard, I quit working for them.'

'Mark, this one is personal. Nothing to do with the agency. And the money is better than good.' Ruby knew, that for the right money, Mark was the ideal man to watch her back – ruthless, resourceful and ready to follow orders.

'Is it now? Want to tell me more?'

And with that Ruby instinctively knew he was game. 'Not right now. You will have to trust me.'

'I do. You know I do.' He chuckled. 'As much as

you trust me. How many times have we watched each other's backs?'

'Often enough. Why else would I call you, Mark?'

'And here I was thinking you called because of my lovely smile and beautiful body!' They both laughed. 'When and where do you want me? And how long will we be gone?'

Ruby's spirits lightened when he said that. 'We move out tomorrow. We should be back in two weeks.'

'That's it, eh? Short assignment.'

'Yep, short and sweet. And lucrative.'

'That's my kind.' A laconic laugh. 'Where are we headed?'

'India, eventually.' Momentarily, the mention of India unleashed a whirlpool of emotions inside her, about her father... *a father who abandoned me... he means nothing to me.* Without realizing it, she made a dubious moue. *Doesn't he?* She pushed away the thought. *Not now!*

'India, eh? Exotic! Sounds good to me.' He made a humming sound. 'Say, boss,' Mark asked, somewhat bashfully, 'we flying coach or...'

'First class, Mark. Nothing but the best for you, mon ami. Your ticket will be in your mailbox shortly. Meet me at Heathrow a couple of hours before the flight.'

She knew it was a happy Mark who'd put down the

phone. He looked happy even now as they came out of Colombo airport and headed towards the taxi stand.

Traffic in Delhi was never easy and these days, with construction taking place all over the city and the massive influx of tourists, it was maddening. To make things worse, Delhi had not seen such heavy rains, not in the last forty years.

As the car laboured through the clogged streets, Ravinder wondered what it was that the home minister wanted to discuss, and hoped there would be no more unpleasant surprises. Their first meeting had been one hell of a shocker. His mind fled back to that day.

'Have you heard the good news, Gill?' Thakur had greeted them with a big smile when Mohite and he entered his office. 'India is hosting the Israeli–Palestinian Peace Summit.'

'We are?' Ravinder was stunned. One glance at Mohite's face and he realized that this was not news to him. *Damn the man! When would he learn to play for the team?* 'The Israelis and Palestinians are talking? That's a surprise, considering the recent terrorist attack on Jerusalem! How did this happen, sir?'

'That's what triggered it off. The Americans – in fact the entire international community – have put a lot of pressure on them. Everyone is tired of the mindless bloodshed.'

'And India will have the honour of playing host,' Mohite chimed in. 'Just imagine! We may help peace return to the Middle East.'

'Yes.' Thakur beamed. 'Isn't it great?'

'When is it?' Ravinder ignored their euphoria, preferring to focus on the practicalities.

'Exactly two weeks from now.' Thakur could not stop smiling. 'This is our chance to showcase India. It may be the most critical and game-changing event of our times.'

'Two weeks?' Ravinder was shocked, but the other two were so caught up in their enthusiasm that they missed it.

'Precisely. It starts on thirteenth October.'

Thirteenth! The number sent a shiver up Ravinder's spine. Too much had happened to him on that particular date, and none of it good.

'But that is exactly when the Commonwealth Games are due to start, sir. Such an event will require massive security and we are already hard-pressed for resources.'

'Resources are always scarce, Gill.' Thakur waved dismissively. 'We have to make it work. Don't you see what this Summit will do for India's prestige?'

'I do, sir, but don't you... I mean, one must account for the fact that terrorist groups will do anything to disrupt it. Palestine is the one cause that all the jihadi groups use to pull in money and recruits. They will never allow this.'

'All that is fine, Gill, but we have to make it happen. Maybe things will be simpler if we can keep it low-key.'

'Sir, with the recent terrorist attack on Jerusalem, the whole world has its eyes on the Middle East. There is no way we can keep such a momentous event secret.'

'Well, we have to make it happen regardless.' Thakur's tone was firm. 'We have no choice – the decision has been made. It is a matter of national pride.'

'What if the Summit gets attacked? The stakes are so high for the jihadis, they will definitely try to strike.'

'No, Gill. Nothing must be allowed to disrupt it,' Thakur retorted. 'I want you to personally take charge of the security.'

'But I am in charge of the Commonwealth Games at the same time, sir,' Ravinder protested.

'No, you are not.' Thakur then sprung the second ugly surprise. 'I have put Ashish Sharma in charge of the Games.'

DIG Ashish Sharma was Mohite's peer and they both reported to Ravinder. Now, to his dismay, Thakur was directly delegating work to officers under his command. Ravinder opened his mouth to protest, but stopped, realizing it was pointless.

'I don't see the problem, Gill,' Thakur continued. 'The arrangements for the Games are in place. Sharma just has to keep things going.'

'Then why not put Mohite in charge of the Peace

Summit, sir? That way I will be able to run oversight on both events.'

'I thought about that, Gill. I trust Mohite totally, but I think the Summit is too important for any one man. Do you have any idea of the consequences if something happens to the delegates? India's reputation would be shot to hell… not to mention the carnage that may be unleashed in Israel. No. I want you in charge. Of course, Mohite will assist you.'

'Of course I will, sir. You know we will never allow anything to happen to the Summit.' Mohite was quick to spot an opportunity, one where he would be able to take credit if things went well, yet not be responsible if there was a screw-up. He turned to Ravinder. 'Am I right, sir?'

Ravinder marvelled at the man's cheek.

'True, sir,' Ravinder replied with a silent sigh. When rape is inevitable, enjoy it, he remembered the physical training instructor at the police academy once telling them. 'How come we get to host the Summit?'

'India was a logical choice since we are on good terms with the Israelis, the Palestinians and the Arab world.'

'They met at Oslo the last time,' Ravinder mused.

'Yes, but apparently both sides feel that Oslo is jinxed. That is why when the PM asked Mr Thakur if we could host it, I advised him to accept,' Mohite jumped in again.

Ravinder resisted the impulse to give Mohite a solid kick. Instead he gave a polite smile. 'Wonderful. I am so glad you are going to help me secure the Summit, Govind.'

'But of course, sir.' Missing the sarcasm, Mohite gave another bright smile.

'So we all agree that we must keep it secret?' Thakur asked, failing to mention that he had already spoken about it to at least ten people in the three hours since the PM had informed him. 'I figured Delhi would be ideal. With the Commonwealth Games taking place, we already have a flood of VIPs and athletes, and security would already be functioning at peak level.'

'That is what I explained to Mr Thakur, sir,' Mohite rejoindered. 'It will make our task so much easier.'

Ravinder looked at both men, doubting even they believed that. But he understood that for Thakur this was a once-in-a-lifetime opportunity to showcase himself on an international platform. And for Mohite, a heaven-sent chance to latch onto the minister's coat-tails and grab some limelight too.

Got to watch my back, Ravinder reminded himself again. Given half a chance, Mohite would deliver him to the wolves.

'I know I can rely on you, Govind.' Thakur gave Mohite a cordial smile, then realizing that Ravinder was present, added, 'and of course you, Gill. Now remember, we simply cannot fail. If anything bad were to happen, it would be a shame for India and it would put an end to all hopes of peace in the Middle East.'

Ravinder was in a sombre mood as he listened to the two men prattle on. Obviously, neither had given any thought to the logistics of securing such an event. The whole thing was fraught with danger.

Ravinder's memory spool ran out as their car halted in the South Block parking lot. He led the way towards the minister's office, wondering what new shock awaited him today.

Watching Mark move into action, Ruby smiled again. The efficiency with which he organized a car and driver made her relax.

A sturdy silver, almost-new Nissan van stood before them. The driver, whose name she couldn't get, spoke more Sinhalese than English, but seemed pleasant, presentable and eager to please. They threw their bags into the back. Moments later they were headed north.

Ruby glanced at her watch. It seemed to be ticking fast. A pulse of urgency raced through her. For the nth time she wished she had been given the heads-up about the Summit sooner. And again she cursed Pasha, the Lashkar-e-Toiba commander who had told her about it and also e-mailed her the gory video of Yusuf's killing. Flashes of that video returned to her every night, leaving her afraid of even turning the lights out.

Those murderous Jews had even chopped his hands off.

Pinpricks of wetness pushed at her eyes. She kept them at bay, knowing she could not allow them to be seen by Mark. In their world, tears were a sign of weakness, and weakness was death.

Shaking off the gory images of Yusuf's dismembered body, Ruby mentally urged the driver to go faster. She needed to be in motion. Motion was important. It kept the nightmares away.

They hit the first security checkpoint on the outskirts of Colombo. Fortunately only a few cars were ahead of them. It took seven minutes to get past it. A second one, a few miles out of town, took a tad longer.

Then the highway stretched out before them. Long. Narrow. Lonely.

Thakur's office was tastefully decorated, in contrast to his abrasive personality. Lemon-coloured walls set off the Persian carpet in the centre of the room. On one side was a burnished teak table with a high-back, deep-brown executive chair and four matching leather guest chairs at the opposite end of the table. In the far corner, a trio of single-seater sofas were placed around a smoked-glass centre table with several books. Large paintings hung on the walls. Ravinder could hear the soft hiss of the air-conditioner and the aroma of room freshener reached out to him.

Lavender. One of his favourites.

'Ah, there you are, Gill.' In his mid-fifties, Thakur wore the trademark attire of Indian politicians, a white kurta–pyjama. A cream Nehruvian jacket completed the look. He did not bother to get up. 'Come, come. How are you two? How are the preparations for the Summit and Games coming along?'

'They are coming along just fine, sir,' Mohite said without waiting for Ravinder to reply. 'We have taken over the top two floors of Ashoka hotel and our teams have started installing state-of-the-art equipment to secure the Summit. We have also started putting checkpoints and roadblocks around the hotel.'

'That's good.'

'We have also broken three terror cells and have information about two more sent in from Pak-occupied Kashmir to attack the Games. We hope to catch them before they get anywhere near Delhi,' Mohite continued.

'Hope to?' Thakur raised an eyebrow. 'No hopes, Govind, just get them.'

'We will, sir,' Mohite said.

Thakur drummed his fingers on the table. 'These damn terrorists never give up, do they?'

'No, sir, they don't,' Ravinder replied. 'The ISI has

given them carte blanche, sir. They will do everything possible to hurt us.'

'Yes, I can see that.' Thakur's smile slipped. The full implications of the threat now dawned on him.

'But don't worry about it, sir. We will not allow anything to happen,' Mohite said, ever eager to keep the boss happy.

'Excellent.' Thakur's smile returned. 'I know I can rely on you, Govind.'

Ravinder held his peace, not wanting to rain on their parade and point out that it was impossible to stop *every* terror strike. Somewhere, somehow, someone would always manage to break through every cordon, no matter how good it was.

'Here.' Thakur pulled out two slim brown files and slid them across the table. 'A list of the thirteen Summit delegates, with their complete details.'

Damn, thirteen again! Ravinder frowned.

The minister's voice intruded. 'Each delegate is accompanied by two personal security officers. Considering the circumstances, we are permitting the PSOs to carry weapons.'

'Foreigners running around with guns in our capital?' Mohite looked up, surprised.

'Yes, Govind. And... oh, that reminds me, to assist us, the Americans and the British have both sent across an agent each.'

'Why? What do we need them for?' Mohite half

rose, his agitation palpable. 'We are more than capable of handling things.'

'Calm down, Govind.' Ravinder waved him down, even though having foreign agents mucking around was the last thing he wanted to worry about. 'We will need all the help we can get.'

'Yes, but…'

'Orders from on high, Mohite.' Thakur glared at him. 'They will be coming to your office later today, Gill. The Israelis are also sending an agent to brief us about the threats they anticipate. He should be here in a day or so.'

'Don't worry, sir,' Ravinder reassured him. 'We will ensure things go smoothly. Anyone and anything that helps us get the job done well is more than welcome.'

'Good attitude, Gill. Now for the most important thing. The PM will be coming on the first day of the Summit – I got the call this morning – and the PMO wants the security plan immediately.'

'Today?'

'Why? Any problem with that?'

'None at all, sir.' Ravinder kept his chin up, knowing the rest of his day was going down the shitter; the PM's personal security was paranoid and would question everything till the cows came home. *Oh well! Maybe that will keep Mohite busy and get him up to speed.*

'Good, then send those plans to me as soon as possible and I'll forward them to the PMO.'

Minutes later they left Thakur's office.

'Let us use this time to firm up the details we have to send to the PMO,' Mohite muttered as he hopped into Gill's car. 'I will ask my car to lead. Too much bloody traffic. The siren will clear the way for us.' Poking his head out, he yelled instructions to his driver.

They headed out with Mohite's staff car leading, its flashing red siren madly whooping, carving a corridor through the dense traffic. Ravinder detested the siren and would have liked to minimize the time he spent with Mohite, but he recognized that he had made useful suggestions. The sound of turning pages took over as both cops went through the profiles of the Summit delegates.

'Did you notice this, sir?' Mohite tapped the file in his hands a few minutes later.

'What about it?'

'Look at the list of delegates. The Israelis are sending Ziv Gellner, Yossi Gerstmann and Shahar Goldstein. From the Palestinian side, we have Hisham Gheisari from the Hamas, Mullah Ghassan Ahmed Hussein, the head imam of Al Aqsa mosque, and Ghazi Baraguti from the Fatah.'

'Interesting,' Ravinder said as he ran through their profiles. *Thirteen delegates... Again that bloody unlucky number.* But he shrugged off the foreboding that snaked through him and nudged his mind back to the profiles.

Ziv Gellner, a former aide of Yitzhak Rabin,

the Israeli premier, was a staunch Kadima man and one of the chief proponents of a peaceful resolution. Originally a hardliner, he'd lost his wife to cancer and later his first-born son David in an Arab attack on the Yitzhar settlement. Mourning his son, he'd adopted Ean, a boy who had survived the raid but lost both his parents to it.

When Rabin was gunned down, Ziv's feelings had converted him into a staunch pacifist. Ziv had been right there, a few feet from Rabin, when he was assassinated. He had seen their hopes for peace disappear, blown away by the assassin's bullet.

'Damn! Did you read this?' Ravinder pointed at Gellner's profile. 'He also lost his adopted son Ean, in the recent terror attack on Jerusalem...'

'Really?' Mohite perused the profile. 'Hmm... I wonder how he will handle this Summit.'

'Another coincidence...' Mohite pointed out a moment later. 'Like Gellner, Yossi Gerstmann also lost his son and wife during the same Arab raid on Yitzhar.'

Ravinder found Gerstmann's resume fascinating. A hotshot intelligence professional, he had been earmarked to head the Mossad. But a counter-terrorist operation led by him went wrong and resulted in a bloodbath, putting paid to a promising career. Now a political advisor, Gerstmann was a staunch right-winger who strongly believed that Israel should not part with an inch of land. He was the obvious choice for the hardliners and a foil for the pacifist Gellner.

The third Israeli, Shahar Goldstein, also known as the Prince, was the son of a former Israeli premier and was a respected Likud man. Due to his legacy, Goldstein carried weight in most sections of Israeli society and could be expected to maintain a balance between the opposing viewpoints held by Gellner and Gerstmann. His presence would ensure that whatever solution was recommended would be acceptable to the Israeli public, who still held his late father in high regard.

Of the Palestinian delegates, Hisham Gheisari, a Hamas man based in Gaza, had done a lot of community development work and made life easier for the Palestinians. He was reputed to be incorruptible and there were a dozen schools and hospitals in Gaza that owed their existence to him. Men like him had helped end the corrupt Fatah regime. Though a staunch Hamas man, Gheisari was also a known dove.

Mullah Ghassan Ahmed Hussein, the head mufti of Jerusalem, respected in all circles – Islamic, Jewish and Christian – would also play a pivotal role with the Palestinians, especially in light of the recent Jerusalem terror attacks. In a way, he was Shahar Goldstein's Palestinian counterpart.

However, the third Palestinian, Ghazi Baraguti, a Fatah man who had been languishing in an Israeli jail until now, was a surprise. For several months there had been talk in Israel about setting him free as a goodwill gesture. But it had ended abruptly when Fatah terrorists made the mistake of capturing some Israeli soldiers and demanding his release. All talks of release had died away.

'Do you see the point I am making?' Mohite asked again. 'From Egypt we have Atef Aboul Gheit, a retired diplomat. Jordon is sending Ghafar Al-Issa, an advisor to their ministry of foreign affairs. Ghada al-Utri, another senior diplomat, is representing Syria, and from Saudi Arabia we have HRH Prince Ghanim Abdul Rahman al-Saud.'

'And from America we have Senator George Polk,' Ravinder added, flipping the page.

'Isn't he prone to marching to his own drumbeat?'

'The very man,' Ravinder replied, double-checking the senator's profile. 'No one can be sure what his stance is, though the odds are that he'd be biased against the Israelis.'

'Surprising. Very surprising.' Mohite made a clicking sound with his tongue. 'Right. And from Britain, it's MP Sir Geoffrey Tang, and lastly we have the Norwegian, Sigurd Gaarder.'

'Like Polk, Tang too is a wildcard, though he's more likely to be sitting in the middle. As for Gaarder, he was one of the original Oslo negotiators and could bring invaluable expertise.'

'Well, yes, but have you noticed something?' Mohite

grinned. 'Each of the delegates has a name starting with G... first or last.' He looked up. 'Even the two of us.' His smile broadened. 'We should code name this the G-string Summit!'

Ravinder could not help smiling. 'Nice, Govind! Now let's work on keeping that damn G-string intact! We've got a lot to protect and not much to do it with. Every damn terror group in the world must be panting to take a shot at us.'

'True.' Mohite's face turned grave. 'Like you said, bringing peace to the Promised Land will take away a major raison d'être for the jihad.' He might be an ass-licking busybody, Ravinder thought, but he was no fool.

The two-car mini-convoy slowed as it turned on to the road leading to MSO Building which housed the police headquarters. The traffic was awful and despite the siren, they were now crawling along.

That was when a man caught Ravinder's attention: medium height, clean-shaven, mid-twenties. Perhaps it was the purposeful manner in which he was approaching Mohite's car. Or perhaps it was because he was wearing such a bulky overcoat. It wasn't *that* cold.

An alarm clamoured in Ravinder's head. Tersely ordering his driver to stop, he pulled out his 9mm Browning and leapt out, even before the car had come to a full stop. Mohite and the driver stared after him, perplexed.

The man was now fifteen feet away. He swivelled

and saw Ravinder rushing towards him. He froze for a nanosecond, then threw open his overcoat and reached inside.

Ravinder saw the coat fly open and spotted the bomb strapped around the man's waist. Instantly his right hand rose up, the gun coming level. Mindful of the crowd, he took aim and fired once. It was enough.

The man came to an abrupt halt, as though he'd run into a brick wall. For a second he was upright, and then fell backwards, his head covered in blood.

Ravinder had gone for the headshot. He could not have let the man detonate the bomb; the casualties on the crowded road would have been horrendously high.

It was over as swiftly as it had begun.

The rest took an hour to sort out.

'He was Mir Kasab, from the Jaish-e-Mohammed. A known terrorist... we have a thick file on him. Came in from POK last week,' Mohite reported to Ravinder. 'We found a map of this area in his pocket and the numbers of three cars: yours, Ashish's and mine. Apparently he had been tasked to take out senior ATTF cops.'

'Looks like the terrorists want us out of the picture at this juncture.'

'I guess so.' Mohite's tone was grim; he was still sweating. Ravinder could see that he was shaken up.

'Don't think too much about it, Govind. It could well have been my car. Or Ashish's... he would have gone for whoever had reached first.' Silence. A shitty feeling. 'The luck of the draw, my friend. Who knows when one's time is up.' Ravinder had to lift the mood, both Mohite's and his own. 'Look on the bright side. We got the bugger before he could get us.'

But the words had little effect on either of them. Both knew that the next time the tides might well favour the other side.

'There is more, sir. He was not alone,' Mohite almost stammered. 'He was part of a cell of three men.'

'Who are the other two? Find any clues on him?'

'Yes, most probably Javed Khan. We already have a file on him. And another guy, an unknown called Aslam. The three of them came from POK together. Most likely the other two are still out there...' Mohite stared out the window, 'somewhere in Delhi.'

'We have to find them.'

'I have already issued an APB and also alerted the Int agencies.'

'We'd better find them... before they find us.' Ravinder thought for a moment. 'Have the guards doubled – at the office and all three residences. And caution Ashish.'

Ravinder knew there was nothing more they could do. Not yet. 'Now let's focus. We have a Summit to secure, Govind. The PM's office is waiting for our security plans.'

Had it not been for the air-conditioning, the seven-hour drive to Vavuniya would have been intolerable. The dust and the pot-holed road added to her misery. But Mark seemed to be handling the heat and dust well. Ten minutes into the drive, he was sprawled against the car door, snoring gently. Ever so often, Ruby saw him smile. He was obviously having pleasant dreams.

Oh well... at least someone is. A mirthless smile creased her face. He looked good, if a trifle uncomfortable, his head knocking against the window every time they hit a bump. *Pity he is gay! All the good ones are... either gay or married.* Ruby sighed; she could do with some comforting. It had been a while since she had been held... not since Chance had gone. Wondering where he was right now, Ruby felt a tug at her heart. She missed him.

For a moment she thought about the differences between Chance and Mark. Physically they had a lot in common – both were tall, well-built and fair, with similar close-cropped hair. But that was where the similarities ended. Chance was sensitive, caring and had a great sense of humour. Mark, on the other hand, was not cerebral and liked to plunge into action without a second thought. Well, that was what she needed right now. Someone who would simply follow orders.

Ruby couldn't sleep; she felt restless, pumped with oxygen. She sat on the edge of her seat, watching the countryside fly past. Barring small green patches of cultivation, she saw only bleak, brown land. As they moved further north from Colombo, the stretches of green grew scarce and the presence of soldiers and army camps increased, grim reminders to the recently-ended insurgency.

The driver stepped on the gas, going as fast as the road allowed. Ruby was finally about to try and catch some shut-eye when they hit another checkpoint. A long line of vehicles waited ahead. The soldiers were searching each vehicle thoroughly.

Ruby sat back, exasperated, watching the vehicles inch forward. Her mind wandered back to Palestine, to a similar checkpoint.

'That day the line at the Huwwara checkpoint was long.' Rehana's oft-told story echoed in Ruby's memory. Her voice was clear, as though it was Rehana, and not Mark, sitting beside her in the car.

The Israel Defence Forces checkpoint at Huwwara, one of the main inner checkpoints of the West Bank, lay deep within Palestinian territory, just south of Nablus, at the junction of Routes 57 and 557. It was located between the settlements of Bracha and Itamar, dividing Nablus from the satellite communities that depended on it.

'About six thousand people pass through Huwwara

every day,' Rehana's narration echoed in Ruby's mind, 'to work, to the hospital, to visit relatives or to do their shopping.'

Like all such checkpoints, passing through Huwwara involved a meticulous process. It was not uncommon for it to take up to two hours to get through. And the rules were never predictable, adding to the confusion and delay.

Men lined up in a closed waiting area, while women and children went through a separate pathway. The area for men was an open shed with a corrugated roof. Waist-high walls demarcated the aisles. The roof trapped the sweltering heat.

'*Wuakef* (stop)! *Jubil aweah* (show me your identification papers)!' the soldiers shouted as each person was processed.

'One by one, the men trudged up to the barred window and handed over their papers. They lifted their shirts and rolled up their trouser legs to confirm that no weapons or bombs were concealed there. The women and children were also frisked thoroughly. Rows of scanners would be at work constantly.

'The procedure for cars was more tedious, with all passengers having to get out while a search was carried out using undercarriage mirrors, detectors and sniffer dogs.'

Bilal, Rehana's brother, thumped the steering wheel, looking worriedly at his mother Salima lying in the back seat. Half an hour had passed and only two cars had been cleared, with three more still ahead of them. Bilal, the eldest and usually the calmest of the three siblings, was getting jumpy; perhaps his diabetes was acting up. It did not help that in their rush to take their mother to hospital, he had not eaten. Eventually, driven by his anxiety, he got out and went to speak to the IDF soldiers.

'You! *Wuakef!* Stop right there!' a soldier yelled at him, the Galil AR multi-purpose rifle in his hand coming up.

'Where do you think you're going?'

'Soldier, my mother is ill,' Bilal replied.

'I don't fucking care,' the beardless soldier yelled. 'Get back into your car and wait your turn. *NOW!*' His rifle pointed straight at Bilal, rock-steady, confirming his willingness to use it. 'Don't come any closer.' He pointed at the security line painted on the road meant to keep the soldiers safe from suicide bombers. The neatly painted *Born to Kill,* shining whitely across the front of his helmet, and his badly accented Arabic added to the menace of the moment.

Bilal walked back to the car, cursing under his breath. Another fifteen minutes slithered by and only one more car had been cleared. A bout of coughing shook Salima and more blood sprayed out. By now the sheet covering her was splattered with red dots.

'Mother had been terribly ill when she woke up

that morning. She had started coughing blood. Her condition was so bad that your uncles Bilal and Yusuf decided to rush her to hospital at once. I too went with them.' Rehana began to cry as she told the story to Ruby. 'By now our mother was barely conscious. The fever had skyrocketed. I could feel her body burning.'

Sitting in the front passenger seat, Yusuf looked explosive, but also on the verge of tears.

Bilal could not take it any more. His breath was short and his hands had begun to shake as the level of glucose in his body plummeted and hypoglycaemia began to take hold. That, coupled with his mother's increasing distress, shattered his control. He jumped out of the car again.

'What the fuck is wrong with you?' *Born to Kill* screamed again. 'Get back inside your car!'

'Come on, soldier,' Bilal yelled back. 'Look! She is losing so much blood. Let us through.'

'Yeah, right!' The anger in *Born to Kill*'s voice matched his raised weapon. 'Get back to your car and wait for your turn!'

'Please, soldier!' Bilal was begging.

It had no effect on the soldier. 'Back in line.'

'She seems to be really sick,' a younger soldier standing beside *Born to Kill* whispered in Hebrew. He had peered inside the car during the heated exchange. 'Why don't we let them through first?'

'You shut your fucking mouth, wimp,' *Born to Kill*

hissed. 'You don't know these bastards. That is exactly what a pregnant woman said to my father. They were about to let her through when she blew herself up, taking my father and four others with her.'

The recruit, Ean Gellner, subsided. This was only his fifth week in uniform and his first day on checkpoint duty.

The other soldiers sniggered.

Their words meant nothing to Bilal since he did not understand Hebrew, but those sniggers were more than he could take. He leapt forward shaking an angry fist.

'Stay back!' *Born to Kill*'s strident yell fell on deaf ears.

'Stand back, you moron!'

The second warning also went unheeded.

'Do *not* cross the line!'

Tension suddenly escalated.

To Yusuf and Rehana, watching from the car, everything happened fast and slow at the same time – too fast for them to do anything, yet slow enough to feel every nuance.

As Bilal crossed the line, the rifle in *Born to Kill*'s hands emitted a sharp flat report. A second later, another shot exploded out.

The gunshots echoed bleakly in the silence, shattered seconds later by Bilal's howl of pain. The first bullet gutted him. He was falling when the second bullet hit him. He swayed, and then slumped to the ground. A shocked Yusuf jumped out of the car and rushed to his brother's side.

Yusuf's move broke the frozen tableau. People scattered about frantically, racing to get out of the line of fire.

Born to Kill stood still, his rifle still pointed at Bilal, a confused expression on his face.

Ean Gellner looked as though he was about to burst into tears.

'What the hell have you done?' a soldier yelled, dismay plastered on his face.

'What could I do? Didn't you see he was rushing me?' *Born to Kill* said, a sick smile on his face and fear in his eyes.

Yusuf, who was kneeling beside his dying brother, looked up and saw the smile. He let out a howl of rage and ran towards the soldier.

Rehana screamed, but Yusuf had already broken past the line.

Born to Kill saw him rush forward. His finger was still on the trigger. The finger tightened and seconds later, half the 35-round magazine had emptied itself.

Two of the bullets slammed into Yusuf's right shoulder, spinning him around and dropping him to the ground. One bullet shattered the windscreen of the car and found his mother's jaw. It decimated Salima's face, replacing the already quivering, blood-stained lips with a gaping red hole. Three bullets found two more victims in the fleeing crowd. The others slammed harmlessly in the cars and the milling dust.

'There was so much blood all around me... I can feel it even now.' Rehana shuddered as she narrated the incident to Ruby. Involuntarily her hands started rubbing against her skin, as though trying to wipe the blood clean. 'No outsider can ever understand why our youngsters are so ready to seek martyrdom. Ruby, they don't understand that we have no choice. We either die in a blaze of glory or slowly, inch by inch, one day at a time, but we die and continue to die...' her voice trailed away. 'And still nothing changes.' Rehana's cheeks were wet with tears, her voice barely audible. 'Nothing changes... nothing. Ruby, *we* have to change this, we *have* to do something...'

Harsh popping sounds shattered Ruby's bloody march down memory lane. The heavy tyres of the Nissan van ground over loose gravel, and pebbles flew from under the tyres with sharp, flat reports as the driver brought the vehicle to a halt. Except for the puffs of dust swirling around, everything was still and silent.

Ruby looked around, befuddled, her mind still trapped in her mother's violent memories. It took a moment for the red and yellow faded signboard outside to register.

'Diya Dahara Restaurant', it read.

'You must try the food here,' the driver said, turning around. 'This place is famous.'

'Why don't you help us with the menu?' Mark took the reluctant driver by his arm and led him to a table below a fan.

'And tell them to go easy on the spices,' Ruby added.

The driver seemed uncomfortable sharing the table with them, but that did not stop him from ordering a big meal.

The service was efficient, not surprising since there was just a handful of customers. They had just cooled off with a glass of chilled King Coconut when the waiter carted in a series of steaming dishes.

'Did you order food for the whole restaurant?' Ruby said and smiled as dish after dish arrived, soon covering the entire table.

'I did not want you to go hungry,' the driver replied, eyeing the food hungrily.

The aroma of yellow rice flavoured with spices filled the air as the waiter removed the lid from the first platter. Next, he displayed fried chicken, crab curry in coconut gravy, devilled cuttle fish, white cashew curry and coconut sambol.

Mark cast several covetous glances at the bottles of Three Coin Beer chilling in the cooler near the cash counter but made no move to order one. He knew Ruby enforced the no-drinking-on-the-job rule.

Ruby couldn't believe it all cost just a little more than what they would have paid for a sandwich back home in London.

'So why are we here again?' Mark asked Ruby when the driver went back to the car. 'I thought you said this assignment was in India.'

'It is, but we first need to meet a man and pick up some equipment.'

'Okay...'

'We also need to recon our extraction route. In case we need to leave India by less... umm... conventional means.'

Mark nodded. That he understood. He liked that Ruby was thinking through to the end. Her recent long silences had made him uneasy.

'Tell me about the team I asked you to put together, Mark... Who are the three guys you picked?'

'Solid, reliable hitters – just the kind you wanted. Experienced blokes who don't ask too many questions. They take orders and have no qualms in executing them.'

'Perfect.'

'Yeah. Not the fancy, brainy, officer types.'

Ruby laughed. 'Any of them have criminal records?'

'Nope.'

'Perfect. Can't have any flags going up when they cross the border.'

'Don't worry about it.' He waved airily, but Ruby

could tell there was something on his mind. 'Say, boss,' he said after a while, 'any chance they won't be coming back at all?'

Ruby shrugged. 'Depends on them and how things pan out… and how they handle them.'

'Fair enough.' He cleared his throat. 'Well, the first two are a couple of Aussies, Gary Boucher and Shaun Ontong, who currently operate in South Africa, and the third, Rafael Gerber, is from Germany. All three are clean and perfect for the job.'

'Did they have any questions?'

'Not the Aussies, but the German did. He is a bit anal, wanted to know who he'd be working with so I had to give him a brief about the Aussies. He was happy to know they're operating in Africa. He's been there for many years and thinks it's the best training ground.'

'Nothing about me, I hope?'

'Not a peep about you.' Mark smiled reassuringly. 'In any case he had but one primary concern.'

'Which is?'

'Wie was das Geld ist?' *What is the money like?*

'Das Geld is gut,' Ruby replied firmly.

'Yeah,' Mark grinned. 'That's exactly what I told him. Half payable on reaching Delhi and the rest when the job's done. He had no further questions.'

'Did you set up the communication protocol with them?'

'I did. They are packed and ready. One text message and they'll move to Delhi.'

'Perfect.'

Twenty minutes later they were off again. The further they moved from Colombo, the A9 highway seemed to get worse. As did the condition of the buildings they passed. It would take time for Sri Lanka to recover from the devastation of the decades-long conflict.

Ravinder and Mohite had finished hammering out the details of the security arrangements for the Summit and shot it off to Thakur when Gyan, Ravinder's office runner, entered.

Gyan had been with Ravinder for several years. Though less than brilliant, Gyan was rock-solid and devoted to Ravinder. The bond between them had grown ever since Ravinder, learning about Gyan's cancer-stricken seven-year-old son, had ensured that Gyan was always posted where the best medical facilities were available and received aid from police welfare funds to care for his son.

'There is a visitor for you, sir.' Gyan's gentle tone was a contrast to his massive size. A moment later a tall, well-built man with close-cropped blond hair and bright blue-grey eyes walked in.

'Mr Gill?' Dressed in a smart grey business suit, he

appeared slightly ill at ease. 'I am Chance… Chance Spillman. I'm with the agency.' His British accent made it abundantly clear which agency.

'Ah! Mr Spillman.' Ravinder extended his hand. 'The home minister told us to expect you. How are you?'

'Very well, thank you, sir. It is a pleasure to meet you.' Chance held out a letter. 'Our director asked me to convey his regards.'

Ravinder took the letter. 'And how is my friend Edward?' He was referring to Sir Edward Kingsley, Director of MI6.

'He is well, sir.'

'Did he mention that we had been at college together in London?'

'I don't believe he did, sir.' Chance smiled. 'Not that I meet him very often.' He grinned again. 'I am still at the lower end of the food chain.'

Ravinder felt himself warming towards the man. 'Right.' Ravinder laughed. Turning to Mohite, who had a frown plastered on his face, he said, 'This is DGP Govind Mohite, my deputy.' The two men shook hands warily.

'When did you get in, Mr Spillman?' Ravinder continued.

'Just this morning, sir.' Then he added, 'Chance is good enough for me.'

'Chance, it is,' Ravinder acknowledged. 'An unusual name, if you don't mind my saying so.'

'Well, that was my dad for you,' Chance said. 'He always believed that everything that happened was purely a matter of chance, and only that.'

'Well, Chance, I want you to know that we really appreciate your government sending you down to help us,' Ravinder said.

'I would like to assure you that I will do my best to make things work in whichever way you want them to. We understand this is your turf and...'

'I am glad you understand that, Mr Spillman.' Mohite made no effort to keep his tone polite. 'India has been fighting terrorism for over thirty years and we don't need anyone to tell us how to do things around here.'

Ravinder groaned inwardly at Mohite's rudeness. But before anyone could respond, there was another knock at the door and Gyan entered. A fair, attractive woman with auburn hair followed him in. She was of medium height, in her late twenties or early thirties, with curves in all the right places. Like Chance, she too was dressed in a grey business suit. Despite her physical attributes and chiselled facial features, everything about her screamed secret agent, only the earpiece and dark glasses were missing. Her nasal twang defined her nationality.

'I am Special Agent Jennifer Poetzcsh.' She shook hands with the three men, a strong handshake, the kind women adopt when working in a male-dominant field.

Ravinder noticed the appraising look she gave Chance. Her gaze lingered on his wedding finger, when they shook hands, noting the absence of a ring. Chance also seemed taken by her.

She presented her CIA credentials to Ravinder.

With that out of the way Ravinder spoke, 'As you both know we have just started preparing for this Summit so may I suggest you two spend the next few days getting a feel of Delhi while we complete the arrangements.'

'Very well, sir.' Chance nodded. 'If there is anything we can do in the interim, please call us.'

'Of course, Chance, thank you.' Ravinder liked the professionalism of the young MI6 man. 'Where are you two staying?'

They named different hotels.

'Then may I suggest you both shift to the Ashoka, since that is the venue for the Summit. Govind will have a word with the hotel. They will give you rooms on the seventh floor, where we all will be staying. We are sealing off the top two floors for the Summit, the seventh for security and admin staff and the eighth for the delegates. You two will have adjacent rooms on the seventh floor.'

'Excellent suggestion, sir. I will shift tomorrow.'

'So will I.' Jennifer nodded. She shot another glance at Chance, clearly pleased to be staying closer to him.

'Lastly, may I also request you to contact your

agencies and get us whatever intelligence they have – anything that may affect the Summit.'

'Well,' Jennifer began, 'we have indications that a terror strike on Delhi may well be underway.'

'Really?' Ravinder asked. 'What's the target? What else do—'

'That's all we know right now,' Jennifer broke in. 'No way of knowing if the target is the Commonwealth Games or the Peace Summit.'

'Anything specific?' Ravinder asked when he realized she was not going to continue. 'What is the source?'

'It's classified,' Jennifer countered. 'Just that we have electronic intelligence to suggest that mercenaries, probably from England, have been hired by Lashkar-e-Toiba. I'll let you know as soon as we have anything more.'

The manner in which she delivered her words created tension in the room. Mohite's face displayed increased hostility. Even Chance looked uncomfortable. Ravinder masked his irritation, though he had half a mind to remind her that terror strikes were something Indians expected almost every day.

The meeting did not end on a great note.

The A9 highway from Colombo to Vavuniya was an unpleasant drive. Ruby saw little cultivation on either side of the road. Barring an odd civilian vehicle and frequent army trucks, there was little traffic.

Lounging in the rear seat, Mark dozed off again. Though tired, Ruby was wide awake, her mind boiling with thoughts and memories that would not let her sleep.

The sight of soldiers and their surroundings felt strangely familiar to Ruby. The bleakness was so similar to what she had recently encountered in Congo...

Again her mind flew back... to the last time Mark and she had operated together. That day, too, they had been in a similar vehicle.

Ruby folded the newspaper she'd been speed-reading and let it fall to the floor of the five-door, eight-seater Toyota Alphard. The engine was running so the air conditioner could beat some of the stifling Congo heat. She threw a glance at the house across the street before checking her watch again. Only an hour had passed. Tired of sitting still, Ruby shifted, trying to make herself more comfortable.

'The wait is always a bitch,' Mark, sitting beside her, murmured; as usual he didn't miss a thing.

'It's these bloody vests,' Ruby muttered, trying to wipe away the sweat that was making the vest stick to her skin.

'Yeah! But I'd rather be hot than not wear these when there's lead flying around.'

Ruby was about to reply when her Motorola handheld, a frequency-hopping piece of work, crackled to life.

'They are coming out now,' Mission Control said in a calm, clipped voice.

The words unleashed a rush of adrenaline in Ruby. Her spine straightened and her breathing ramped up. Her fingers clutched her weapon.

Like Mark, she was carrying a 5.56x45mm NATO, 30-round Heckler & Koch G36K. She loved its heft; it was a lightweight and low-maintenance weapon, constructed almost entirely of tough carbon fibre-reinforced polymer. Its barrels had been exchanged to give it a carbine profile, making it more useful for close quarter use. The fight ahead was likely to be up, close and personal. And bloody.

'Nitpickers?' Mission Control again, asking and alerting them simultaneously. The code word showed MC's kinky sense of humour.

'Ready to nitpick.' Chance Spillman's voice carried the undercurrent of a man ready for action. Despite its tautness, it ignited a storm of feelings inside Ruby. Desire. Regret. Confusion. The nagging feeling of something left unfinished, unresolved.

Ruby had always worked to ensure no one ever got under her skin. She had always kept her distance. But

Chance had managed to touch her heart. Being around him just reminded her of the feelings she had for him. She knew she wanted him back in her life, but…

'He is the enemy, Ruby,' her mother's voice tugged at her. Rehana had been miffed when Ruby had told her she was moving in with Chance. 'You are forgetting your purpose. He will never understand or accept what our people have suffered.'

'But I love him, mom.'

'More than your people? More than our cause? You are ready to throw everything away, everything that we suffered to ensure you are trained and ready when the time comes for you to act.'

Unsure, conflicted, Ruby had faltered. Love, an intense feeling of care and longing she had never experienced before, had pulled her to Chance. Love for her mother and her cause pulled her away from him. It had torn her apart.

She knew she needed to sit down and talk with Chance. So many unsaid, unfinished things hung between them.

Wandering minds get people killed, she remembered. Too many people had drilled that into her. She focused on the mission and checked the deployment again.

Chance was one of the five MI6 agents there, the one controlling the four snipers ranged around the house. She thought it was a clever deployment and congratulated herself mentally since she was the designated Operational Commander for this mission and it had been her plan.

The target house was a dilapidated bungalow on the outskirts of Kinshasa, the capital of Congo. Known until 1997 as Zaire, Congo was the third largest country in Africa by area and the fourth most populated. Torn apart by warfare since its inception, the vast land had made no progress, and was one of the poorest countries in the world. Estimates were that about 1,250 people died daily due to war and related causes like hunger and malnutrition.

In better times, the bungalow, with its red tiled roof, would have housed some high-ranking Belgian official. But most of the tiles had fallen or were broken, leaving ugly gaps in the roof, like missing teeth. Now it was occupied by a handful of Lord's Resistance Army terrorists.

The LRA, despite its grand name, was a small rag-tag group of about one hundred men, women and adolescents, who usually operated in Congo's north-eastern province of Orientale. The group had come to the attention of MI6 because it had kidnapped the British ambassador and his wife, and was now holding the couple hostage for a large ransom and for the freedom of their colleagues in Congo jails. The kidnapping had been a stroke of luck for the LRA and the result of sublime stupidity on the part of the ambassador, who had disregarded basic security procedures.

And now we're in this hellhole to bail out the idiot and his wife.

Ruby's fingers instinctively checked the weapons load to make sure it was set on single-shot fire mode. Her feet began to flex inside her black, rubber-soled, lace-up loafers, getting ready to run towards the target. Her fingers checked the weapon's magazine again.

The door to the bungalow opened and two men emerged. Both were young, one barely out of his teens. Both toted AK-47 automatics. Cheap and easily available, this was the weapon of choice of Terror Central. They halted on the porch, surveying the area.

The porch ran right around the house. It was surrounded by an unkempt garden that ended in a six-feet-high wall, which, like the rest of the bungalow, was also in disrepair. Beyond it ran the road on which Ruby and her teams were deployed. The road was bereft of traffic. A short distance away, a handful of children played, their occasional shouts of laughter blowing in the wind.

'Bloody amateurs,' Mark said, noting that the scouts had their rifles casually slung on their shoulders and not in the half port position, so they could swing into action instantly, should the need arise.

Ruby nodded in agreement. This was no place for amateurs.

The two kidnapper scouts did not venture onto the

road. Even if they had, it was unlikely that they would have spotted the two concealed cars, one on either side of the road. The vehicles on the other three sides of the bungalow were also safely tucked away.

Breathless minutes ticked away as the two scouts completed their half-hearted security scan. Then the younger one went back inside, again with that same casual swagger. It was another minute before he emerged with two more gunmen, also barely out of their teens. The new pair held their rifles in battle positions and appeared more alert.

They would die first. She was certain that Chance, controlling the snipers, would ensure that. It would be operationally expedient to do so.

A portly Caucasian man came out next. He had his arm around a short, plump Caucasian woman. From her halting gait and how the man supported her, she seemed to be sick. Or wounded, Ruby noted.

'That's our man,' Ruby muttered as she recognized the ambassador. No one replied. Everyone was now readying for action. They knew the signal would be coming any second.

Eight more gunmen emerged. And a couple of gunwomen too. They arrayed themselves around the hostages and moved towards a yellow minibus parked outside the gate. A handful seemed alert, but none was very careful. Sure, no one would have known where they were had it not been for one of their lot who had turned Judas for the silver thrown at him by MI6. Ruby wondered which one of them it was.

Would he live to enjoy the loot?

'Now!' Ruby half-whispered as the LRA gunmen and the hostages stopped near the minibus, trying to pre-empt Mission Control. Once they got into the vehicle, the job would become much more difficult.

'Sun down.'

The code word cracked out of the radio.

A scant second later, the sharp crackle of the team's sniper rifles rang out and four kidnappers fell.

Four down. Eight to go.

That was the last thought in Ruby's head as she levered open the door and flew out, holding the gun in her left hand, which was not her master hand but that did not bother her, She had trained herself long ago to marksman standards with both hands.

She had barely exited the Toyota when a battered maroon van turned the corner and began to nose its way down the pot-holed road.

At the same time, three women on foot came around the bend to the left; they hit the road metres away from the terror cluster.

Ruby cursed under her breath. Collateral damage would not go down well on her record.

She was on her third stride when the first shot left her weapon. Though almost flying, her shot did not miss. Beside her, Mark's weapon spat lead a millisecond later. Another kidnapper fell.

The team's sniper rifles crashed out again. More terrorists fell.

The ambassador had dropped to the ground, dragging his wife down with him.

The terrorists' lack of training was evident. They were firing blindly before they had even registered their targets.

Ruby and her team raced in.

The maroon van, seeing all hell break loose ahead, screeched to a halt and began reversing as fast as it could. The three women were huddled on one side of the road in a screaming cluster. One went silent as a passing bullet found her. The screams from the other two grew louder, but they were lost in the thunder of gunfire and screams of the dying.

By the time Ruby fired her third shot, all twelve terrorists were down. A thirty-something man and one of the younger women lay writhing on the ground. She shot both of them, putting a bullet through each head, as she weaved past them to the ambassador.

He was huddled in the dust, his arms wrapped around his wife. She was screaming, a ululating, keening sound that set Ruby's teeth on edge. Controlling the urge to slap her, Ruby reached down to grab him. She did not notice the beardless teenager, fallen beside the ambassador, reach for the pistol in his waistband.

She became aware of him only when Mark's weapon crackled to life behind her and he died with a scream.

Ruby cursed herself, even as she gave Mark a grateful look. He gave a fleeting salute as he continued checking the others for signs of life.

Ruby hoisted up the ambassador. His wife followed in tow as he clutched her. They hustled towards the Toyota, which had raced forward as soon as the sound of the last shot faded away.

The two women on the roadside had stopped screaming. The sound of the playing children had faded away. The maroon van had vanished. Barring the thrumming of Toyota engines, the silence was complete.

Just eighty-seven seconds had elapsed and twelve kidnappers had forfeited their lives.

Score one for the home team, Ruby thought triumphantly as she did a quick visual check and saw that her team was intact. Losing someone always hurt. Nor did it look good on the Operational Commander's scorecard.

Seconds later the Toyota was racing away with its twin prize safely seat-belted inside. The ambassador's wife had finally stopped screaming and lapsed into the never-never land of shock but Ruby did not care. She only had to get them back alive.

The Toyota raced past the spot where the children had been playing. Ruby spotted one of them staring open-mouthed from around the corner of a hut. He would have stories to tell for a long time.

Or maybe not. This was Congo, he was likely to have seen worse.

They had gone half a mile when the other five vehicles caught up. The convoy pelted down the narrow, potholed road.

'We have them,' Ruby heard the driver bark into the radio as she replaced the half-empty magazine of her weapon and began to reload. Beside her, Mark was doing the same.

'Jolly good show,' Mission Control intoned, his Brit stoicism intact. 'Extractors inbound.'

Minutes later, the vehicles pulled off the road and ground to a dust-churning halt in a flat, open field. The vehicles drew up in a wide circle. Kevlar-clad agents spilled out and took position behind their vehicles, all facing outwards. Not that they expected trouble, but security drills were what kept them alive.

The dust had yet to settle when three choppers swept in. Two of them headed straight into the secured clearing while the third, its guns ready, started circling overhead in a wide loop, to ensure nothing on ground interfered with the extraction. And, though the agents could not see them, high up in the sky, a sortie of RAF fighters ran a protective Combat Air Patrol (CAP).

The ambassador and his wife were hustled into the first chopper with Ruby's team. She saw Chance and his sniper team jump into the next one as hers lifted off.

Mission complete!

There were smiles all around.

Ruby leaned back and let the stress drain away. Momentarily, the faces of the downed terrorists flipped through her mind. She shrugged.

The fuckers should have realized what they'd signed up for. The thought induced a shrug. *They are wrong. I am right. Well… if not right, at least on the good team. Wasn't that reason enough for me to pull the trigger? Was it?* The thought troubled her only briefly. *Of course, it was. That is all there is to it… nothing to fret about.*

Closing her eyes, she shut out the clamouring roar of the rotors.

As the Nissan van halted again, Ruby was startled back to the reality of Sri Lanka.

The man whom Ruby and Mark had travelled halfway across the world to meet was waiting for them outside a seedy hotel in Vavuniya.

Barely five feet tall, the dark-skinned Chanderan was rotund, and like most men Ruby had seen on the streets, wore a checked blue-and-white cotton lungi and a white cotton half-sleeve shirt, its buttons undone almost to the midriff. He proudly led them to the reception desk – a tiny wooden table adorned with a large, well worn guest register and a pink flower vase with plastic flowers in it. Like the table, both the flowers and the vase had seen better days.

'It is all taken care of,' he announced grandly. Though afflicted by the typical islander accent, his English was all right. 'I will wait while you freshen up.'

'No worries.' Ruby was in no mood to tarry. 'Come on up to the room with us.' She threw a glance at Mark, making it clear that he was to stick with her.

The first-floor room Chanderan led them to had a queen-sized bed in the centre, and a small wooden table and chair near the window overlooking the noisy street. The bed was covered with a flowery, cotton bedspread. A stale smell hung in the air, making it obvious that the room was hired by the hour, and it had been a while since it had seen any housekeeping services. With the three of them in it, the room felt claustrophobic. Mark threw an amused look around. No air conditioner, just an ancient looking fan slowly rotated overhead. Ruby thanked her stars that they were staying just the one night.

'Our mutual friend said we could depend on you to get us what we need,' Ruby said to Chanderan once Mark had closed the door.

'He is most kind. I will try my best.' There was nothing about him that convinced Ruby that he had been the primary weapons supplier to the Liberation Tigers of Tamil Elam (LTTE), the terrorist group that had held the island captive for two decades. Of course, with the group now decimated, Chanderan's business had nose-dived. Ruby had been given these inputs by Yusuf uncle when he had last called her from Dubai.

'This is what I need.' Ruby handed over a short list to him. He scanned it, all at once mutating from a bumbling hotel manager to a seasoned arms supplier. Ruby could see why he had survived so long in this deadly trade.

'The rocket launcher and the rockets will not be a problem.' Chanderan looked up. 'The Glocks will take time.'

'How much time?'

'At least two weeks. Maybe more. I will need to check. New stuff stopped coming in a while ago, ever since...' He shrugged.

'I don't have that much time.'

'Maybe I can give you something else in that category?'

'No.' Ruby shook her head – the Glock 17s were crucial. With seventeen per cent of it made of high-tech plastic polymers, the Glock 17 was almost undetectable. When passed through a metal detector, unassembled, it required an expert to ascertain its presence. And its seventeen-shot magazine capacity offered a huge advantage. She needed that kind of firepower for the thirteen targets to be taken down. Not to mention the security men between her and the targets.

Chanderan was about to say something when Mark spoke. 'Boss, can I have a word with you?'

Chanderan took the hint. 'Why don't I organize some refreshments while you two discuss things.' He left.

'How badly do we need them Glocks?' Mark asked softly as soon as they were alone.

'We need them for sure.'

'I know a guy who can get them for us in India, and he is way bigger and more organized than him.' He nodded towards the door through which Chanderan had exited.

'You sure?'

'As sure as I can be. I have dealt with him. Anyway, what have we got to lose? This guy can't get us any in time. So even if the chap in India doesn't give it to us, we go for the next best option.'

Ruby nodded. 'All right.'

'We can even get the rest of the stuff in India. Why cart it all the way from here?'

'We need him to get us out if things go wrong,' Ruby explained. 'This guy is also taking care of our fallback escape route, so this is money well spent.'

'Makes sense.'

After Chanderan returned, it took another twenty minutes to seal the deal. Ruby did not bother to negotiate the price even though she knew he was over charging.

'But, for that price,' Ruby said flatly, making it clear that her demand was non-negotiable, 'you will need to deliver our materials to India and also organize a boat for us.'

Chanderan obviously needed the business; he agreed without a murmur.

With everything going as per plan, Ruby should have slept well that night but she didn't. With sleep came the recurring dream.

The faceless, formless man appeared, urging her on, pleading with her. She woke up with a jolt, feeling nauseous. Gulping down a glass of water, she drew on her inner resources, the way they had taught her during training. It was a while before her calm returned, bringing with it a renewed sense of purpose.

When she finally fell asleep again, it was a deep, dreamless sleep.

By the time Ravinder finished checking the Games' Village security and returned home, it was almost eleven. The road leading up to his house was in near darkness, the power supply had failed again.

Ravinder noted the two additional security guards, one patrolling along the boundary wall and the other backing up the gate guard. They seemed alert. Mohite had got this one right.

First thing tomorrow I must caution Simran and

Jasmine to be extra careful till those Jaish terrorists have been captured.

Ravinder let himself into the dark house. He had already called Simran earlier that evening to let her know he'd be late and knew she wouldn't be waiting up for him.

Day Two

Ruby woke up feeling rested. The bright Sri Lankan sun streamed in through the thin curtains, warming her face. Sometime in the night, her mind had scaled a plateau. She felt alive again. There was a spring in her step as she left the seedy hotel room.

Mark noticed her changed mood. He did not say a word, but he was relieved. Her brooding silences were new to him and he had begun to worry.

After a hurried breakfast they left for their next destination. Chanderan sat toad-like in the front seat. Filled with purpose, Ruby could not keep still. She kept up a barrage of questions about everything they drove past but that did little to dispel the tension that rode with them.

Simran was in the living room when Ravinder came down. The Gill family lived in a two-level government bungalow on Satya Marg, allocated to Ravinder by virtue of his position as ATTF chief. They could have stayed at their farmhouse in Chhattarpur – a huge eight-bedroom bungalow with a swimming pool, tennis court and gym – but Ravinder preferred it here. It was easier to commute and spared him the hassle of explaining to everyone how he, a cop, could afford such an extravagant lifestyle.

On one wall of the rectangular living room hung a bright, cheerful painting of a young boy running with a kite. The painter had caught the boy's excitement well. On the wall facing it was a sombre, dark mountainscape with small huts caught in the dying rays of the sun. On a third wall was an array of photographs – ancestors in their regal finery, the large family home in Patiala, men in uniform, the family crest clearly visible. Ravinder referred to this as the family's vanity wall, a reminder of their royal legacy. A massive Persian carpet, two big, well-polished brass lamps – one on either side of the sofa – and an abundance of antique wooden furniture added to the room's aristocratic feel. Ravinder liked this room but rarely got a chance to spend time in it. In fact, barring the monthly dinner that Simran hosted for close friends and family, he found himself with little time to unwind.

Dressed in a fawn sari that had an intricately embroidered border, her waist-length hair neatly tied in a bun, Simran was an elegant woman and carried her years well, despite the few extra inches. An elaborate tea service was placed on the coffee table. Scattered around were some photographs and papers. When Ravinder strode in, she was scrutinizing one of them, her lips puckered in concentration.

'You are just in time.' Simran looked up. 'I want your opinion.'

'On what, my dear?'

'You never listen to me,' Simran said, sounding exasperated. 'I have been telling you that we need to find a suitable groom for our Jasmine.'

Ravinder's sigh was inaudible. He knew he was again going to be drawn into the running battle between his wife and daughter.

'Simran,' he said, sitting down beside her, 'why bother? You should know your daughter by now. Jasmine is not going to agree to a marriage proposal. Let her finish her studies and...'

'What does she know? She wants to finish her law studies, pursue her master's degree, and then work. Girls from our family don't do that! This is the age for her to settle down. She is a child. It is our job to make sure she follows the family traditions.' She waved her hand at the clutter of papers and photos. 'Don't you realize that these boys are the best we can find... and they are all from a royal lineage...'

'The pick of the litter, are they?' Ravinder could not resist the quip. It earned him a cold, angry glare, and he regretted it immediately.

'Be serious! Our daughter's future is at stake.'

'Sorry,' Ravinder said, but before he could go on, his mobile chimed. Grateful for literally being saved by the bell, he walked out to the garden to take the call.

'Good morning, sir.' Mohite sounded angry. He launched off without waiting for Ravinder to respond. 'I have no idea how to deal with these bloody foreign agents.'

'What happened, Mohite?'

'I spent all of yesterday going over the security arrangements at the hotel with them, but that bloody Spillman is not satisfied with anything!' he exclaimed. 'And that woman, Jennifer, I have never seen anyone nitpick so much… she has a problem with every bloody thing.'

'Okay.' Ravinder knew that Mohite was prone to exaggeration and that he needed to get him focused. 'What were their concerns?'

'There were so many,' Mohite spluttered, 'where do I start?'

'Start with the big ones, Govind.'

Ravinder spent the next twenty minutes listening. As expected, the issues had more to do with Mohite's hostility towards the two foreigners than any practical concerns. Ravinder diplomatically talked Mohite through them one at a time.

'You're asking me to give in to them on everything.' Mohite complained.

'Govind, this is not about them or us, it is about ensuring the damn Summit goes off smoothly. Remember how much Thakur sahib trusts you? Can we afford to let him down? How would he feel if these guys complained to him?'

There was a pause at the other end. 'Right, sir, if that's what you want, I will do it.' Mohite did not sound happy.

'So where are they now?'

'I told them to take a hike and go see the city for the day… while I fix the problems,' Mohite replied, now in a satisfied tone.

Ravinder wondered why they called people like him civil servants. There was hardly anything civil about Mohite and no desire to serve anything but his own interests.

But we have to work with what we have. No point in bitching. Just deal with it.

'Fine, you work on the issues we have discussed. I will swing by later, once I've met Ashish.'

By the time the call ended Ravinder felt drained, and the day had only just begun.

'Don't forget we have to go for Navjyot's wedding reception tonight,' Simran said as he walked back inside and picked up his laptop.

'Navjyot?' Ravinder gave her a blank look.

'My cousin's daughter, Ravinder!' Simran said with an exasperated cluck.

'Oh, that's tonight?' Ravinder thumped his forehead.

'Yes, 8 p.m. at the Claridges. Come straight there if you're getting late.'

'Right, I think I'll do that.' Ravinder waved a hurried goobye as he headed out of the house.

'I know, I know. It's too much to expect you to come home and go with us.' Her exasperation followed him to the door.

Chance and Jennifer were already in his office when Ravinder walked in. Chance was sitting, but Jennifer was pacing the room, her agitation evident.

'Mr Gill,' her frustration burst out. 'You really need to look into this. Mr Mohite does not seem to understand the basics of security... and he is so rude.'

Ravinder kept calm. 'Why don't you take a seat, Jennifer? Would you like a cup of tea? Or coffee?'

'That might be a good idea, Mr Gill,' Chance interceded. 'Jennifer.' He pushed the chair beside him towards her, trying to calm her.

'These guys had better get their act together,' she muttered as she sat down.

'Right, so what is the precise problem?' Ravinder asked after instructing Gyan to get some tea for Chance and himself and coffee for Jennifer.

'We don't want to be difficult, Mr Gill,' Chance took the lead, 'but Mr Mohite is not sharing any information.

We have no idea what your security plans are. So how can we confirm to our superiors that our people will be safe? Please understand, our agencies will hold us accountable if anything goes wrong.'

'I understand, Chance.' Ravinder met his gaze evenly. 'Let me assure you that I will personally look into matters and make sure you are kept in the loop at all times. Give me a day to sort things out.'

'Fair enough, Mr Gill.'

Jennifer looked unconvinced, but she caught the look on Chance's face and subsided.

'While I do that, why don't the two of you do some sightseeing? Delhi has a lot to offer...' He smiled.

'Seems like a good idea.' Chance returned the smile.

Once they left, Ravinder sat down and began to work out how he would resolve the issue without ruffling any feathers, neither Thakur's nor his crony Mohite's.

The paperwork put together by Ruby, passing them off as volunteers working with a British aid group, got them through the checkpoints easily, but the constant delays irritated her.

It was past noon when they entered Vellankulam, a clutter of houses and huts – some of brick, but mostly mud-walled – amidst clusters of palm trees.

The sun was almost directly overhead, but the

heat was mitigated by a sprightly sea breeze as they alighted outside a small house by the sea, with faded wooden doors and windows. Several windowpanes were missing, the gaps boarded over with cardboard and yellowing newspaper.

On Sri Lanka's eastern coast, Vellankulam was historically an illegal jump-off point to India. During the war years it was established as a staging post by the terrorist groups for men and war-like materials. So it abounded in fast moving speedboats and men who plied this risky trade. It was to meet one such man that Chanderan had brought them there.

He was waiting for them when their vehicle navigated through the narrow wooden gate. He seemed to be a taller and heavier version of Chanderan. No time was wasted in pleasantries and introductions.

The cargo sought by Ruby was already loaded on the speedboat lashed to the jetty. Mark checked each item. The rocket launchers were Swedish 84mm Carl Gustaf, easy to use and effective. Both were wrapped in oily polythene. Accompanying them were two containers of rockets – the first had two High Explosive (HE) rockets and the second two High Explosive Anti Tank (HEAT) rockets.

'Everything seems to be in order,' Ruby told Chanderan when Mark gave her the thumbs up.

'Of course it is.' He smiled. 'Should we move, then?'

Ruby nodded. They clambered into the speedboat, covered the items with a tarpaulin and took off.

The sun bounced off the water, blindingly bright. There was a lively breeze, but that did not affect the high-powered boat, since it was skimming the surface of the water.

For the first few minutes, Chanderan tried to point out places on the coastline, but the wind made talk impossible. And neither Ruby nor Mark was in the mood for a guided tour. They were aware of the dangers of being intercepted by the Sri Lankan or Indian coastguard, even though Chanderan had assured them they could outrun anything that either government could throw at them, but that had not been particularly reassuring. Outrunning another boat was one thing, outrunning bullets was another.

But reconnoitring the escape route was important, and it was worth the risk.

Soon the sun was dropping towards the horizon, casting a deep red glow over the waters. As darkness closed in, lights began to flicker on the approaching Indian coastline.

Ruby's mind had again begun to spiral away when they made land and the engine was cut. Though slowing, the boat slid forward due to the momentum. Chanderan and his taciturn accomplice leapt into waist-deep-water and hauled the boat ashore.

Ruby felt pain and anger jab at her as her feet hit

Indian soil. *The land of my father...* this was not how she'd ever imagined coming here. It was an unsettling feeling. Confused, she pushed it away.

It was a quiet and deserted beach, perhaps cleared by Chanderan's local contact, a spot often used by smugglers and so avoided by locals altogether. Fishing nets had been hung out to dry here and there. A yellow light from a nearby temple cast eerie shadows all around.

A man emerged from the shadows and helped them offload the cargo.

'He will have them trucked down to Delhi and stored. They'll be there by the end of this week. You can collect them from the address I have given you,' Chanderan told Ruby.

'Have you told him about our return?'

'Of course. He will wait for you at the guesthouse in Chennai. It is perfectly safe... my cousin owns it. You just reach there and he will get you back.'

'And him?' Ruby gestured at the boatman.

'He will wait for you here for four days starting October fourteenth. Remember this temple,' Chanderan pointed. 'It is an easy landmark... just ask for the Devipattinam temple.'

Mark and Ruby took note of the long, unfamiliar name.

'Right. That's it then. Let's go.'

Minutes later they were heading back to Vellankulam. Their escape route had been physically reconnoitred and their weapons were being delivered to Delhi.

By now the darkness around them was almost complete. Barring the rhythmic throbbing of the powerful Yamaha outboard motor and the sound of water swishing past, silence surrounded them. It was almost spiritual. The dark skies, the overwhelming magnificence of the ocean, and the wind zipping past, all came together in harmony. Soon, the glow of the dying sun also vanished and darkness gathered strength, broken only by the twinkling lights of some distant coastal village or passing ship. Their boat rode without lights.

Ruby felt a comforting calm. It began in her heart and slowly spread through her, enhancing the positive feeling she had woken up with that morning. Despite that, somewhere deep inside, the sight of the receding Indian coastline unsettled her. She knew that somewhere out there, in that massive land of millions, was the man who had abandoned her – her father.

Where is he? Will I run into him?

Does he think of me? Ever?

All at once she wished they would never stop moving.

But they did.

Soon they were rushing through the night, back to Colombo. They had a flight to catch to Delhi. Ruby did not want either of them to enter India illegally.

It was pushing midnight when the cab brought them back to Ashoka hotel. Chance paid the driver and followed Jennifer in. Both had rooms on the seventh floor, in the zone that was being secured.

The encounter with Mohite that morning had soured the start of their day. But then, realizing they needed to give Ravinder time to sort things out, they'd taken his advice and gone sightseeing.

They'd had an exciting time traipsing through the Qutub Minar. Though access to the upper reaches of the world's tallest brick tower was no longer allowed, they had fun walking around it. Jennifer tried to embrace the famous iron pillar after their guide told them that anyone who managed to encircle it fully would have his wish fulfilled.

Watching her, Chance wondered what she was wishing for. Then, out of the blue, the thought of Ruby dropped into his mind. He wondered where she was... how she was doing... what *she* would have wished for.

What would I have wished for?

That caught him by surprise. It was an uncomfortable thought. He pushed it away, declining to try the pillar when Jennifer asked him to.

The ultra modern Lotus Temple was a change from the historic Qutub Minar, its exquisite construction and serene gardens leaving them enthralled. An hour's drive later, they reached the Jantar Mantar, a collection of architectural astronomical instruments built by Maharaja Jai Singh II. They were amazed at the sophistication of the 18th century monument. Then they spent a few hours wandering through Jama Masjid, Delhi's oldest and most famous mosque, built by Emperor Shah Jahan, who had also built the Taj Mahal. They were exhausted by the time they arrived at the Son-et-Lumiere, the sound and light show at the Red Fort, but felt rejuvenated by the time the brilliantly choreographed show finished. The evening ended with an authentic Indian dinner at Karim's, a restaurant near the Jama Masjid, in one of Delhi's oldest markets – the ambience as exotic as the food.

As the day progressed, Jennifer's attempts to get closer to Chance became obvious. It began with small gestures, a brush of his hand, a touch on the shoulder, and by evening they were holding hands and strolling through the Red Fort. Though uneasy, Chance made no attempt to free his hand.

The ancient fort with its sprawling, lush gardens had an irresistibly romantic aura. Chance felt it even though he didn't want to. It had been a while since he'd been with a beautiful woman. Still, he felt confused responding to Jennifer's flirtations. He was unsure where he stood with Ruby, and this made him feel uncomfortable. Almost guilty.

'Would you like to come in for a nightcap?' Jennifer asked as they halted outside her room.

The hint of desire in her eyes tugged at him. But

Chance hesitated. 'Not tonight, Jennifer.' Realizing he may have been too abrupt, he added, 'I am very tired. It has been a long day. Maybe tomorrow.'

'Maybe.' Jennifer gave him a light peck on his cheek and went inside.

Chance stood in the corridor, wondering if he should knock on her door and tell her he had changed his mind, but he couldn't bring himself to do it.

On the other side of the door, Jennifer sighed as she heard him walk away.

Ravinder was feeling drained by the time they managed to get away from the clutch of relatives at the wedding. It was not the ideal way to end a stressful day at work.

Jasmine too was feeling the pressure. These days, weddings were not high on her list of favourites, especially with Simran using every occasion to have one or the other of her sisters and cousins try and talk her into settling down. Several times Ravinder had seen Jasmine surrounded by a gaggle of aunts, looking hurricane-hit. More than once he'd even worked up the courage to wade in and rescue her.

Simran, of course, was thriving. She loved the hustle and bustle of these functions.

By the time they finally got free and hit the road, it was near the witching hour.

Ravinder was almost asleep when he remembered.

He had again forgotten to tell Simran and Jasmine to remain cautious. And he'd also forgotten to check on the latest with Mohite, about the hunt for Javed Khan and Aslam. The APB that had been put out yesterday and the request to Int had yielded several leads that Mohite was following up on. He thought of waking up Simran and Jasmine and cautioning them, but it had been a long day.

Tomorrow. First thing tomorrow, Ravinder promised himself. *We have to find those bastards before…*

Day Three

Ruby woke up as the plane began its descent towards Delhi's Indira Gandhi International Airport.

She checked her watch, a Cartier Tank with an ivory dial, blue metallic hands and black Roman numerals encased in a stainless steel body, a steel bracelet with yellow-gold links forming the strap. It made her smile. Rehana had saved up for it and gifted it to her when she had finished her MI6 training.

Well beyond my pay grade, Ruby thought with a wry smile.

As the aircraft hit the ground with a thud, bounced once and then settling down, roared down the runway, Ruby came back to reality.

Seven days to the Summit.

The ops clock in her head started ticking louder. It happened before every mission. Her spine stiffened and shoulders squared as she got off the plane.

Battle mode was on.

The massive, recently commissioned Delhi airport was bustling with energy. Mark and Ruby cleared immigration without any hassles and caught separate cabs. Mark made his way to the Radisson, a short hop from the airport and within striking distance of the target.

Ruby checked in at the Hyatt Regency, a short run from the Ashoka, where the Summit would be held.

She settled into her room and reached for the phone.

Ravinder was getting ready to leave for the office when the phone suddenly rang. He paused for a second, one hand still trying to push the links through his shirt cuff, deliberating if he should take the call.

'Good morning, sir. The man from Mossad is here. He wants to know when he can brief us.' Mohite's voice crackled through the phone.

Ravinder glanced at his wristwatch and mentally worked out his calendar – it would be another chock-a-block day. But this briefing could be important. 'Can he make it at twelve?'

'Of course he can. What else is he here for?' Mohite declared with his usual tact. 'I will tell him to come to the office at noon.'

Ravinder shook his head. He thought of telling Mohite that this was not the way to go around making 'friends', but didn't have the energy. And, knowing Mohite, it would be futile.

'And Govind, please request Chance and Jennifer to be present for the briefing.'

'Why?'

'Because they are here to help us secure the Summit. They need to be kept in the loop... that's why,' Ravinder replied patiently.

'But...'

'And just in case they are not in their rooms, leave a message with the front desk *and* send them a text,' Ravinder cut him off. He was about to end the call when he remembered. 'Oh, yes, what's the latest on Javed and Aslam? Any progress?'

'Nothing so far, sir,' Mohite replied, suddenly subdued. 'We drew a blank on seven leads. False alarms.'

'How many leads are there?'

'Nine, so far. Three from Int and six public sightings. I'm having the remaining two public sightings followed up today.'

'Keep me posted. And no matter what happens, keep up the publicity on these buggers. Radio, television, flyers, posters... the works. That will keep them on the run and not give them time to sit down and plan their strikes.'

Ruby tapped her feet impatiently, waiting for the phone to be answered. She had already called five times.

'Damn it, Mark! Where the hell have you been?' Ruby realized she had spoken more sharply than she had intended. She added, more gently, 'I need you to confirm with that guy about the remaining equipment.'

'I had gone down for breakfast and then I was just taking a shower, Ruby. It was a long flight. And I had to go out to call our man… I didn't want to do it from the hotel.'

'And?' Ruby knew he was right about taking these precautions, but she was itching to find out if he'd made any progress on procuring the Glocks.

'Anyway, he is out of Delhi and can only meet us the day after.'

'No way he can make it sooner?'

'I tried to get him to, but he says that's the earliest he can get back.'

'Damn! Well, in that case, let's focus on the reconnaissance for now.'

'Where do you want me?'

'Not with me. Not yet. The less we're seen together, the better. But there are some places I want you to check out on your own.'

Chance and Jennifer were already there when Ravinder walked into the conference room. So was Mohite. He sat beside a well-built, fair, serious-looking man at the other end of the table.

'Good afternoon.' The newcomer held out a large hand. 'I am Ido Peled.' His English was only slightly accented.

Ravinder brought the meeting to order and Peled began his briefing.

'My government has asked me to give you a detailed account of the Jerusalem attack and the people responsible for it, since we believe they will try to disrupt this Peace Summit too. I will also give you details of all delegates and try to answer any questions you may have.'

'The delegate profiles,' Mohite asked loudly, 'how are they relevant? Does your government believe that some of them may also attempt to disrupt the Summit?'

Ravinder acknowledged that the question was valid, but winced at Mohite's tone. Jennifer looked at Mohite sternly. Chance, more in control of himself, simply looked away.

'We have no reason to believe that the delegates could be involved in an attempt to sabotage the Summit, Mr Mohite,' Peled replied non-committally, meeting his gaze evenly.

'I see.' Mohite appeared inclined to discuss this further.

Ravinder intervened. 'Fair enough. Please tell us about the terror strikes.'

'Our investigations confirm that fifteen people were

involved in planning and executing the terror strike on Jerusalem, though only twelve women carried out the actual strike. These women had four things in common.' Peled, clearly a fluent communicator, had practised his presentation.

'First, none conformed to the profiling systems of most security agencies post 9/11. They appeared to be well-integrated members of society and thus were the ideal undetectable recruits.

'Second, all identifying dental work and body marks had been removed, and every stitch of clothing on them had been procured locally. Barring false passports, they carried nothing that could reveal their identities or show which group they belonged to.

'Third, all twelve were prepared to die as readily as they were to kill.

'Finally, they had all been trained thoroughly, especially the six women who arrived last. The first six entered Israel from various points in Europe. The other six, also of European origin, came from Pakistan. However, since passengers from Pakistan are subjected to extra scrutiny by most countries, this lot too was routed in through European cities. They had been handpicked from amongst 185 women trained for two years at two special Lashkar-e-Toiba camps at Bhimber and Kotli in Pakistan-occupied Kashmir.' Peled paused for a sip of water. 'This was done so that the planners could pass off this attack as a Zionist conspiracy.'

Mohite interrupted, 'Considering the efforts taken to prevent all this from coming out, you seem to know an awful lot.'

'Yes, because we pieced the whole thing together from camera footage at the airports, from the targets, eyewitness accounts and forensics.' After a pause he added softly, 'Also because we captured one of them alive.'

'You did?' Jennifer couldn't contain her surprise. 'But that was not in the news.'

'We don't want the people behind the strike to know we are onto them.'

'Good thinking.' Ravinder gave an approving nod. 'So you know exactly how the raid was executed?'

'Yes, we do.'

'Please share it with us. I am sure there can be major lessons in it for all of us.'

Peled gazed at Ravinder. Then he began his story. 'The strike on Jerusalem began at precisely ten-fifty that morning.'

As he spoke he held a wireless controller in his hand. Powered by his laptop, footage from a security camera began to beam onto a screen at the far end. It showed dozens of tourists milling around, along with several security men.

'The attack started innocuously enough, but escalated so rapidly that our security was initially swamped. By the time we recovered and started a counter-attack, the raiders had gained a foothold, a tenuous one, but enough to ensure that the damage inflicted was substantial.'

His four-person audience listened in rapt attention.

—•—

A security camera zoomed in to show three women walking up towards the Al Aqsa mosque. All seemed to be in their mid-twenties and blended into the touristy crowd with ease. They held travel books in their hands, big cameras slung around their necks, and water bottles peeped out of their backpacks. Their heads were covered with scarves and they wore full-sleeved shirts and trousers, ensuring there was no indecent display of skin.

In retrospect it was easy to see that their eyes were not still; they constantly darted around, like the advancing scouts of a rifle section. They had divided the area into zones, so between the three of them maintained a total view of the surroundings. This heightened awareness was mostly due to the Benzphetamine pills they had taken a few minutes ago.

It was at the Al Aqsa mosque that the Holy Prophet was given the commandment to pray five times a day for the following sixteen-and-a-half months, with Jerusalem as the Qibla (direction of prayers), though today Muslims face Mecca while praying.

The Dome of the Chain marks the central point

of the Al Aqsa, which like most mosques has four minarets, three square ones and a cylindrical one from the Mamluk period. Recognizable by its lead dome, which replaced the aluminium covering built in 1964 in order to restore it to its original cover, Al Aqsa comprises three distinct parts: narrow arcades running along one end, a huge atrium, and a covered area to the south.

Signs of damage done to the mosque in 1969, when a fanatic Jew set fire to the covered area, are still visible. Amongst the numerous sad losses was the loss of the beautiful handmade pulpit from Aleppo made of over 10,000 interlocking pieces of wood, ivory and mother of pearl, held together without a drop of glue or a single nail, and considered one of the most beautiful pulpits in the world.

'If the plan that had been developed for these terrorists had fully succeeded, the damage would have been much more severe.' Ido's tone was sombre.

As the three women approached the main entrance of the mosque, they appeared engrossed in animated conversation. They were fifty feet from the entrance when a motorcycle sped past on the road in front of the mosque. About twenty metres from the main security post, the motorcycle lost control. Since the camera feed was not backed by an audio track, they could only imagine the loud thud with which the motorcycle hit the road. It would have been followed by a nerve-grating, screeching sound as metal scraped along the tarmac. The rider's helmet broke loose. When the bike screeched to a halt she lay still – a young woman in her mid-twenties with blood covering her face.

Two of the six security men stationed at the monument's gates ran forward to help even as the attention of the other four remained focused on the fallen rider.

Ravinder realized that the security men had been lured into a trap.

Converging on the motorcyclist along with the security men were another nine or ten eager-to-help passers-by. The soldiers reached the crash victim first. This lot was decimated by the forty kilograms of high explosive strapped onto the motorcycle. The fuel tank's explosion added to the carnage.

'The explosion was so powerful that it was heard miles away, which is what it was supposed to do, since it not only created the diversion for the main assault force, it also triggered the next phase,' Peled explained.

While a cloud of motorcycle parts, blood and bones billowed upwards, the security camera caught the three women suddenly pull weapons out of their knapsacks and run forward purposefully.

'All three were wielding Micro Tavor assault rifles.'

Of Israeli design, with a length of just 23 inches, the MTAR 21 is possibly the shortest 5.56mm assault rifle, shorter even than the Uzi, but more accurate due to its relatively longer barrel.

They headed straight for the main gate.

People only became aware of the attack when the terrorist leading the charge hurled a grenade at the security post spanning the main gate.

'It landed behind the sandbags, which ensured the attackers were safe from the shrapnel,' Peled said, his tone dispassionate. 'None of the security personnel survived.'

'Charging through the carnage, Raiders One and Two,' Peled pointed at two women on the screen, 'headed for the solitary door on the western side that opened into the covered area of the mosque. Meanwhile Raider Three, who had thrown the grenade, continued towards the security post on the west to prevent the guards from interdicting her teammates.'

It was happening so fast that the security men on that side were caught unawares. All three died.

'Then Raider Three whipped around and headed for the sentries at the next gate on the west.' Peled traced her path on the screen with a laser pointer.

The camera footage was grainy, but Ravinder could see her expertly flip her magazine as she ran. She fired at the two security men but one of them managed to put a bullet in her, high on her left shoulder, before he collapsed.

Ravinder saw her falter briefly. She collected herself,

spun around and headed for the next security post. By now the guards were ready to engage. She fell to a hail of bullets. For a moment everyone froze. A soundless explosion spread across the screen. She had triggered the explosive in the camera around her neck. Parts of her body were hurled up and outwards. The amount of explosive was enough to decimate her upper body, which was deliberate, to keep the identities of the attackers obscure.

'Her objective was the same as the woman who had crashed her motorcycle, to provide the primary pair of raiders an opportunity to get into the main mosque.'

The camera feed switched to show Raiders One and Two racing into the mosque, firing in short, ammunition conserving, two- or three-round bursts, gunning down everyone in their way – tourists, people in prayer and security guards.

The camera feed switched again, now showing two more women. Raiders Five and Six, emerging from the crowd between the Al Aqsa mosque and the Temple Mount. They ran towards the solitary door on the east, which led into the covered area of the mosque, gunning down everyone in their path.

The security forces here, however, were on full alert.

Raider Six fell to a hail of bullets halfway to the mosque. Her final act was to trigger the bomb in the camera slung around her neck. Two bystanders were blown up with her. The chaos created by the explosion allowed Raider Five to slip into the mosque.

'By now three terrorists had penetrated the inner sanctum of the mosque.'

The screen went black as Peled switched to the feed from the security cameras inside the mosque.

Raiders One, Two and Five could now be seen selectively rounding up hostages. A majority were Muslims – a deliberate part of the plan. Only two of the fourteen hostages were non-Muslims, both men in their late forties, and both Jewish from their dress and demeanour. 'One was a schoolteacher,' Peled said, pointing at a meek looking man. 'The second was his American cousin on a sightseeing tour.'

Raider One stood guard while Raider Two secured the hands and feet of the hostages. All this while, Raider Five could be seen moving from window to window. Every so often she would raise her weapon and fire.

'A few hundred metres to the north, the next pair of terrorists, who we now know were called Raiders Seven and Eight, opened fired at the tourists milling around the Dome of the Rock. Most guards fell to the initial onslaught. The two who survived managed to put bullets into the attackers, but failed to prevent them from entering the monument. So, with Raiders Seven and Eight inside, both monuments were now in control of the terrorists.

'As you will note from the proximity of the two

buildings,' Peled indicated the area between the buildings with the laser pointer, 'it was now extremely hard for the security forces to undertake cleansing operations from here, since they'd be in range from one or both the buildings.'

His audience nodded. The predicament of the IDF was obvious.

'Despite the speed with which the attack developed,' Peled continued, 'the IDF's reaction was fast.'

Having studied the lessons of the Mumbai Ghazwa (raid), Ravinder knew it was imperative to dislodge the terrorists before they got firmly entrenched. Given time they would not only secure more hostages or kill more people, but also take up good defensive positions and lay booby traps.

'By now our counter-terrorism units were racing in,' Peled resumed. 'Our biggest problem was that no operation could be carried out without damage to the monuments. Considering their religious significance, any damage would incite massive anger in Muslims the world over.'

Ravinder could see the others trying to figure out how *they* would have reacted.

'Meanwhile the remaining terrorists swung into action. They had also learnt the lessons of the Mumbai attack and planned on attacking multiple targets simultaneously.'

Once again the screen sprang to life with the footage

of another set of cameras. Raiders Nine and Ten, another pair of pretty girls in their early twenties, could be seen hauling out Micro Tavors from their knapsacks and firing at the tourists at the Tower of David.

Raider Nine was running towards the security post as she fired. She got two guards before the others gunned her down. She too disappeared in an explosive thunderclap as Raider Ten raced into the monument.

'The one who went inside gunned down everyone she came across.' Peled's tone hardened. It was impossible not to feel his anger. 'Her job was not to secure the monument, it was to inflict maximum casualties and also force us to go in and get her, thus diverting our forces from their primary target, the Al Aqsa.'

Everyone in the room was riveted.

'As soon as information about this latest attack reached headquarters, a section of the IDF response team rushing to Al Aqsa split and headed to the Tower of David. Post Mumbai and due to the changing nature of urban jihad, we were now geared to handle simultaneous, multiple threats.'

'At the same time as the Tower of David was attacked, eight kilometres to its north, the final pair, Raiders Eleven and Twelve, two more young women, also armed with Micro Tavor assault rifles and grenades, headed for the security post guarding the Chapel of the Ascension.'

Peled clicked the controller and the feed from another set of cameras showed two girls racing forward, firing. They gunned down guards and raced towards the Chapel.

'Here also they simply gunned down everyone in sight.' Peled now was having trouble keeping his emotions in check. Ravinder knew how he felt. Though Peled had started with a well-rehearsed presentation, now the words were coming from his heart. Very raw. Very poignant.

'As soon as we got word of this attack, another section of the counter-terror unit racing towards Al Aqsa broke off and headed to the Chapel. And seeing that the threat had enlarged, headquarters began to scramble more forces.'

The footage returned to Al Aqsa and the Dome of the Rock. The units could be seen rushing in and taking position to secure the perimeter.

The camera feed changed and commando detachments could now be seen arriving at the Tower of David and the Chapel of Ascension.

'Within minutes of getting there, we began the operation to regain control of the monuments,' Peled said, again using his laser pointer. The units could now be seen deploying sensors and sending in probes.

Ravinder knew their first step would be to gather maximum intelligence. The security forces would already know the layout. Also, in most such buildings there are cameras and security sensors. The security forces use these for real-time combat intelligence, which is vital to ensure that the building can be retaken with minimal loss of life. Ravinder was glad he was not in the shoes of the IDF commander.

'There is no doubt that the planners of this strike were veterans of such dark ops. They had carefully planned to enhance the psychological impact of their strikes.' Peled's voice stayed low and intense. 'They left all audio surveillance, motion or heat sensors intact. Pinpointing and destroying them would have taken too much time. But they destroyed all the surveillance cameras they could find. These would not only give away their strength but also their equipment, location and condition. However they left the cameras in the inner sanctums of the mosque intact. The terrorists wanted to make sure everyone saw the gory finale.'

The screen showed footage of the inside of the mosque.

The raiders could be seen moving rapidly from one firing position to another, keeping up a barrage, doing everything to deny operational intelligence to the security forces and keep them at bay.

At the Tomb of David, Raider Ten kept firing till she was down to her last magazine. As the first commando broke in, she ran forward and detonated her camera bomb. Both were annihilated.

'The Tomb of David was back in our control. Barring the area around the explosion, the damage was within manageable limits. But eleven people lost their lives.'

Peled's words rang bleakly through the room.

'At Ascension, Raiders Eleven and Twelve kept the initial probes of our forces at bay, but they too were running out of ammo. They were setting up explosive charges when IDF commandos raced in and gunned them down. They too detonated the bombs but the damage to the Chapel was minimal. Our loss here was much higher. Four security men and seventeen tourists gunned down.' Peled's voice had a brittle edge to it.

The footage flipped again as it returned to the Dome of the Rock.

Both terrorists had been wounded, Raider Seven so badly that she couldn't move at all. Raider Eight could move, but slowly.

'That is why their shoot-scoot-shoot strategy did not work. Minutes later the Dome was back in our hands. However the death toll here was a shocking twenty-six, including three commandos. The damage to the building was also more severe. But, as you will see now, our problems were far from over.'

Once again the footage changed. The inner sanctum of the mosque came into view. It showed twelve panic-stricken hostages. The three terrorists were racing from window to window, keeping up a rain of fire on the forces outside. The fourteen arches, twenty-seven marble columns on the eastern side and the same number of stone piers on the west afforded them cover to switch positions.

Suddenly Raiders One and Two raced back to the hostages. The security camera caught Raider One as she switched on her BlackBerry and began to record a video. She was in direct sight of the camera, which revealed the tension on her face.

At Peled's command, the feed now fragmented into two.

On the second half of the screen Raider Two could be seen lining up the hostages. Starting from one side she began to gun them down, delivering one shot each to their faces, ensuring that they screamed as they saw death coming. Acrid gun smoke furled up in the air.

As Raider Two proceeded, the killing became more brutal. She shot the sixth hostage first in the lower jaw. His soundless scream rang out. Only then did she put one between his eyes. The eighth was shot twice in the knees before her coup de grace. The eleventh, the American cousin visiting Israel, was begging for mercy when she put the muzzle against his stomach. There was a soundless click as the firing pin slammed down on an empty chamber. The kneeling hostage looked up in shock. Then he vomited.

By now Raider Two was directly in front of the security camera overhead. Probably she was aware of it and had positioned the hostages to ensure it caught every bloody detail. Dropping the now empty assault rifle, she unsheathed a knife from her ankle holster.

The hostage was still vomiting when she reached

down, grabbed his hair and yanked his head back. The knife moved in a quick diagonal slash across the throat. He gurgled and then slumped forward. His blood rained out in droplets on Raider Two's hands. She licked her lips as she wiped the dagger clean on her pant leg.

On the second half of the screen, recording all this on a BlackBerry, Raider One was moving in tandem with Raider Two. They saw an odd expression on her face, as though she wanted it all to end, yet was fascinated by what she was seeing. Her mouth was parted a little and her chest heaved. Now and then her tongue forayed out and moistened her lips.

By the time Raider Two moved to the twelfth man, her breath was coming in rasping gasps, her eyes blazing, and splatters of blood pockmarked her.

The final hostage did not scream. There was an amazing calm in the way he stared at her, perhaps a touch of pity. His lips were moving as though praying for her.

The surge of anger on Raider Two's face at his lack of fear was palpable. Perhaps that he was a Jew fuelled her anger. Shifting the knife's angle, she sliced out his right ear. The hostage screamed now. Though no sound emerged, each viewer could hear the animal-like howl of pain.

The scream goaded Raider Two on. She sliced off the other ear too. Then reversing her hold on the knife, she drove it into the hostage's right eye. The scream ended abruptly as the knife entered the brain and drove the life out of him.

Raider Two stood frozen, still holding the knife buried in the hostage's skull. She seemed depleted. As though it was not just the hostage who had died. As though something inside her had died too.

Ravinder felt his breath thud to a stop, unable to believe the brutality he had witnessed.

Watching it on the BlackBerry's screen, Raider One smiled. She began tapping something on the keypad. Then she watched impatiently as the file uploaded slowly.

A moment later she gave a satisfied nod and was putting the phone away when a stun grenade smashed through a nearby window. It exploded with a blinding flash.

Moments later, the IDF commandos raced in and unleashed a hail of bullets.

Their mission complete, the two terrorists triggered their camera bombs and death claimed them.

'The BlackBerry handset was destroyed so we'll never know whom she sent that video to.'

Peled's comment was cut off as Raider Five raced into the central hall. She saw that her teammates were down and reached for the trigger of her camera bomb.

A commando had heard her run in and shot at her twice even as her hand was reaching for the camera bomb.

His first bullet missed. The second grazed her temple. It bit deeply enough to make her reel and clutch at the wound.

In a flash the commando was on her, hammering her into the ground, disarming her and pinning her down, making sure her hands got nowhere near her camera bomb.

The carnage was over.

The silence in the conference room was complete, though the footage on the screen rolled on.

The task force commander now raced into the mosque. He came to a stunned stop as he surveyed the bodies.

'The last hostage killed was Ean Gellner, the son of Ziv Gellner, who is one of our delegates for this Summit,' Peled said softly.

On the screen, the task force commander turned and said something to the commando who had captured Raider Five.

'I knew we had to keep her capture from the media,' Peled said.

'*You?*' Chance asked wide-eyed. 'You were the task force commander?'

'Yes,' Peled replied. 'I also did most of the post-event investigation. That is why I was asked to come down and brief you all.'

A long silence followed his words.

'Who were the others involved?' Jennifer's voice broke the moment.

'The mastermind was a Qassam Brigades commander.'

'Who?' Jennifer asked again.

'We are still not sure,' Peled replied with a straight face. No way Israel would officially admit to Yusuf Sharbati's involvement, not after he had been disposed of in Dubai by a kidon team barely a week ago. 'But we do know that the Qassam commander was funded by someone from the Lashkar-e-Toiba.'

'Not surprising,' Ravinder remarked. 'They've been looking for a way to up their profile in global terror for years. Of late, they've become frantic because their refusal to take up arms against their sponsors – the Pakistani government – has tagged them as betrayers of Islam.'

'True,' Mohite agreed. 'That is why they are under huge pressure to redeem themselves in the eyes of the "ummah", the community. Not to mention that they want to exploit the gap in leadership of Terror Central, with Osama dead and other senior Al Qaeda leaders having gone underground.'

'That could also explain the similarities of the Jerusalem strike to the 26/11 LeT ghazwa on Mumbai,' Chance pointed out. 'Mumbai was also their doing.'

'Yes,' Peled nodded. 'We have certain leads about this man but have yet to ascertain his identity.'

'You know, we have a very extensive database on all LeT commanders,' Ravinder offered. 'We have suffered because of these lunatics and their ISI handlers for decades now. Let us know if we can help.'

'That is kind of you, sir.' Peled gave a grateful smile. 'We shall take you up on that.'

'Just share your leads with us and Mohite will help you dig up possible matches.'

'Right, so...' Again, it was Jennifer who brought them back to the present. 'Twelve women and two guys... that takes care of fourteen people. You said there were fifteen. Who was the fifteenth?'

'There was a thirteenth woman,' Peled replied.

Damn! Thirteen, again! Ravinder swore under his breath. It had become a recurring theme with this damn Summit.

Peled continued, 'We do not know much except that she is probably Caucasian. The terrorist we captured caught a glimpse of her and heard her talking when she came to meet the Qassam commander. She says she heard a British accent. As of now, that is all we know.'

The others were listening, but did not catch the unspoken. Ravinder did. He sensed that Peled knew more than he was telling.

At that moment, barely thirteen miles away, the thirteenth woman, dressed as a tourist, complete with camera, hat and water bottle, approached Ashoka hotel.

Ruby carried out two runs to and through the hotel. The minute she entered it, she knew she had no hope of going past the main lobby or the restaurants. Disappointed, but not surprised, she surveyed as best she could.

On her first run she studied the layout and identified ingress points. On the second, she confirmed the observations she had made, double-checking to ensure she was correct.

By sunset, Ruby had every detail of the venue embedded in her head. Satisfied with the day's work, she returned to her hotel room and began to work out attack combinations.

It was not going to be easy. She'd seen cops crawling all over the place, in plainclothes and in uniform. Most inner areas in the hotel had already been cordoned off. Roadblocks had been set up on all approaches and there were security posts at both hotel gates.

It did not take her long to realize that a frontal assault would fail. It would have to be a covert attack – though a frontal assault *could* be a useful diversion. In fact, a critical one, if delivered right.

A couple of hours later, her plans tentatively complete, she called it a night. Though exhausted, her sleep was hampered by her anxiety about the meeting with Nanda, the arms dealer, the next morning.

I hope that bugger can come up with the Glocks. That was her last thought as she fell asleep.

Dinner was drawing to a close when the phone began to clamour. Simran frowned as Ravinder wiped his hands and got up to answer it.

'We have two candidates, sir,' Mohite sounded excited. 'It took a while, but...'

'Candidates for what, Govind?' Ravinder cut in.

'Oh!' Mohite checked himself. 'I was helping Peled to sift through our database on the LeT commanders and we have two possible suspects. The first is Pasha.'

'Hmm. Give me a moment while I get my laptop out.' Ravinder retreated to his study. Booting up the device, he pulled up Pasha's profile. The screen showed two photos, the only two they had of him.

The first, taken by an Indian intelligence operative, showed a clean-shaven man in a neat and obviously expensive steel-grey business suit. He carried the suit well, as though used to it. Short and diminutive, he looked like a jockey. A small but prominent pear-shaped scar marked his right temple.

The second, taken by a Taliban turncoat, showed a different man, heavily bearded with shoulder-length hair, now dressed in a typical black Pathani kameez and ankle-high salwar. There was little resemblance to the man in the first photo.

Ravinder scanned through the man's profile. Born Khalid Abbas Khawaja, he had been a Wing Commander in the Pakistan Air Force. No one knew whether he had retired or had been ordered to retire, or if it had been made to look like he had retired. Mysteriously, one fine day Wing Commander Khalid Abbas Khawaja had just vanished.

He appeared to have little in common with the man who surfaced in Afghanistan a year later, the year the Taliban had begun to make its presence felt. The crew cut and sharp pencil line moustache had been replaced by an unruly beard and shoulder-length hair. This slightly built man, with an AK-74 in one hand and a radio or satellite phone in the other, soon became a fixture in the entourage of the one-eyed leader of the Taliban. He now piloted people, not planes, tweaking their destinies and ensuring they served just one purpose, the jihad.

However, as he had been ordered to do, Pasha stuck to the shadows. He feared the powerful generals in Islamabad. He knew they would throw him to the wolves if he dared cross them.

It was Pasha who had planned and executed the 26/11 Mumbai terror attack. This much was known – or at least strongly conjectured.

'Who is the other suspect?' Ravinder asked.

'Well, if it is not Pasha then it could only be Saeed Anwar.'

Ravinder opened Anwar's profile. There were many photos of the portly, skullcap-wearing, bearded, bespectacled man. Clad in white, he was fond of leading public rallies and was a primary fundraiser for the LeT. He had helped Osama plan and execute the 9/11 strike and was known to have transferred 100,000 US dollars to the hijackers just before the attack.

Yes, he too is a strong possibility. In fact, considering the others in the LeT leadership, it seems certain that one of the two would have been behind the Jerusalem attack.

'Good work, Mohite. What does the Israeli have to say?'

'He said his boss would be talking to you soon.'

'All right.' Ravinder rang off.

Sure enough, an hour later his phone rang again and on the line was Meir Dagan.

Though he had met him only once, Ravinder could easily picture Dagan, the current head of Mossad. Known to be the antithesis of M, the James Bond spymaster, Dagan, an avid student of history, a no-frills man who clocked eighteen hours of work every day, was famous for his bull-headed doggedness, and commanded respect, both within Mossad and outside.

Though Ravinder did not know it yet, the reason Dagan took an hour to finally call him, was because he first needed to get the Israeli PM's sanction. Ordering a kidon hit was not something Dagan had the authority to do on his own.

To have Pasha and Anwar taken out, he had to first get their names added to the 'execution list.'

Given the severity of the Jerusalem attack, Dagan had little doubt that the sanction to place Pasha and Anwar on this list would be accorded. However, as per protocol, such a request could be confirmed by the Israeli PM only after a go-ahead by the designated judicial investigator, a person whose identity is so secret almost no one has heard of him. The judicial investigator must have been clocking serious overtime that day since he had given his approval quite fast.

'Do you agree with the possibility of these two being the most likely candidates?' Dagan came to the point immediately.

'Well, the chances of it being one of them are high. None of the others seem to have the authority to organize something of this magnitude,' Ravinder replied. 'Also, you can assume that if one is involved, the other will be too. These two buggers are thick as thieves.'

'In that case, we have a favour to ask of you,' Dagan said. 'We would like to deploy a team to bring them in. We need you to help us with a firm base and some logistical support. I know it is a lot to ask, but given the geography, we have no other option. Not if we want to do this fast – and we do.'

'Bring them in, or take them out?' Ravinder asked.

'Whatever is possible, Mr Gill.' Dagan did not hesitate. 'We cannot – will not – allow such a heinous attack on our country to go unpunished.'

'I understand. I really do, but I will need to speak to my boss first.'

'If you want, I can request our PM to talk to yours,' Dagan offered.

'I will let you know if that's required.' Ravinder knew that the Indian PM would prefer not to know; plausible deniability was much sought after. 'Let me clear this with my boss.'

It was with great satisfaction that Ravinder returned Dagan's call an hour later. It had taken him that long to root out the home minister and get him to speak to the PM. For once, Thakur had delivered.

'You will see that our role in this matter remains totally secret?' That had been Thakur's primary concern.

'You can rest assured about that,' Dagan confirmed.

Even before either of them retired to bed, a team from Mossad's kidon unit was headed to Delhi.

Ravinder felt content as he fell asleep that night.

It took a long time for Ravinder to realize that it wasn't just a dream – the phone was actually ringing.

'Sorry to bother you so late, sir, but I thought you'd like to know.' Mohite sounded shaken.

'What happened?' Ravinder asked, still groggy with sleep.

'We just missed them… Javed and Aslam… the two remaining Jaish terrorists.'

'What?' Ravinder was wide awake now. 'What happened?'

'You remember I'd told you about the remaining two leads? Well, I'd ordered the SHOs of the concerned areas to follow up on them. The SHO of Friends Colony just called me. They raided a suspected house a while ago and discovered that the bastards had been staying there. Apparently Javed and Aslam stepped out minutes before the raid. They *just* missed them.'

'Missed them by chance or had they been warned about the raid?'

Mohite was silent. He had obviously not thought of that. 'Let me look into it, sir.' Pause. Then he added dubiously, 'But Sher Singh, the SHO, is a loyal guy.'

'He is, but ask him to double-check his staff… everyone who knew about the raid. Could be a coincidence, but no harm in checking.'

'Wilco, sir. I agree. And they're interrogating the owner of the house now. He appears to be a supporter… let's hope they come up with something. I'll rest easy only when we have the bastards behind bars… or six feet under.' Ravinder could sense his tension. 'Damn! To think we almost had the bastards!'

'Don't stress about it, Govind. Shit happens. We can only try.'

Even to Ravinder the words offered no solace, knowing he was one of the three people the terrorists had been sent in to kill. He knew exactly how Mohite was feeling – lousy.

Day Four

Ruby arrived at Dilli Haat half an hour early for her meeting with Nanda. She spent it casing the area, watching for anything out of sync. She spotted nothing unusual, no one loitering around surreptitiously with those giveaway earpieces or bulges under their coats. She wasn't expecting trouble, but she wasn't about to leave things to chance.

Satisfied, she returned to the cream coloured Toyota Innova she had hired and waited. The driver, Kishore, was a polite young man about five-and-a-half feet. His grey Safari suit was well-maintained and as clean as his car. He left the air conditioner on for her as she waited, and stood beside a tree a short distance away.

After a few minutes she saw Mark emerge from a black Hyundai sedan that pulled up in a slot three cars away. Ruby was pleased that he too had arrived early and was in top form. She wondered if the men he had hired were as good. She hoped they were – their lives and, more importantly, the mission, depended on it.

Ruby saw Mark survey the area, sweeping it quadrant by quadrant, just as she had done.

At ten thirty on a weekday morning, Dilli Haat, the famous arts and crafts market, had yet to fill to its potential. A short hop from the Hyatt, the colourful market, with its tiny stalls and regional, multi-cuisine food stalls, was popular with locals and foreigners alike.

Fronted by an elaborately carved stone gate, manned by armed khaki-clad cops and a set of massive doorframe metal detectors, the market had a bright red stone wall around it. By now the ice-cream vendors, balloon sellers and ladies in bright Rajasthani skirts selling bangles and applying the traditional henna, had started setting up shop outside the gates.

It would not be long before the market began teeming with people. That, in fact, was why they had chosen to meet Nanda here – crowds always offered safety.

The cream suburban to your left, Ruby shot off a text to Mark.

Mark spotted Ruby's car and then headed over to the counter. He bought an entry ticket and walked across to the food stalls at the end of the Haat, the designated meeting point.

Half an hour later, he walked out, a portly, balding man with him. In the midst of the casually dressed holidaymakers, he looked incongruous in his Armani suit. A gold watch and several golden Cross ballpoint pens in his breast pocket lit up his attire. The two parted ways at the entry gates, both heading for different parts of the parking lot.

Mark watched Nanda climb into a blue Mercedes 300 as a chauffeur held the door open. The chauffeur was as smartly dressed as his boss, his white uniform and cap giving him a regal air. Once the car pulled out, Mark made his way to Ruby.

'All taken care of.' Mark opened the door and poked his head in. 'We will have the stuff on Wednesday.'

That was three days from now. And three days to D-day.

'All four Glock 17s?'

'All four Glock 17s.' Mark nodded. 'Ammo and spare clips.'

'You think he is reliable?'

'He won't let us down,' Mark reassured her. 'Not for the kind of money the bastard is charging us. If he started double-crossing his customers, I don't think he'd last long in this business.'

Parked near the parking lot exit, Sanjeev Nanda was watching from the rear window of his Mercedes. He saw Mark walk over to an Innova and speak to someone inside, but he was unable to see who it was. It seemed to be a woman, but he was not sure.

He knew he had spotted an opportunity: a foreign mercenary looking for four deadly, high-capacity weapons which were hard to detect. The Commonwealth Games was around the corner and a dozen Pakistan-based terror groups had declared that they would not allow them to take place. The cops would pay through their nose for this one.

Nanda, lost in his thoughts, did not notice Mark walk away from the Innova and drive off. He was startled when he heard a loud tap on his window. Mark was staring at him hard. Nanda knew his suspicions had been aroused.

Powering down the window, Nanda conjured up an explanation. 'I am waiting for my driver.' Luckily, a few minutes back Nanda had sent him to buy a packet of cigarettes from a shop near the gate. Just then, the driver returned, got into the car and handed over a packet of Davidoff Lights to Nanda.

Grabbing the pack, Nanda snarled at him, 'Drive.'

Mark watched Nanda go. He had a feeling that things were not so kosher.

Ruby was still in the car after Mark left. With her reconnaissance complete and most of the preparatory work well under control, she wondered what to do next.

May as well get in some sightseeing. Who knew when she'd come to India again?

Will I even survive this mission? The thought halted her. She shrugged. *It does not matter if I don't. My life has no meaning. Not if the delegates survive and the Peace Summit succeeds... they'll slice up Palestine.*

Pushing the thought away, she bought herself an entry ticket to the Haat. She took the ticket and opened her wallet to keep the change back, failing to see a man approaching behind her. Arms closed in around her waist and her body automatically moved to counter the assault. She was about to raise her hands to break the hold when he spoke.

'Ruby Gill, I presume.' The familiar voice shocked her into stillness.

She spun around to find Chance Spillman's smiling face inches away. An overwhelming memory of the past took over her and something inside her snapped. She leaned forward and kissed him. For one brief moment she felt herself in another time, as their lips came together. The magic was back.

Then someone passing by giggled and the moment disintegrated. Reality returned.

'What on earth are you doing in India?' Chance released her. That tentativeness, that withholding, so frequent in the last few months that they had been together, returned. It stood between them once again.

But Ruby could not help smiling. She was thrilled to see Chance. Seeing the feeling mirrored on his face warmed her heart.

Looking at him, in dark blue jeans and a white linen shirt, with that cocky smile on his face, Ruby felt her knees go weak. She felt the urge to kiss him again. She might have done it, but just then Chance spoke.

'So? What on earth are you doing in India?' he repeated.

She remembered why and that Chance was also an MI6 agent.

How long has he been here? Has he seen me with Mark? That would be disastrous.

Chance knew Mark well. He also knew that Mark was now freelancing.

'What are *you* doing here?' she countered, struggling to regain her composure.

'Security for Sir Geoffrey Tang,' Chance replied, surprising her with the ease with which he divulged that. Ruby knew he tended to be pretty anal about security. The son of a senior SAS officer who had been killed in counter-terror operations in Ireland, Chance had a personal axe to grind with terrorists. Perhaps he was talking as one colleague to another.

Or perhaps he is as shaken by our meeting as I am.

The name struck a chord in Ruby's head; the name of every Summit delegate was imbedded in her. 'Tang is here?' she asked innocently. 'How is the cranky old bugger?'

Both laughed. Sir Tang had given Ruby hell when she rode shepherd on him during a state visit to

Pakistan. It had happened when she was living with Chance.

'Same old, same old.' Chance smiled.

'What's he doing here? A bit far from the House of Lords, is he not?'

'An important meeting… but mostly for the Games.' Chance's natural secretiveness had reasserted itself. 'So … what brings you here?'

'The Games.' Ruby eagerly grabbed at the excuse Chance had provided. 'And I just needed to get away for a bit.'

She studied him and decided it had been an innocent question. He stood with his head cocked slightly to the right, a smile dancing on his face, his bright blue eyes taking her in. The sight made her heart beat faster. It was that smile that had first ignited desire in her.

Ruby's mind flipped back to the first time they had met.

They had been working on putting down an Iranian spy ring which counter-intelligence had chanced upon during an audit of the British nuclear facilities. They'd identified four British scientists who were involved. A British-bred Iranian lawyer who operated out of Kensington had recruited them; he was obviously the spymaster. Chance and Ruby were part of the MI6 team keeping him under surveillance.

At first Chance had come across as a slick lady-killer type, the kind she detested. It took her a while to realize that he was anything but that. It was the delicious fajitas he bought for their third stakeout that broke the ice.

'Lovely,' Ruby said as she took another bite. 'Where did you buy these?'

'I didn't,' he replied between mouthfuls, his eyes still fixed on the spymaster's house. 'Made them myself.'

'Yeah, right.' Ruby laughed, then seeing that he was serious, changed tack. 'You cook very well.'

'Thanks.' He smiled. 'Never had an option, you see. Mum died when I was eight. So just dad and me,' he said, his attention still on the house. Ruby was surprised at the ease with which he opened up. 'And dad!' Chance laughed. 'He had a soldier's palate. He'd eat anything put in front of him. Not me… I couldn't handle the tripe he churned out, so I learnt to cook. No option.' He laughed softly at the memory.

They both focused on the fajitas. The silence was companionable. It lasted longer than the fajitas did.

It was during those long stakeouts that they had come to know and like each other. The more time they spent together the closer they became. Ruby certainly did, and he reciprocated. But both were also smart enough to know that office romances were frowned upon. Things would not have progressed if it hadn't been for the way that assignment had ended.

It so happened that the lawyer–spymaster had picked up on the surveillance – perhaps one of the agents had slipped up, or he was smarter than he seemed. But the lawyer made the mistake of calling up his controller before attempting to leave the country. Alerted that he was going to make a break for it, both the MI6 teams on watch were ordered to bring him in.

Chance and Ruby were watching the front of the house and neither expected the bugger to come out shooting, but he did.

They were approaching the front door, Chance a step ahead of her, when the spymaster flew out. Ruby saw him first, but by then he was almost upon them. She saw the gun in his hand and knew they were too late. It was up and levelled at Chance.

Ruby shouted and threw herself straight into the line of fire. The bullet hit her bullet-proof jacket. The Kevlar stopped the bullet, but fired at point-blank range, its high velocity impact pummelled her into the ground. Then a thunder of gunfire drowned out everything.

When she opened her eyes, Chance was standing above her, smoke curling out of the pistol in his hand. The lawyer lay dead a few feet away, two neat holes in his head.

It took Ruby a long time to realize that she was still alive. Chance could not look away from her. 'You jumped into the line of fire...' he said over and over again. He had not been wearing a body vest.

After hours of tedious paperwork, after-action reports and de-briefing, they were silent as he drove her home. When he stopped outside her apartment, she made no move to get out. They sat in silence for a while.

'May I come up?' Chance finally asked. There was a wild look in his eyes. His lips were slightly parted and his eyes shone with desire.

They stood beside each other as the elevator rode up, close but barely touching. The minute the door to her apartment closed, Chance's mouth found hers. It was a compelling, urgent, demanding kiss. Her lips parted as his tongue probed inside her mouth, and her arms enveloped him. She shivered as his hands slid down her back, caressing her buttock. He drew her closer.

Buttons and zippers gave way till there were no clothes left between them. Ruby felt his lips caress her neck, and then her breasts, pulling at her nipples, at first gently and then with urgency. His tongue made its way down her body, licking her below her breasts, in her navel, and then lower still. It inflamed her. Grabbing his hair, she pulled him up. 'Take me, now ...' Her voice was a strident, hoarse whisper.

He did. On the carpet, just a few feet from the door. Her breath came faster. Ruby moaned as a wonderful sensation ripped through her. His orgasm came a moment later.

A short while later they found each other again in the bedroom. And then, later, in the shower. Each time was more beautiful than the last.

Ruby's foray into the past shattered as Chance spoke again. 'Sorry, you were saying?'

'I said I can understand why you needed to get away. I heard about your mother when I got back from Kabul.' Chance's smile had vanished. 'I'm terribly sorry for your loss.' He reached out and touched her cheek gently. It overwhelmed Ruby.

'How are you coping?'

'Fine.' It came out as a choked whisper. Ruby was fighting to stem her tears. Without warning, the secret agent was overwhelmed by the woman inside.

'Is there anything I can do? If there is, you know you have only to ask.' His imploring face conveyed his sincerity. Ruby knew he meant every word.

She shook her head, unwilling to trust her voice. She could feel her mind starting to torque away and fought to control it. 'I needed to get away,' she whispered again. Slowly, the avenging warrior within began to regain control. The fragile thread lay broken again.

'I understand.' Chance, at a loss for words, was searching for something to say. 'Did you finally meet your father? I remember you telling me he was from India.'

'No, I haven't met him yet.'

'Why not?'

'I don't know. I have to. That is another reason I chose to come to India. But...' Ruby improvised, 'I am working up the courage to meet him.'

'You? Working up courage? Since when?' Chance could not hide his amusement. 'The Ruby I know would just pick up the phone and call him.'

The Ruby you know... you knew... Ruby held that thought at bay. Instead she forced a sheepish smile. 'I will call him tomorrow.'

'Great!' He smiled. 'Speaking of calling people, this is my hotel number.' He scribbled it on the ticket stub in her hand. 'You must call me. Don't hesitate if there is anything I can do.' She felt a touch of awkwardness as he paused, as though he had run out of words. 'There is something I...'

'There you are!' Jennifer interrupted Chance, as she walked up to him.

Ruby felt a spasm of irritation and then surprise as she took a close look at the newcomer. She got the eerie feeling that she was looking into a mirror.

Barring the newcomer's fair complexion and auburn hair, her resemblance to Ruby was uncanny. The woman even wore her hair the same way – pulled back in a high pony.

Then Ruby saw the smile on Chance's face and felt a pang of jealousy. The smile on the newcomer's face disappeared as the two women assessed each other and within seconds their instincts confirmed that they were rivals.

'Ruby, this is Jennifer... Jennifer Poetzcsh.' Immune to the subtle exchange of womanly vibes, Chance turned to Ruby and introduced her. 'Jennifer, this is my friend and colleague Ruby Gill.'

The two women shook hands warily. 'Jennifer is with our cousins,' Chance added, making it clear she was CIA.

'Ruby Gill,' Jennifer murmured with a tight smile. 'You are the second Gill I've met since I got here.'

'Yeah! You are right!' Chance laughed. 'Funny, isn't it?' He turned to Ruby. 'The guy from Delhi Police who is helping us with the conference is also called Gill... Ravinder Singh Gill.'

Ruby froze. The name hit her instantly. On the rare occasions that her mother had spoken about him, she had mentioned that Ruby's father was in the Indian Police Service, but Ruby had never imagined that he'd be the one to... *There couldn't be many people with that exact same name, could there?*

Ruby realized that Chance and Jennifer were staring at her, waiting for her to respond. 'What a funny coincidence,' she blurted out.

'Mr Gill mentioned that he'd been in London

in college with Sir Edward, so I know he lived there for a bit,' Chance added. 'Wonder if you two are related?'

Ruby had recovered by now. 'I guess all Gills are? That is what my mom used to say!'

An awkward silence now fell upon them. Just minutes ago, Chance had shared an intimate moment with her. Or had she imagined it? *Had it just been concern for a colleague… an old flame?* She was no longer sure.

'Hey,' Chance intruded again, 'we were planning to spend some time here. I believe it's a great place. You feel like joining us?'

Ruby almost laughed as she saw the expression on Jennifer's face.

Just to spite Jennifer, she felt the urge to agree, but realizing the danger of prolonged contact, she declined. 'You guys please go ahead.'

'Why don't I get the tickets while you two…' Jennifer walked off towards the ticket counter.

'She is a very nice person,' Chance said as he watched her go.

'Is she now?' Ruby murmured, her jealousy getting the better of her. 'Trying Pepsi instead of Coke, are we?'

He gave her a puzzled look but before he could say anything Ruby reached up, pecked him on the cheek and walked away, half regretting the remark.

'Even if he is annoyed, damned if I care,' Ruby muttered, her head reeling. She was still grappling with the fact that Chance had left her... just like her father had left her mother... *and her.*

'Men!' she growled as she got into her car and told the driver to take her back to the hotel.

Chance watched her walk away. He had never been able to figure Ruby out, to understand why she had always held a part of herself aloof from him... from them.

He felt angry at the Coke–Pepsi jibe.

Am I attracted to Jennifer only because she resembles Ruby?

He toyed with the idea of going after her but remembered what he'd heard on the agency grapevine, about her nervous breakdown when her mother had died, and realized that he should cut her some slack. He knew she'd been close to her mother. Even when they lived together, she and her mother would talk, if not meet, almost every day.

'I got them.' Jennifer returned, holding up two tickets. 'Let's go.' She reached out and took his arm as if claiming what was rightfully hers.

Chance was more than a little distracted as he took Jennifer's arm and they entered the Haat.

Jennifer looked up at him and smiled. And Chance was struck by her similarity to Ruby.

'It's hot.' Jennifer fanned herself. 'And I'm thirsty. Would you like some Coke?'

Chance was unable to enjoy the afternoon, consumed as he was by thoughts of Ruby. A part of him hoped she would call. Another part hoped he would never see her again.

Once their initial burst of lust had subsided and the reality of sustaining a relationship had sunk in, Chance had realized that Ruby was always holding back a part of herself.

But the fact that she had saved his life had kept him from walking away. Which is why he had been so relieved when the agency sent him to Afghanistan. They had slowly but steadily drifted apart. Things had ended but there was no closure.

And Chance had been on the verge of bringing it up when Jennifer had walked up to them.

Ruby paced her hotel room, conflicting emotions churning through her. Finally, she sat by the window, the mess of thoughts in her head as chaotic as the traffic on the road running past her window.

Think different! The massive billboard advertisement across the road caught her eye.

Just do it! The equally massive Nike advertisement next to it exhorted her.

Out of the blue, things clicked.

Ruby now knew that to get to the Summit delegates she would have to fight her way past her father and the man she had loved.

They abandoned me.

If one of them stood in her way, would she pull the trigger?

The question frightened her.

Would I have taken on this mission had I known that my father was the one... or did I come to India subconsciously hoping I'd run into him?

The pain of not having an answer to these questions grew almost physical. She let out a low, petrified cry for help.

Think different! Her eyes were pinned to the billboard. And her thoughts continued to clash unchecked.

By late afternoon these worrisome questions had coalesced into a pounding headache. Pangs of nausea began to wrack her. She was exhausted by the time she lay down. Sleep came almost instantly. So did the nightmare.

The man who had been haunting her dreams was still faceless. He had blood running down his face. Suddenly, Chance emerged from behind him. He, too, had blood on his face, oozing out from a neat, round black hole between his eyes.

'Why haven't you spoken to your father yet? Just pick up the phone and call him,' he was saying, over and over, his voice a broken whisper. He sounded like

Chance but different. 'Why are you hesitating? Don't you want to know how he is, what kind of a man he is, why he left your mother... and you?' His tone was sharp and insistent.

Ruby awoke with a start. Her heart was pounding and she was bathed in sweat. She reached for the water bottle on her bedside table and took a long swig, draining it. Still thirsty, she got up and pulled another bottle out of the minibar and drank that too.

She lay down again, but this time sleep was driven away by a new need to find out about her father. To understand who he really was. For so many years, she had taught herself not to think about him. She had convinced herself to hate him. But now she knew she could not live without knowing any longer.

Why? Why did you leave? What did I do to grow up without a father?

The room was pitch dark. Though the curtains were drawn back, not even a speck of light filtered in. The darkness outside felt as deep as the darkness within her. She longed to reach out and talk to someone. Anyone. But who? Chance?

Her hand reached for the phone. But she stayed it. *No.* She did not need the aggravation of feeling her way through whatever still existed between them... *if* anything still did.

He's met my father... He'll know what kind of a person he is.

What about my father? He *was* her father after all. Ruby dwelt on that for a long time.

But he abandoned us. Not even once, over all these years, did he bother to check on me... come looking for me... hug me... hold me... talk to me... to find out if I was alive.

Ruby felt confusion, hurt and resentment building up. She fought them; damned if she would allow herself to cry over a father who did not even care whether she was alive or dead.

Did he? Her mind was playing tag with her again, as it often did when she was upset. *Did he really not care?*

She gave up trying to sleep. She *needed* to talk to someone. Scrabbling through her bag, she retrieved the ticket stub with Chance's number.

She hoped Chance would be happy to hear from her.

The phone at the other end began to ring.

Chance had just entered the bathroom and unzipped when the phone began to ring. He called out to Jennifer, who had joined him for a nightcap after another exhausting day of sightseeing. 'Could you get that, please?'

'Sure,' Jennifer called out, reaching for the phone.

'Hullo.' Ruby had heard it only once before, but she immediately recognized the nasal twang. 'Hullo,' Jennifer said again.

Ruby almost spoke. She would have, but her eye fell on her wristwatch. It was past midnight.

Chance has moved on.

She cut the call and returned to her lonely, restless vigil by the window.

He has left me too.

Tears pricked at her eyes. With an effort she pushed them away.

'So, what's new? Men do that all the time,' Ruby said out loud, as though she needed to hear it to believe it. Her father had done that to her mother. Chance was no different.

Then she cried and cried, till she could cry no more.

She felt angry with Rehana. Why had she always avoided talking about her father, about what had happened between them?

Ruby remembered asking her often when she was young, 'Where is daddy? How come he never comes home... or goes to my school, like other fathers?'

'How do I explain to you, my darling? You're too young to understand.'

But Ruby was always old enough to know that her father was not there for her. She remembered the nights she had cried herself to sleep, as she longed for her father to hold her and protect her. The pain had been so intense, so hurtful, that she had tried to stop thinking about him.

That pain now returned. Even after all these years, it was still sharp. Perhaps sharper, since it had been ignored and suppressed so long.

And now you have left me too, mom.

As Ruby hit the end of her tether, Rehana reached out from beyond and pulled her out of the abyss.

'Did I not always tell you, my child?' Ruby heard the constant rejoinder echo in her head. 'Chance will never understand. Just as your father never did. No one will... our cause is our own... that is the way it has always been. Nothing will ever get better, not unless we fight for it. *They* will not allow it to.' She would thumb towards Chance's photo on Ruby's bedside table. 'Men like him. They are the ones who killed our family... who have been killing our people all these years. It was these bloody Brits who started it all. If not for their support, the Jews would never have had the guts. I am telling you, Chance will use you and dump you... just as your father did to me. Remember that.'

The words seemed prophetic now.

A clap of thunder boomed out. Lightning lacerated the sky, intermittently lighting up the road outside.

Just do it! The Nike advertisement tugged at her.

And just like that, it all became clear to Ruby.

I will show you... all of you... The transition from

confused woman to committed freedom-fighter was swift.

Large drops of rain began to hammer on the windowpanes. The drumming sound eventually dulled her into a deep sleep.

'Why didn't you tell me, sir?' Mohite asked, peeved.

'About what, Mohite?' Though it was past midnight, Ravinder spoke patiently.

'About the Israeli commando team that has reached Delhi and is now on its way to Amritsar.'

'Who told you?' Ravinder asked, even though he already knew.

'I had gone to meet Thakur sahib and he mentioned it.'

'You didn't need to know, Govind.' Ravinder hardened his tone, just enough to let Mohite know who was in charge.

'Foreign agents are running around all over our country with guns and I don't need to know? Thakur sahib thought it fit to let me know.'

'Then from now on, I suggest you ask him to keep you informed!' Ravinder slammed down the phone.

Day Five

Dawn was lighting up the horizon when Ruby woke up. The rain had stopped but the sky was overcast. A stubborn sun struggled to make its presence felt.

Her eyes strayed to her wristwatch.

Five days left for the Summit.

Suddenly she was bursting with energy, as though the night's rain had washed away her confusions. She thrust herself out of bed. She knew what she needed to do.

The foul aftertaste of last night's conversation with Mohite was still in his mouth when Ravinder heard his mobile ring. He was in no mood to talk with that arsehole again... not first thing in the morning, at least. He checked the calling number. It was an unknown.

'Good morning, Mr Gill.' It was Ido Peled. 'We have heard from one of our sources in Pakistan that Saeed

Anwar is going to be at a safehouse near Lahore. Our director asked me to let you know that we would like to send our team in now.'

'Be my guest, Ido. I'll put out the word.' Ravinder suddenly felt lighter. 'And all the best.'

'Thank you, sir.' Peled rang off.

I hope they get the bastard... dead or alive... one less problem for us to deal with. The phone rang again. This time he picked it up eagerly.

The conversation with Sanjeev Nanda was brief. Ravinder knew that if Nanda said they needed to meet, it was important.

'Delhi Gymkhana,' he told the driver as he settled into the official Scorpio SUV. The red light whirled as the car inched through traffic. Ravinder was not too fond of it. He winced as the driver blew the horn long and loud. Despite this, the drive took about thirty minutes.

'Whatever he has to offer, it better be good,' Ravinder muttered as he entered the club.

Nanda was at the corner table in the Gymkhana bar where they usually met. Ravinder had to smile as he took in Nanda's snazzy Armani suit, the gold Rolex and his diamond embedded tie clip. *He has definitely changed,* Ravinder reflected. *Who says crime doesn't pay?*

He remembered the first time they had met.

Ravinder was in Narcotics. All of five weeks in the

department, totally green behind the ears, but full of energy. Nanda was the first croak he had ever turned.

They nabbed a Nigerian drug peddler with two kilos of cocaine but Ravinder decided to take a gamble and let him go. In the subsequent weeks, the Nigerian led them to ten others selling the stuff. Eager to take down the kingpins, Ravinder had them all put under surveillance. They led him to Sanjeev Nanda, who was caught with enough coke to lock him up for a very, very long time. Ravinder then took another risk. His intuition told him that Nanda was not the big man and that he was weasel enough to shop the main guy to save his own hide.

'You will not peddle again,' Ravinder warned as they cut the deal. 'If I ever come to know that you are, all bets are off.'

'Never, sir.' Nanda had crossed his heart theatrically. 'I swear on my mother's soul.'

Nanda's patently false sincerity made Ravinder sorry for his mother's soul.

'What else do you have to offer?'

'You tell me, sir,' Nanda said smugly, assuming the cop was expecting a bribe.

'I want you to keep your eyes open and an ear to the ground,' Ravinder said, surprising him. A clean cop was a rarity. And honesty was certainly not a career enhancing attribute, not in this profession. 'Whenever you come across something big, I want to know.'

Nanda felt uncertain. If the others ever found out that he was a snitch, he would have a short life and a most unpleasant end.

Ravinder sensed his fear. 'This will remain strictly between you and me. No one else needs to know... ever.' Nanda looked a little calmer. 'And you will be paid. I will ensure that.'

That had sealed the deal. And so, every now and then, Nanda called Ravinder. Every meeting had proved to be worthwhile for both. Nanda enhanced his riches and Ravinder acquired the reputation of a ferocious crime-buster.

'You are looking well, sir.' Nanda stood up and offered his hand.

'Not as well as you, my friend. Certainly not as well as you.' Throwing a quick look around, Ravinder sat down opposite him. 'So, what do you have for me today?'

'Straight to business as usual, sir. You haven't changed a bit. A cup of tea or coffee first?'

'Not today, Sanjeev. Tell me... what's up?'

Ravinder's face was sombre as he listened to Nanda's narrative. And his excitement escalated. *Could this be the big attack that Jennifer had mentioned?*

'There are two of them?' he said finally.

'Yes, sir. Mark, the Irish guy who got in touch with me, and then the second one he went and met with right after that – a woman, I think, but I cannot be sure. The car windows had dark film on them.'

'Anything else you can tell me? Which car she was in, the registration number?'

'Sorry, sir.' Nanda gave a sheepish smile. 'I was too far away, but it was a cream-coloured Toyota Innova.'

Ravinder couldn't mask his disappointment. There were thousands of those in Delhi.

'This guy, Mark? What's his full name? Where is he staying?'

'I don't know, sir.' Another sheepish smile. 'I've dealt with him just once before... a while ago... it was a small, cash-and-carry deal... so...' He shrugged.

'But you're sure that's his real name?'

'Well...' Nanda pulled a dubious moue. 'Not really. But that's what he called himself when we met.'

'When are you handing over the guns?'

'Day after. Wednesday.'

'Where?'

'He said he'd call me.'

'You have the number he calls you from?'

'I did check on that. He used a public phone both times.'

'The same one?'

'No. Different both times – from different parts of the city.'

Ravinder nodded, disappointed but not surprised. It had been a long shot. 'Fine. Call me as soon as he gets in touch with you.'

Nanda hesitated. 'Sir, I am going to make the delivery personally... I hope your people will be careful when they...' He trailed off.

'Don't worry. I will oversee the assignment myself.'

Ravinder was feeling elated, yet a trifle anxious as he headed back to his office. This could be the break he had been hoping for. He only wished he could be sure what their target was – the Games or the Summit?

Oh, well. Ravinder shrugged. Even this was heaven-sent. He knew that Thakur, keen to show the PM he was doing well at his new assignment, would be thrilled when they caught the terrorists. He called Mohite and brought him up to speed.

'Could this be what that CIA woman Jennifer was talking about? She said the Lashkar had hired British mercs to strike Delhi.'

'They may well be the same... though she said British and this Mark guy is Irish.'

'Yeah, yeah. British, Irish, what's the difference? These firangis are all the same.'

'Never mind, Govind.' Ravinder sighed.

'This is fantastic!' Mohite was excited. 'Thakur sahib will be very pleased.'

'Yes, but keep this under your hat for now. Let's only talk to him about it once we nab them.'

'I agree. Like a surprise gift.'

'Yeah, like a surprise gift.' Ravinder tried to contain his sarcasm. 'Have a team on standby from tomorrow night. They should be ready to move at short notice. I will go with them. And you will accompany me.'

He got out of the car as it halted outside his office.

The sun had vanished again. The sky was the colour of concrete. Growls of thunder were making their presence felt.

'There is someone here to meet you, sir,' Gyan said sheepishly as he waited for Ravinder at his office door. 'I tried to tell her that she could not meet you without an appointment, but she insisted. She said she is...'

'Who is it?' Ravinder frowned as he pushed open the door. Then he came to a dead stop.

'Oh my God! *Ruby*.' The stunned whisper was a half-question. 'You look just like your mother.'

'Yes, father, that is what everyone says.'

There was a tense silence as the two strangers stood looking at each other.

'You used to call me daddy... always.' Ravinder's voice was a strangled whisper.

'I know. And you called me princess. But then you left us.' Ruby couldn't conceal her bitterness.

Her words stabbed him like a hot knife.

He took a step towards Ruby; he was aching to embrace her. 'No! I didn't.' He halted, uncertain.

'All these years...' Her voice shook. 'I waited for you to come looking.' She could feel tears begin to build. The crafty, focused fighter who had planned this visit was furious for displaying the slightest hint of emotion.

Reining in her tears, she began again. 'Every morning I would wake up and hope you would come back. Every day, I would come out from school and hope to see you there. Every night I used to pray...' She started to cry.

'Ruby, I did look for you, but...' Ravinder could not go on, nor could he stem the tears that had begun to trickle down. He realized that Gyan was still standing behind him and wanted him gone. Without turning, he said, 'Gyan, get us some tea.'

He walked up to Ruby, but instead of embracing her as he was aching to do, he took her by the arm and said, 'Come... please sit down.'

Ruby felt a rush of emotion. Despite all her planning, the warrior and the woman, both had been blown off their feet.

Her eyes fell on two mahogany photo frames placed on Ravinder's desk. One photo had Ravinder posing next to a regal looking woman, a pretty teenage girl between them. The one on the right caught Ruby's attention.

A little girl in a pink frock was standing on a chair, smiling, a huge three-tier cake with a princess on top placed in front of her. The princess too was in a pink frock.

It was the same photo she had forced her mother to have enlarged. And the only one Ruby had ever hung on her bedroom wall.

Ravinder followed her glance. 'That was on your third birthday,' he said softly.

'I know. I remember. That was the last one all three of us spent together.' She looked away. 'Then you left. Just two weeks before my fourth...' Her voice broke.

'No, princess, I did not leave.' Ravinder's voice choked. 'I don't know what your mother told you, but it was not I who left.'

'No one told me anything. And today you can say anything you want, there is no one left to tell the other side of the story.'

'Ruby, you must believe...' Ravinder broke off when he realized what Ruby had said. 'What? What did you say?' He paused, suddenly afraid. 'Where is Rehana?'

'She is not with us any more.'

'W-what happened?' He could barely speak.

'Does it matter?'

'Yes, it does!' Ravinder was shocked, but he could see how terribly she was hurting. He wanted to hold her tight... the way he had done when she was small. 'Ruby, I really, really loved her.'

His words struck Ruby like hammer blows. That wasn't what Rehana had told her.

'Rehana meant the world to me,' he repeated.

Just then Gyan entered with a tray. They sat in silence as he poured the tea and placed a plate of biscuits between them. The aroma of freshly brewed tea filled the room. Ravinder waited for him to leave.

'I hunted everywhere for both of you when Rehana left, but...' The phone rang. Ravinder felt a surge of irritation, and then remembered they were in his office. He gave Ruby an apologetic look and took the call.

'We cannot talk here,' he said to Ruby when he had finished. 'There will always be something or the other interrupting us.' He thought for a moment. 'Tell me, where are you staying?'

'At the Hyatt Regency.'

'Not any longer.' Ravinder had made up his mind. 'You're coming home to stay with me – with us.'

'Are you sure?' Ruby asked, looking at the family photograph on his table.

He nodded. 'That is my wife Simran and my daughter Jasmine.' He paused. 'I remarried a few years after Rehana sent me the divorce documents and... that was the last I heard from your mother.' The pause this time was longer and more awkward. 'It will be okay with them.'

'Okay.' Ruby felt a flash of triumph run through her – she was in.

'Okay, then.' Ravinder scribbled his address and handed it to her. 'When should I expect you?'

Ruby looked at her watch. 'Would it be okay if I get there by about five?'

'That will be perfect.'

He followed Ruby to the door. She was almost out when his voice stopped her.

'Ruby, there is a lot unsaid between us,' he began hesitantly. 'I do not know what Rehana told you about what happened between us. No matter what you believe, I want you to know this – I loved you then, Ruby, more than you can imagine, and I love you now. I am grateful God has given us this chance to be together again. And I will do my best to make things right. I do not want this opportunity to pass… not without giving it my best shot.' He broke eye contact, feeling wetness creep into his eyes. 'But I don't know where to start, Ruby… will you help me? Please?'

Ruby could not speak, her throat was choked with emotion. A part of her knew that this man standing before her, the father she had once loved and doted on, meant every word he was saying. 'I don't know either, father… I am not sure if I am big enough to forget… or forgive.' She drew a deep breath. 'But I will try.' The double agent had no idea when the girl within slipped those words past her.

Then Ruby was gone, leaving Ravinder in a whirlpool of emotions – happy, but also uncertain. He took a couple of minutes to gather himself before heading for his car.

He was opening the door to get in when Gyan came running out. 'Sir, there's an urgent call for you. Minister sahib wants to talk to you immediately.'

'What is this I am hearing, Gill?' Thakur sounded in a foul mood. "The American and British agents are complaining that they are not getting enough cooperation from your people.'

'I am afraid I have heard nothing about this, sir, but I will look into it right away.'

'How come you don't know what's going on in your department? Mohite knows. He was just telling me about it.'

Damn that son of a bitch. 'Don't worry, sir. I will take care of the problem.'

'How can I not worry? You don't seem to understand how important this Peace Summit is for me... for India. The whole world will be watching. This is our chance to...' Ravinder tuned out as Thakur took off. He was waiting patiently for the call to end when something Thakur was saying caught his attention.

'... it is very important that we capture these terrorists alive. Mohite was telling me they could be the key to a much larger operation. Have we found out anything else about them?'

Realizing that Mohite had blabbed about the tip Nanda had given him, despite having been told to keep it under wraps, Ravinder decided it was time to put Mohite on the firing line. He'd keep him so busy that the idiot would have no time for squealing to the minister behind his back. 'Not yet, sir, but we are working on it. In fact, since we all know how critical it is, I am putting Mohite in charge of this operation.'

'Good idea, Gill. We should allow Govind to live up to his potential.' Thakur sounded pleased. 'That man has promise. He will go places.'

Yeah, sure! Ravinder grimaced. Especially with you watching out for him.

Ravinder headed back to his car. He needed to talk to Simran before Ruby reached home. It was not a conversation he was looking forward to, but it had to be done. He wished all this was not happening right now. Not when he needed to focus on the Summit and the Games. *But...* he shrugged fatalistically... *things happen when they are meant to.*

There was a loud thunderclap and it began to rain. Soon a thick curtain of rain enveloped the car, making it even harder to see things clearly.

When Ravinder walked in, the house was in an uproar. The maids, the gardener and the driver were running around with buckets and mops. Standing in the centre of the living room, Simran was busy supervising.

'What happened?'

'What else?' Simran replied with an exasperated cluck. 'These damn government houses! Some new problem every day.' She paused to instruct a maid before turning to him. 'Now the upstairs bathroom drain has choked. We have water seeping into the kitchen from every corner.'

Ravinder opened his mouth to suggest something when he realized he was out of his depth with this one. 'Should I have someone from my office look into it?' he finally asked.

'What for? They'll take forever to respond and by then my kitchen will be a total mess.' Simran was miffed. Ravinder sensed that there was something else bothering her too. 'And by the time they fix it, something else will break down. Why can't we stay in our own house instead of this dump?' She was referring to the luxurious farmhouse in Chhattarpur that Ravinder had inherited. 'It is lying empty as it is... such a waste.'

'Simran, we have had this discussion.' Of course they had. Many times. But despite his best efforts, he had been unable to make her understand that it would not sit well with the powers-that-be, for him to be living in such an ostentatious place. Not to mention that the remote farmhouse would be much harder to secure... something he needed to worry about with those two Jaish-e-Mohammed lunatics still on the loose.

'The Sharmas have no problem,' Simran sniffed,

referring to his colleague who headed Delhi Traffic. '*They* are happily staying in his wife's grand family home.'

'What they do is their call,' he pointed out patiently. 'In any case, their house is in Model Town, literally a stone's throw away from his office.'

'Yeah, yeah! I know! *We* are always the special ones... we can never do anything normal.' Simran's anger was simmering. 'I can never understand why you had to opt for the police when you had the option to join the Foreign Service.'

Ravinder sighed. He had no response that would mollify her. Anything he said would only prolong the argument. Even after twenty-four years of marriage, she had not stopped griping about his career choice.

He understood where she came from. Born into a Punjabi royal family, one not very different from his, she had expected to go on living as she had been used to, even after marriage. In those days it was considered prestigious to marry a civil servant. He remembered her fury when he, despite having topped his course, had chosen to opt for the police rather than the more glamorous foreign service. He knew that Simran would have called off the marriage if not for the ignominy that would have led to. There was, of course, also the fact that there were not too many men from a royal lineage available any more.

Despite all this he *did* love her, but there was always a gap between them they had never been able to bridge.

They were different people with different beliefs and ideas… and somewhere, somehow, Rehana had always managed to stray between them.

They had married when he had returned from London. His parents, especially his mother, had forced him to come back when she heard he had married a Palestinian girl.

He would never have returned if Rehana had not vanished, taking his darling Ruby with him. It had driven him to the edge. He had run around like a madman through the streets of Birmingham and London, chasing down every possible lead, but Rehana had disappeared, as though the earth had swallowed her up. He finally gave up and returned home to India.

Even today, Ravinder was not sure what had hurt more, the fact that Rehana had left him or the fact that she had left without explaining why. Later, he realized that in the weeks before she left, she had been moody and withdrawn.

No. Rehana had always withheld a part of herself from me… from our marriage.

'Even if you had to join the police, why couldn't you manage your postings the way others do?' Simran's voice intruded on his memory. 'Four years in the faraway hills of Nagaland with not one decent shop for miles around and… and…' Spluttering, she waved an angry hand. 'Now finally we get to Delhi and you agree to take over the Anti-Terrorist Task

Force. Couldn't you have tried for an easier job? With a normal life?'

'I didn't ask for it, Simran, you know that. When Menon died, they had to move fast with the Games and all happening, there was no time to waste.'

'And of course you were the only one they could find. No one else was good enough... or silly enough...'

'Simran.' Choking off a retort, Ravinder waved his hand placatingly, trying to calm her. 'Could you please stop? I need to talk to you about something urgent. Will you please listen to me for a moment?'

'What can be more important than this?' she said, but gestured to the servants to leave the room. 'What is it?'

Ravinder did not know where to start. He had tried to think of a way on his drive back, but hadn't found one. He decided to go it straight.

'Do you remember me telling you about Ruby? My daughter from...'

'From *that* woman.' She hated for this topic to be brought up even after all these years. 'Yes. What about her?'

'*That* woman is dead,' Ravinder said softly.

'Oh,' she said, her face inscrutable.

'Ruby is here in India.'

Simran blanched. 'Why has she come here?' She suddenly sat down. But ramrod straight, on the sofa's edge, as though on guard.

'To see me, I guess.'

'To see you or to lay claim to your property?'

'Simran,' Ravinder was irritated, but he had to retain his cool or this could all blow out of proportion. 'The girl has just lost her mother. Is that not reason enough for her to want to meet her only surviving parent? Please… let us give her a break.'

'How do you know?' Simran pushed back an errant hair which had come loose and fallen on her face. *A very un-Simran-like gesture*. Ravinder could tell she was nervous. 'You are so gullible. You believe everything everyone tells you,' she continued.

'She has not said anything to me about property. She just came to the office to see me, that is all. I invited her to come and stay with us.'

'You invited her to come and stay with us?' Simran enunciated each word clearly. 'Here? At *our* home?' Her tone spiralled upwards, almost out of control. '*Are you crazy?* Do you know what will happen to our chances of getting a decent match for Jasmine if people come to know?'

Ravinder had to let her vent for a while. When she halted to draw a breath he spoke again, his tone even and non-confrontational, yet firm. 'You must understand that she is also my daughter. I cannot – *will not* – ignore her.'

Simran could hear the steel in his voice. It emerged rarely. 'How long will she stay?' she asked in a resigned tone.

'For a few days, I think.' Ravinder saw her collapse into the sofa. He drew a deep breath. The battle was over, but he felt no satisfaction. Her anguish saddened him. 'I did not get much of a chance to speak to her, but I guess it will be for a few days only.'

'What will we tell Jasmine?'

'Jasmine knows I was married earlier, Simran.'

'Yes, but knowing something and having it shoved in your face like this are two different things.'

Simran was on the edge of tears, as her carefully constructed world began to crumble. But she held herself together.

Ravinder's heart went out to her. When he spoke again, it was gently. 'I agree, but I trust Jasmine enough to know that she will handle it maturely.' He reached out and took Simran's hand.

'So you say.' Simran freed her hand and put it back in her lap. She kept looking down at her hands, as though something precious had trickled out from between her splayed fingers. A moment later, her fingers closed into tightly clenched fists, the knuckles white with tension.

Ravinder did not reply. There was nothing else he could say to make it easier for her.

'When is that girl coming here?'

'Ruby will be here,' Ravinder checked his watch, 'in another hour.'

'Today?'

Ravinder nodded.

Simran gave him a long look. 'Fine,' she muttered through clenched teeth. 'But promise me that you will not mention this to anyone else.'

He nodded again, knowing that the views of society, especially of their relatives, mattered a lot to Simran.

'Let me get the guest bedroom ready.' Simran got up. 'But I am not going to sit around chatting with her, be clear on that. Keep that girl out of my way.'

Ravinder sighed.

Now Jasmine.

He steeled himself. Knowing that Jasmine was due to return from college soon, he got up and went into the garden, hoping that she would come before Ruby did.

Throwing another look at his watch, he began to pace the garden. His body needed to be in motion. His mind needed rest.

Ruby got to work the minute she got back to her hotel room. First she called Mark. She had been dying to call him from her mobile while in the car, but did not want the driver listening in.

'How's it going?' Mark sounded upbeat. India seemed to be suiting him.

'It's going well. Listen carefully now. I am checking out of here in a couple of hours. I will be staying with...

at a friend's place... not far from here. Make sure you don't call me. I will call you.'

'What if there is an emergency?'

'Send me a text... something personal... like asking me out on a date or something.'

'I like that!' Mark laughed.

'Yeah, right, but don't get too excited,' Ruby could not help chuckling. 'I'm a woman, remember?'

'Pity. What a man you'd have made.' He laughed.

'Have you got hold of the team?'

'Yep. All three will be here tomorrow night. The Aussies at Maurya Sheraton and the German at Taj Mansingh. All booked.'

'That's perfect.' She noted down their room numbers. 'They'll have enough time for a thorough recon then.'

'Yes... umm... they asked about the payment.'

'It will be waiting when they get here,' Ruby replied, making a mental note to call one of the financiers Pasha had informed her about. 'When is the stuff from Chennai due to reach?'

'I spoke to the transport guy. He said it's en route... by tomorrow for sure.'

'Fine, then we're on schedule.' Ruby felt satisfied. 'Now you have to let me know when and where we meet your man.'

'I'm still thinking about the venue.' Mark hesitated,

unsure whether he should share his misgivings about Nanda.

But Ruby picked up on them. 'What is it?' she probed. Mark told her what had happened after the meeting with Nanda.

'I don't know what exactly he was up to, but I have a bad feeling...' He broke off. 'Well, maybe not bad, but I don't have a good feeling about this bugger now.'

Ruby understood. It was something all operatives encountered every so often in the field. She had found it was always a good idea to trust this feeling. 'I hear you, Mark,' Ruby empathized. 'And I agree... we need to be careful.'

'That's why I've got to ensure it's a safe place.'

'What do you have in mind?'

'Nothing yet, but I am going to recon a couple of places today. Public parks, monuments... that kind of thing.'

'Good idea. Let me know.' She was about to end the call when it hit her. 'Does he know where you're staying?'

'Are you kidding me? He doesn't even know my full name. Just Mark.'

'Well, as long as he doesn't treat you like one, we're good.'

It was almost four by the time she checked out and headed for Ravinder's house.

Colourful banners dotted the roads and huge billboards with advertisements and Bollywood stars added to the frenzy of a city preparing to host the Commonwealth Games the coming Monday. With Diwali also around the corner, the madness was complete. But Ruby hardly noticed any of it. The stress of how Ravinder's family would react to her mounted as the car nosed its way through the crazy traffic.

Ravinder was pacing the garden when a Toyota Innova halted outside the black gates. One of the security guards went out to check while the other two covered him, their weapons at the ready. Ravinder was pleased that they were alert. Mohite was obviously ensuring that the duty officer briefed them daily.

The rear window of the car slid down and Ruby's face emerged. She was about to say something to the guard when Ravinder called out, waving at the guards to allow her in.

The gates swung back and the car drove in.

She immediately spotted the harried look on Ravinder's face and felt a wave of morbid satisfaction. She had no intention of being taken in by his tall tales now, with Rehana no longer around to tell her side of the story. Yet, a part of her felt his pain. And Ruby again regretted that Rehana had never spoken to her about what really happened between them.

'Take the luggage to the guest room and then get us some tea,' Ravinder told the servant as he held the door open for Ruby. 'Come, let us sit in the garden for a while… it's a lovely day.'

Ruby looked around – it certainly was. The rain had melted away and the sun, now on its way down, bathed the garden in a red glow. Rows of colour-coordinated flowers bordered the neatly tonsured grass, separating it from the high yellow brick boundary wall that ringed the house. The grass was still wet with rain.

On one side of the garden was an old banyan tree, its leafy branches providing an umbrella-like shade. Under it was a wrought-iron garden table, with matching iron chairs with bright cushions and an ornate garden swing to one side. At the far end, she could see an aluminium ladder with a pair of garden shears balanced on the top step. The gardener who must have been using them was nowhere in sight.

Despite the road being only a few metres away, the bungalow was enveloped in a peaceful silence, broken only by the occasional car driving past. A tranquil picture, in contrast with the turmoil gripping most people here.

Ruby followed Ravinder to the garden table. Then skirting past it, she went to the garden swing and sat facing him.

Before either of them could speak, a servant came out with the tea.

An elaborate silver service was placed in front of them. Along with it came some delicately cut cheese and cucumber sandwiches, an assortment of biscuits and some walnut cake. Simran had ensured everything was just right. Ravinder could see her peering out from the dining room window, curious to see Ruby, but too proud – or insecure – to come out.

Ruby was slowly rocking the swing back and forth. She finally broke the silence.

'Will you tell me what happened, Father? Back then?'

'It's a long story.'

'I have waited a long time.' Her bitterness reached out to him.

Despite his fears and her anger, he mustered the courage and sat down on the swing beside her. A world of gentleness was in the hand that reached out and stroked her hair.

Ruby felt herself tearing up. The woman craved the contact, the warrior resented it. She blinked, trying to fight it off, but not quite managing. The woman fought back harder; the woman who wanted to know more about her past, the life she should have had, without an incomplete childhood, those untold bedtime stories, birthday parties, family picnics, and all those dreams that had been snatched away.

'Mom never spoke to me about all this... about what

happened between you two. I think I need to know... I deserve to know.'

From inside the house, the whistle of a pressure cooker sounded, clear as a bell in the silence between them. It subsided abruptly.

'Yes.' Ravinder looked away and nodded. 'Yes, you do.'

'So, why did you leave?'

The pressure cooker whistle exploded again.

'Is that what Rehana told you?'

Ruby pondered before she said, slowly, 'No, she never actually said that.' Ruby searched for the right words. 'But that is what she always implied.'

'I did not leave, Ruby.' His voice went soft. He felt bad having to discredit Rehana. 'Your mother did.'

She cringed away even though somewhere, deep inside, she instinctively knew he was telling the truth. *This had to be why Mom was always reluctant to talk about it.*

'Why?' she whispered. 'What happened between you two? And whatever it was, why did I have to pay the price?'

'You should not have had to pay the price. I am not sure what happened but I think the rift between us began when I came home one day and found her hosting a meeting of Palestinian activists; an unsavoury bunch. I knew that, sooner or later, they would get Rehana into trouble. She got worked up when I forbade her to have such people in our house again.'

Ravinder paused, feeling his way through the fog of distant memories and trying to recall that day.

'She did not say anything to me, and I did not even sense it then... but later... when I thought about everything, I realized that from that day something about her changed. She began to shut me out more and more. And then,' Ravinder was having trouble talking, 'one day I came home and found she was gone, and so were you. She had left me a note, which really said nothing.'

Ruby teared up as memories of that horrible day trickled back to her.

Rehana had bundled her out of the house right after Ravinder went out that morning. Two suitcases were already packed. Brushing aside Ruby's questions, they had gone straight to the airport. Ruby was excited by the surprise adventure, but later she began to tire. She soon wanted to go home, and she wanted her father.

'Why is daddy not with us?' The first few times she asked, Rehana had fobbed her off. Eventually, when Ruby did not stop, she lost her patience.

'He is not.'

'Why? I want him to tell me a story.'

'I will tell you a story if you stop crying.'

'No! Daddy always does that.'

'Well, he will not do that any more.'

Ruby could remember how much that had hurt.

'Though Rehana had been uneasy for some weeks, I had no idea she was so upset. I never actually came to know what had happened.'

They lapsed into silence. Neither knew where the conversation was headed, but both knew whatever it was, it needed to be out in the open now.

'Where did you guys go?' Ravinder asked.

Ruby was about to reply when she realized that she could not tell him that Rehana had taken her to Palestine. She sensed that it must have been the cause of her people that had made Rehana leave. She had always placed that far above everything else – *even me*.

'We moved so often... before we finally settled down in London,' Ruby said carefully. Rehana's love for her cause and the manner of her death were two facts that might well make Ravinder sit up and take notice – even question Ruby's sudden arrival here.

'Yes, I thought so,' he said, 'since the divorce papers were from a lawyer in London. I asked him several times where you two were but he refused to tell me anything. And all the letters I sent came back unopened.'

'You did not contest the divorce?' Ruby asked. But even as she spoke, the realization that Rehana had lied about all this dawned on her.

What else did she lie to me about?

'How do I explain to you what things were like for

me in those days, Ruby? With you two gone, I was devastated. And my parents were giving me hell. In fact, it was my mother who received the divorce documents. I was not at home, and she only told me about them after the court dates had passed and the divorce was a done deal.'

Ruby, relieved that the conversation had steered away from dangerous territory, changed the subject. 'How did the two of you meet?'

A slow smile lit up Ravinder's face. 'It started as one of those regular evenings,' he began, now hardly aware of his solitary audience. 'I was coming back from college and decided to go to a pub with some friends. We came out after a couple of beers and were strolling down the street when we heard a loud scream.'

Rehana was walking a couple of steps behind her aunt Zahira – more to avoid conversation than anything else, an arrangement which suited the aunt as well since she had yet to figure out a way to handle the high-strung Rehana.

Two muggers erupted out of an alley and faced Zahira and Rehana. One of them slashed the air menacingly with his knife.

'Give me your money, bitch!' he hissed.

The second one gave Zahira a hard shove, dropping her on the pavement, then threw himself on her and bit her gold ear bobs off. Zahira screamed as blood spurted out. The mugger went for her other ear when a volley of shouts rang out.

'Hey! What's going on here?'

They turned to see three young men rushing towards them. The muggers fled, vanishing into the gloom.

Moments later, a patrol car pulled up near the women.

'We need to get you to a hospital, ma'am,' the cop said after one look at Zahira's torn off ear lobe.

He was helping her to the patrol car when Rehana noticed one of the rescuers. In his twenties, he was dressed in jeans and a light wool jacket that set off his broad shoulders and contrasted with his navy blue turban. He was staring at her as though struck by lightning. Flustered, she gave him a brief, grateful smile.

That was all it took.

Ravinder gave a happy, mellow laugh. 'She was standing there with flushed cheeks and long, lush hair blown all over her face, still breathless and shaken. Then she looked at me and smiled.'

Ruby smiled.

'How can I explain to you what Rehana was like in those days, Ruby?' He gave her a long look. 'She was just like you. The same smile... just the same...one look and I was a goner.' He laughed again. Ruby could not help laughing with him.

'I am Ravinder,' he introduced himself to Rehana at the hospital. 'Ravinder Singh Gill,' he said in clean, pristine Queen's English, a hallmark of those educated in top-notch Indian public schools. His gaze was fixed on Rehana, as if looking away would be unthinkable.

'Rehana,' she replied, taking his proffered hand.

Ravinder held it, and kept holding it.

She gave him a sharp look, which softened into an amused glance as she realized it was an innocent gesture. The adoring look Ravinder bestowed upon her was starting to unsettle her, but in a good way. Rehana realized that she liked it.

'My hand,' Rehana pointed out softly with a smile.

He let go with an embarrassed start. 'I did not...' Then he ran out of words. After a few false starts he repeated, 'I am Ravinder Singh Gill.'

'Yes, you told me.' She smiled back, mischievously now. 'I am Rehana.'

'Rehana,' he repeated. 'It is a lovely name. I like it.' He blushed. 'What does it mean?'

'You should know. You're an Indian.'

'How did you know?' Even as the words left his

mouth, he realized it was a stupid question and he turned even redder.

Rehana smiled, giving his turban a pointed look. 'You guys are everywhere.'

'Yes.' He laughed. 'I guess we do get around.'

'And how. I don't think the Brits had any idea when they quit India that you guys planned to follow them home… and take their jobs.'

This time they both laughed.

'So… what does Rehana mean?'

'It means a handful of sweet basil.'

'Basil? Hmm… I like basil.'

'Do you now?' She gave him a mischievous smile.

Of course Rehana did not know it then, but in the days to come, he would do everything he could to woo her.

Rehana loved it. For once there was a person who had no agenda but to pivot his existence around her. The next few weeks were full of walks in the park, trips to the theatre, lunches and dinners and soon, stolen kisses and long, fevered embraces. He swept her off her feet.

Anyone who met Ravinder in those days would have found it hard to believe that just a while back he had been a dedicated and hardworking law student. His parents, who had sent their firstborn to London with heavy hearts, would have been aghast.

But Ravinder and Rehana didn't care. Their world was perfect. Even the London weather was behaving itself.

To Rehana's uncle's annoyance and her aunt's confusion, Ravinder became a fixture in their lives. They were irritated by the unabashed attention he was giving to their niece. That he was not Muslim bothered them, but not too much. And that he was a well brought up young man from a family of means did not escape their attention either. The sudden change in Rehana baffled them. Usually withdrawn, sullen and taciturn, she was now cheerful and constantly smiling. Zahira was blown away to find her helping with the housework and being pleasant about it too.

But the uncle worried. At his wit's end, he threw the ball at her brother Yusuf in Ramallah.

Yusuf's decision came hard and fast. 'There is no way in hell you are going to continue seeing him!' he screamed at Rehana on the phone.

He should have known better. Rehana was as stubborn as he was.

When Ravinder's parents came to know, their reaction was equally predictable.

'She is not Sikh?' His grandmother, who held sway over family matters, raised an aristocratic eyebrow. Despite her age, it took a brave man to stand up to her. That one raised eyebrow and her cold, derisive smile were generally enough to send people scooting for cover.

'She is Arab,' Ravinder's father, the head of a small princedom in India's northern state of Punjab, who had just spent an hour reciting the sordid tale, reiterated patiently. 'From Palestine.'

'A Muslim?' Ravinder's mother, whose hot Punjabi blood would often surge past the wall of royal snobbery, wrung her hands in despair. 'How could he do this to us? What will people say?'

An expression of disgust crossed his grandmother's face. That was about as far as she would go to respond to her daughter-in-law's plebian display of emotion.

'Maybe he is just sowing some wild oats.' The grandmother sounded more hopeful than convinced.

But they were all shocked when they learned that Ravinder was not just sowing wild oats, he was planting royal seeds as well.

'I think it was the resistance from both families that decided things for us. Now, don't get me wrong, Ruby. We did love each other. I am – was – madly in love with her. For me the sun rose when she did and set when she slept.'

Ravinder could clearly remember the day their relationship had moved to the next level. He was walking up to her house when he saw her returning from the other end of the street. There was a Dalmatian pup on the leash with her, a friendly looking thing.

'Cute dog. I didn't know you had one,' he said as she came up.

'It's my aunt's... so I guess he is kind of like my cousin.' Rehana grinned. 'She just got him.'

'Does he bite?' Ravinder leaned forward to pick up the pup.

'I doubt it. Loves attention too much.'

'Does his cousin bite?' Now this was not the usual Ravinder. Today, with his spirits fortified by two large whiskies, he was feeling daring.

'She might.' Rehana giggled. 'Guess you will just have to find out.'

And they did – that very evening. And the cousin did bite. Deliciously.

Ruby noticed a soft expression on her father's face.

Could it be that even now he was still in love... The thought was uncomfortable. Ruby pushed it away. That would rock the foundation of her mission. *Unthinkable.* Ruby reminded herself of her mission, of what her mother had said to her everyday – *you will be the one to avenge us.... To avenge all these years of injustice we Palestinians have suffered.*

'You see, the family resistance simply crystallized things.' Unaware of her turmoil, Ravinder continued, 'We ran away to Birmingham and got married.'

'Why Birmingham of all places?'

'I had friends and relatives there.' He gave a sheepish smile. 'You see, when I told my parents I was going to marry Rehana, they cut me off. I was just a student, so money was a bit of a challenge.'

'You didn't think of getting a job?'

'Nope, I was too used to the royal thing back then.' They both laughed. 'Yes, those were mad, mad days. But I would go through it all over again...' He broke off, and it was a while before he resumed. 'Rehana looked so gorgeous that day, bedecked in bridal finery. I tell you, Ruby, it felt as though we were living in a fairytale.'

'Dad!' A sharp cry intruded on them. '*Dad*!'

Ruby looked up to see a young woman come rushing up to them. She was about five-feet-four, slim, and wore black pants and a white shirt, the typical attire of law students in many Indian colleges. Her clear skin was unblemished by make-up. *She doesn't need it*, Ruby thought enviously.

Ravinder spotted apprehension writ large on the girl's face. He understood that Simran would have briefed Jasmine on the phone. He felt a chasm opening up between them and instinctively moved forward to close it. 'Jasmine, how are you, kid?'

She did not reply, but sailed into his arms and buried her face in his chest. Ravinder held her close, willing her turmoil to seep into him.

'Mom called me,' Jasmine whispered. 'I want you to know that it's okay with me... I understand.'

Ravinder felt a gush of love flow through him. He held her shoulders and pulled her away, wanting to look at her, wanting her to look at him, *needing* her to know that nothing had changed between them. That he was proud of her for understanding. He became aware that Ruby was watching them closely, and suddenly felt awkward.

'Jasmine, I would like you to meet Ruby. Your half... your elder sister.'

Momentarily Jasmine stayed close, clutching his hand. Then she turned to Ruby and smiled. A tentative smile, yet friendly and welcoming.

Suddenly Ruby realized, for some reason she could not yet fathom, that it was important for Jasmine to accept... no, to like her. Ruby gave her warmest and most reassuring smile and extended her right hand.

'Hi, Jasmine, I hope we can be friends.' She heard a nervous plea in her voice.

Jasmine's smile broadened. Brushing aside Ruby's extended hand, she reached out with open arms. Ruby felt a lump in her throat as she hugged her.

'Of course we can,' Jasmine said. 'We share our father, the same family name... nothing can take that away from either of us.'

Ruby could not trust herself to speak. She felt overwhelmed.

Watching them, Ravinder too was shaken. He was about to speak when his mobile trilled to life. Reluctantly, he reached for it.

'Sir,' Mohite sounded excited. 'I think you'd better come to office right away. I think we have just had a major breakthrough.'

'Tell me what happened, Govind.'

'I just got a call from Thakur sahib. Apparently the Israeli team managed to get hold of Saeed Anwar.'

'That's fantastic. Where is he now?' Ravinder masked his annoyance over Thakur once again bypassing him. He stepped away, moving out of earshot.

'Dead as far as I know, but the important thing is that Anwar confirmed that it was Pasha who financed the strike on Jerusalem. He also confirmed that Pasha has hired a British mercenary, a woman, to carry out a strike in Delhi.'

'How do we know that?'

'Easy, because Pasha had asked Anwar to alert one of their money men here to be ready to hand over cash to the mercenary when she contacted him.'

'What is the target?'

'Anwar did not know that. I assume it's the Summit.' Mohite's voice now lost some of its shine. 'Could be the Games too, though,' he added.

'I see. Excellent. Put a surveillance team on this financier immediately.'

'I am doing that right away. I messaged Peled and he has e-mailed the name and details of this guy to both of us.'

'Fantastic. Good work, Govind. I am still to check my mail.'

'Well, I have and I've also activated a team to watch the guy. We may be able to catch them both red-handed.'

'We don't have an option, Govind. We *have* to. We have to catch the mercenary when she meets him.'

'Yes, sir. That was why I was asking if you wanted to come down and brief the team. Though I am going to personally supervise this operation.'

Ravinder figured that Mohite wanted him involved so that he could pass on the blame if things fell apart. *Well, so be it.* 'Hang on. I am leaving right now.'

'Good. I also wanted to know if we should preemptively start rounding up single British women in the capital.'

'Are you nuts, Govind? Do you know how many there would be with the Games around the corner? The Brits will blow a bloody gasket if we pull stunts like that.'

'Well…'

'Hang on, Govind. I will be right over. Brief the surveillance team, but don't start on anything else.'

He ended the call and threw a quick look at the girls. 'I have to go to the office… something important has come up.' He hesitated, wondering how Ruby would feel about being left alone.

'Don't worry about Ruby, dad,' Jasmine sensed his

worry and jumped right in. 'I will take good care of her.'

Ravinder blew her a kiss and rushed towards his car.

There was silence between the two girls for a while after Ravinder left. Ruby felt puzzled by this new situation that she found herself in.

'Would you like to go out for dinner with me?' Jasmine was giving her an expectant smile.

'Sure. That would be wonderful.' She smiled back. 'It is very sweet of you to...'

'Nonsense.' Jasmine cut her off. 'I have never had a sister to go out with... till now.' She broke off, suddenly embarrassed. Ruby reached out and gave her hand a squeeze. 'Would you like to settle in first? Come, let me show you your room.' Jasmine took Ruby's hand and led her inside.

Neither noticed Simran watching from the kitchen as they crossed the living room and went up the stairs. She was still holding the kitchen knife she had been using to slice sausages when she heard the girls come in. Her fingers were wrapped so tightly around the hilt that they had begun to hurt.

Ruby was still getting ready when Jasmine walked into the guest bedroom. She was wearing a mauve silk sari with a black border and a black blouse. The sari was slung low, displaying a slim, fetching waist. Her tiny sleeveless blouse made the best of her breasts. She also wore a diamond pendant held close to her long neck by an almost invisible golden chain. Matching diamond earrings sparkled in her ears.

'My! You are certainly dressed to kill.' Ruby gave an approving smile. Her own black and red dress looked dowdy in comparison.

'I don't usually wear saris... in fact, I just learnt how to wear one,' Jasmine giggled, 'but I thought tonight should be special. After all, how often does one meet a sister one has never met before?'

'Very true. Not often.'

'Say! Why don't you wear a sari too?' Jasmine cocked her head to one side and studied Ruby. 'That dress is lovely, but won't it be fun for both of us to wear saris?'

Ruby laughed, shaking her head. 'I wouldn't be able to put one on or hold it up for...'

'Don't worry. I will drape it for you,' Jasmine replied excitedly. 'What fun! Come!' Grabbing Ruby's hand, she led the way to her bedroom down the corridor. Suddenly they were just two young girls, two sisters, out to have fun.

Half an hour later, Jasmine stood back and surveyed the results of her effort.

'You look gorgeous.'

The deep blue Kanjivaram sari with a black border

set off her Mediterranean features. With straight black hair framing her face, Ruby looked stunning. Looking in the full-length mirror, she could not believe it was her. She looked so different.

I even feel different, Ruby thought with surprise.

'I am nervous.' Ruby swivelled around slowly, clutching the folds of the silk sari. 'What if it falls off?'

'The men will be in for a treat then!' Jasmine chuckled. 'You don't do that,' she said, removing Ruby's hands from the folds of the sari. 'Just let it be. Don't worry. It won't fall off. Now try to walk.'

Ruby took a few tentative steps. Then realizing it was not flimsily tied, she walked more confidently.

'Better? Think you can manage?'

'Much better,' Ruby nodded.

'Then shall we, Ms Gill?' Jasmine gestured at the door with a big smile. Ruby nodded and picking up her clutch, got ready to follow.

'Wait. Something's missing...' Jasmine frowned. 'I know! You need something to set it off.' She walked over to the dressing table and pulled out a pearl necklace and earrings from her jewellery box.

'There is no need for that, Jasmine.'

'Nonsense. We are going to paint the town red! Let Delhi know that the Gill sisters are out tonight!'

Ruby tossed her hair back coquettishly. 'Okay! Let's go get them, girl!'

Ruby was turning away from the dressing table when she spotted a pistol in the open jewellery box.

'You keep a gun?' she asked, surprised. 'Why?'

'Oh, no, I hate guns.' Jasmine gave a shudder. 'That's not mine. Daddy put it there. He even made me learn how to fire it.'

'What on earth for?'

'Ever since we moved here and he was put in charge of the ATTF, there have been threats. He says it is not a problem, but just in case... He even makes me carry pepper spray when I go out.'

Ruby was silent.

'Well, it's not so bad. You should have seen mom's face when he made her go for firing practise. She was fuming!'

Her giggle broke the sombre mood. Jasmine held Ruby's hand as they descended the stairs. Ruby found the gesture strangely natural. It made her feel sad. She realized that this was what life would have been like if her parents had still been together. She suddenly stopped and gave Jasmine a big hug.

'Thank you, Jasmine. Thank you very much.'

Jasmine's eyes were moist. Then she forced a laugh as they headed out. They were at the door when Jasmine remembered. 'Oh! I need to tell mom when we will be back.' She went to the base of the stairs and called out, but there was no response. Jasmine headed up.

When she returned, her smile had vanished.

'She is upset?' Ruby murmured, lightly touching her arm. Jasmine looked away. 'I can understand. Anyone would be.'

They did not exchange another word as they got into Jasmine's car, a silver Tata Vista hatchback, and drove out. The silence was awkward. Suddenly a car alongside swerved and cut them off, diving in front of them.

'Screw you! Moron!' Jasmine flipped her middle finger at the errant driver. She saw Ruby watching her with a smile and giggled. 'That's your first lesson in driving in Delhi.'

They both laughed and the awkwardness vanished.

'What kind of food do you like?' Jasmine asked as they hit the roundabout near India Gate.

'All kinds. Tonight, you decide.'

'Fine. Chinese it is then!' Jasmine giggled. 'I can never get enough of it.'

'I like Chinese a lot, too.'

'Strange, isn't it?' Jasmine said. 'How similar people can be? Despite being so different. Look at us. I'm an Indian, born and bred. You are half Indian-half Palestinian, brought up in London. And yet, we both love Chinese food!'

Yes. We both laugh when we are happy. We cry when we are hurt, or sad. We bleed when we are cut. Then why so many differences?

Jasmine turned the car into the Oberoi hotel and

handed it in for valet parking and walked towards Taipan, the Chinese restaurant.

They entered a large, well-lit room, with tables placed comfortably apart, and sparkling with crystal ware. Snow-white linen lent a pristine touch to the ambience. Soft oriental music was playing in the background, audible but not intrusive. Despite it being a weekday, the restaurant was almost full.

'I love Chinese food, but am not very good at ordering,' Jasmine said as they sat at a table in the corner. 'Would you like to do the honours?'

'Just go ahead and order what you like,' Ruby smiled. 'I am sure it will be perfect.'

'At least help me pick the wine, please. I rarely get to drink. Mom doesn't like me drinking alcohol.'

'Let's not have wine then… no point upsetting your mother…'

'Nonsense! Of course we will have wine today.' She consulted the waiter and ordered a Mao Tai, a fiery 55 proof concoction.

Ruby watched the young girl as she ordered the food. She seemed child-like, innocent, secure.

'Didn't you get a bit carried away?' Ruby asked when the waiter left. 'Are you sure we can eat all that?'

'Of course we can. Just you wait… the food here is excellent. It's not the usual "Chindian" stuff you get in Delhi.'

'Chindian?'

'Chinese–Indian. Like Chilly Chicken Manchurian. I bet most Chinese have never even heard of it, till we invented it for them. Sometimes I think they'd wage war on us if they realized what we've done to their cuisine!' They both laughed.

Jasmine noticed two young men at the next table throw suggestive glances at Ruby. Her hackles rose and she exchanged places with Ruby. Jasmine's angry glares soon turned the men off.

'I *can* take care of myself, you know,' Ruby chuckled, touched that Jasmine felt so protective about her.

'I'm sure you can, but you shouldn't need to, not here, not on *my* watch.'

Ruby laughed again.

Soon they were biting into pan-fried scallops in barbeque sauce. Seared in hot oil for just the right amount of time, their crusts were thin and crisp, and yet tender.

'So,' Jasmine asked when the waiter had served them. 'Tell me about yourself.'

'What would you like to know?'

'Whatever you feel like telling me. Seeing that I know nothing about you, whatever you tell me will be new.'

Ruby was struck by the reality of who she was and why she was here, but kept a smile on her face and gave a bland synopsis of her life, steering clear of her true profession and of Rehana.

'Your mother never pestered you to get married?'

'No. Not really.' Ruby shrugged. 'I needed to devote myself to my career first.'

'See.' Jasmine sat back with a sigh. 'That's exactly what I keep telling my mom.'

'She wants you to marry now? But you are so young.'

'She says it's our family tradition.'

Ruby remained quiet, sensing Jasmine might not take it well if she commented on her mother's views.

'I keep telling her that I need to finish my law degree first, but... it's this damn royal blood...' She stopped when she saw Ruby's puzzled expression. 'Didn't you know? Both dad and mom are from royal families.'

'No, I didn't know that. I thought all that went out with the British.'

'Yes, but you wouldn't know it to hear mom go on and on... that I'll die an old maid. And my aunts are even worse... they pump mom up every time they meet her. Luckily dad's on my side or I don't know how...' she trailed off.

'Do girls marry young in India?'

The waiter interrupted them as he served the braised bean curd with crab claw and steamed cod with garlic and preserved vegetables. Ruby felt she was in culinary heaven.

Jasmine resumed, 'They don't marry so young any more.' As she picked her way through the cod, she said,

'If they're career-minded, they study as much as they want and work on their professional lives. It is just like in your part of the world. I have so many friends…' She broke off again. 'There I go, rambling on about myself. Tell me about yourself. Do you have a boyfriend?' she giggled.

Ruby felt reality tug at her again. 'I am not sure right now.' She was surprised to find herself answering truthfully, as though happy that she was finally able to share her thoughts with someone.

'What does that mean? You either do or you don't.'

'Is it that simple?'

'Isn't it? He is either there or he isn't.'

Ruby pondered her beautiful simplicity. 'Then I guess I don't.'

'What happened? You two had a fight?'

'No. Not really.' Ruby gave a wistful laugh. 'I don't know… somewhere, something just went off track.' She fell silent.

Jasmine asked. 'Did your mother like him?'

'No! Mom never liked him.'

'Fortune hunter?'

'What?' Ruby laughed. 'No. No fortune to hunt. Not in my case, at least.'

'According to my mom there are only three kinds of men. Fortune hunters, sex maniacs and the right ones.'

Ruby asked after she had finished laughing, 'Okay, the first two I get, but who are the right ones?'

'My mom says the "right one", firstly, has to be from a royal family... with more than a drop of blue blood. Secondly, he has to be as rich – if not richer than us.'

'I see. Fair enough.'

'Oh, but there's more.'

'Go on, please,' Ruby smiled.

'Thirdly, he has to be as educated, if not more. And lastly, he must be a Sikh. Trust me, Ruby. *That* is a heavy-duty checklist. It seriously trims the field down. In fact, sometimes I wonder if there is anyone still left in the world.' They laughed.

'By the way, I did want to ask you, do you go to the mosque or the gurudwara to pray?' Jasmine asked. Realizing she may have strayed into sensitive territory, she quickly added, 'I mean, because dad is Sikh and your mother is – was, sorry – Muslim.'

Ruby almost chuckled, but controlled herself, realizing that Jasmine could feel offended. 'Neither, actually. You see, mom was a devout Muslim, but she never forced me into it.' Suddenly sombre, Ruby looked away, her mind in a tailspin, sharply aware that she could only allow Jasmine to enter so far into her mind. Her... *their* father was the enemy. She could not allow herself to forget that. 'And I guess I was too busy trying to fit in with the others at school and in the neighbourhood. I mean,' she saw Jasmine's puzzled expression and explained, 'most were Christians, you see. Though we also had a lot of Jews... and some

Buddhists and Hindus, and of course a number of freethinkers.'

Jasmine gave an understanding smile.

'So I kind of grew up freewheeling. I mean, I do believe there is a god, but to my mind religion, well… most preach love and brotherhood, but in reality it's the cause for so much hate and destruction.'

'I agree with you.' Jasmine gave a grave nod. 'But you have to have some religion… or what will they do at the time of the final rites?'

That broke the tension and got them both laughing.

'I guess I'll cross that bridge when I come to it,' Ruby said playfully. 'Though of course I'll have much less control over what they do to me once I am gone! I just hope they select the most eco-friendly option!' They laughed louder.

'Okay, maybe the last rites argument was a lousy one,' Jasmine resumed. 'How about this – what rites will you follow for your marriage ceremony?'

'I guess I'll worry about that when I find the "right" man.' Chance returned to her mind unbidden, and she fell silent.

'Me…' Jasmine said between mouthfuls. 'I wish I could find someone as good as daddy. He is so amazing. You know, he is my best friend.' Jasmine could not imagine the impact her words were having on Ruby and continued innocently, 'I feel so lucky… he is the best father a girl could want. He is so caring.'

Ruby felt a pang of regret. The dried Hashima that she was eating turned to ashes in her mouth.

'I don't know anything about him,' she said. 'I just remember that he used to call me princess when I was little.'

Jasmine nodded animatedly. 'That's what he has always called me too.'

Ruby's pain turned into jealousy.

Jasmine rambled on, 'You know, once I was very ill… I think when I was four or five, I don't remember, but I was very ill and daddy never left my side even for a moment. He would hug me and sleep next to me. In fact whenever I've been ill or have got hurt, he has always been there. Mom gets upset that I cling to him, but he has always been cool about it. He said that whenever his princess is ill or hurting, he'll be by her side.'

Ruby burned with resentment.

The bill arrived and Ruby reached for it.

'No,' Jasmine plucked it out of her hands. 'Please, allow me.' She threw a look at it and gave a low whistle as she pulled out a credit card. 'Wow! That wine was expensive.'

'I can afford it, Jasmine.' Ruby held out her hand.

'Dad can too, Ruby.'

'I didn't know that Indian cops are so well paid.'

'They are not.' Jasmine shook her head. 'But I told you, dad's family is loaded. So is mom's, for that matter.'

She signed the charge slip with a flourish. 'Might as well make the most of it is what I say.' She laughed. 'Otherwise what's the point of having a rich dad?'

'I wouldn't know.' Ruby hated the grim tone of her voice. *Why did I say that?* She felt ashamed... or was it a feeling of inadequacy? Betrayal? Anger? *What had I done to be so deprived?*

Jasmine fell silent.

The uneasiness between them grew as they left and waited for the car. The valet must have switched the car radio on, because it crackled to life when Jasmine started the engine.

'We lose direction, no stone unturned', Elton John's song, 'Sacrifice', started to play. 'No tears to damn you, when jealousy burns...'

Neither wanted the song to go on, but both were grateful for the sound filling the awkward void between them. The song finally ended and it was followed by Doris Day's 'When I was just a little girl I asked my mother... que sera sera, whatever will be, will be...'

Jasmine felt hurt about the change in Ruby, but was unsure of how to deal with it. Ruby made no attempt to make things better. On the contrary, something inside her made her want to nurture her yet-to-be-defined but decidedly ugly feeling.

They bid each other a muted goodnight at the top of the stairs and Ruby retreated to her room. Her resentment stayed with her as she lay down in the cold, strange bed.

Of course I have been cheated of a complete childhood, a childhood that can never be returned to me.

Outside it began to rain again. No thunder, no lightning. Just sheets of rain.

Ruby was crying when sleep finally claimed her.

Somewhere in the darkness of that long night, the dream reached out to her again, bringing with it the same faceless man who had been calling out to her all these nights.

Suddenly, his face became clear. Ravinder looked much younger, the way she remembered him in her childhood. She knew that face so well, it was embedded in her heart. He had a loving smile and was searching the house, every now and then calling out in a singsong tone, 'Ruby, my princess, come out, come out… wherever you are…'

Suddenly his face vanished again. Slowly a new face emerged from the darkness. It was her uncle, Yusuf. He was calling out to her, pleading for help… the gaping cut in his throat was like a hideous smile. He was desperately trying to attract Ruby's attention, struggling to point out something to her, but his dismembered arms lay limp beside him.

Ruby knew where he was telling her to go. She did not want to go, but moved helplessly down the long, dimly-lit passage into a cold, dark room. She was trembling. Now she stood in the darkness alone. Before her were the charred remains of Rehana – alive and pleading, crying. Tugging at her.

Ruby howled in pain but no one heard her mewing cries for help. The thick walls of the room and the violent drumming of the rain contained them.

Ruby was soaked in sweat when she jolted awake. Drawing a deep breath, she reached for the water on her bedside table. The jug was empty. She got up and went down to the kitchen with the empty jug in her hand.

Barring trickles of light from the windows, the house was dark and silent, though she could hear the faint rustle of security guards moving near the gate. Then she heard the clang of metal against metal… perhaps the guard's rifle butt had collided with the gate. It was followed by a murmur of voices.

Her eyes gradually adjusted to the dim light and she finally located the refrigerator in one corner of the kitchen. She pulled out a bottle of water and refilled the jug.

On her way back to the room, she noticed a flicker of light coming from the room across the living room. The dim light emanating from the room cast eerie shadows on the wall. Ruby felt as if someone was hiding there, watching her. Her grip on the jug tightened; the filled jug was heavy, it would make a potent weapon.

Could it be an intruder?

'Ever since we moved here and he was put in charge of the ATTF, there have been several threats,' Jasmine's warning echoed in her ears.

She considered raising an alarm.

'Who is it?' she called softly. There was no response. Hefting the jug, Ruby ghost-footed forward, ensuring she was clear of the door as she circled to bring the inner room into view.

The culprit was a laptop. It lay open on the study table, facing away from the door. The light from the screensaver flickered, casting scary shadows on the wall.

Ruby was not sure why she went up to it. Possibly only to close it and put it in sleep mode. But when she touched it, the screen came to life and displayed Ravinder's inbox. Ruby hesitated only briefly before she put down the jug and leaned forward to read his e-mails.

The first mail was from a Govind Mohite. It confirmed that Mr Thakur, the home minister, had been informed about the LeT financier identified by the Mossad agent named Ido Peled. It went on to say that the financier – Rizwan Khan – had been placed under surveillance to enable ATTF to identify everyone who came to meet him, including the British woman terrorist they had been warned about.

Ruby's blood ran cold. Rizwan Khan was one of the two names Pasha had given her. He was the one she had meant to call earlier that day.

Ruby drew a deep breath. For a moment she wondered if Pasha knew that the Mossad was on to his financier. Then a second realization – *a British woman... So they knew a hit was coming.*

She had just clicked open the next mail when the clapping patter of slippers hit her ears – someone was coming down the stairs. Swiftly shutting the lid of the laptop, she snatched up the jug and returned to the living room. She was halfway there when she saw Ravinder with a pistol in his right hand, level, ready for action. He gave a start when he saw her and thrust the pistol into his gown pocket.

'Oh! It's you. I thought I heard something...'

'I came down for some water,' Ruby said calmly, even as her heart pounded.

'Okay. Did you girls have a nice time tonight?'

'Yes, we did, thank you.' Ruby smiled. In the dim light he did not notice that only her lips had moved; her eyes were cold and still.

'I'm glad. Jasmine was telling me that you enjoy different types of cuisine. So I was thinking, why don't I take you for lunch to this really nice place where they serve north-western frontier cuisine? It has been a while since I ate there, but it is supposed to be very good.'

'I would like that. Thank you.'

'You're welcome, princess.' Now that once-precious word did nothing for her. 'Tomorrow is bad because...' he broke off, not wanting to talk about his work. 'No, actually it would be perfect since I have to go to the same hotel for work in the morning. I will finish by one. Is that okay with you?'

'That would be nice.'

'Great. So be ready by noon. I'll send the driver back to get you to the Ashoka hotel. They have this lovely restaurant called Frontier. Okay?'

Ashoka hotel! Ruby was thrilled. Now she would get in there again; she knew Ravinder would be going to check on the security arrangements.

'Don't worry about sending the car. I'll get to the hotel on my own.'

'If that works better for you.' He hesitated, then decided to speak. 'We never got a chance to talk properly... there is so much we have to catch up on.' He paused. 'What did happen to Rehana? When and how...'

'It's a long story, father.'

'It feels strange... you calling me father. You always called me daddy. Don't you remember?'

'Sorry. I will try to remember that.'

'No worries.' He gave a tiny smile. 'I understand. It's been a long time.'

'Yes, fath—daddy. It has. I was hardly four when you left.' Ruby's tone was brittle.

'You still don't believe that it was not I who left, do you?'

'I don't know,' Ruby replied bluntly. 'You told me your story. Mom told me something else. I am not sure whom to believe.'

'I understand.'

'Do you?' Ruby asked bitterly. 'And does it matter whether you left or she did? You did not come looking for me, not once in all these years.'

'I did, Ruby.' Ravinder struggled with the reply. 'In the beginning I really did, but then I thought... maybe Rehana wanted me to leave you two alone...'

'You're a cop, how difficult could it have been for you to find us?'

'Not very,' Ravinder replied softly. 'But I didn't want to intrude. Rehana's lawyer made it very clear that she wanted no further communication. And then, as time passed, I thought maybe you guys had started a new life... I didn't think it right to...'

'Because you certainly had started a new one,' Ruby cut him off.

The ensuing pause was growing unbearable. Ravinder felt compelled to fill it. 'So what happened to Rehana?' he asked.

'Like I was saying, *dad*, it is a long story and it has been a long day. Some other time?' There was no way she would tell him where and how Rehana had died. It would only make him suspicious about the timing of her arrival… *especially now that they are looking for a female mercenary from England.*

'You are right. I didn't realize… seeing you has brought back so many memories, so many questions. For you too, I'm sure. Sleep well then, princess.'

The words sounded hollow to Ruby.

He gave her a hug as they parted ways at her bedroom door. It was a tentative one. And she was in a hurry to get away.

As she returned to bed, something kept nagging at her. It was something to do with the second mail she had just opened when Ravinder came down. She thought hard, but could not figure it out.

Day Six

Ravinder woke early the next morning, raring to leave for the office. Ruby's arrival had energized him and the guilt he felt towards Simran pushed him to leave the house sooner.

When he entered his study to pick up his laptop, he noticed a round water mark on the table. It irritated him. And then he remembered Ruby holding a jug of water the night before. *Could Ruby have been in my study last night?*

He was looking at it, perplexed, when he heard the gate grate open. He saw Ruby come jogging down the drive, her maroon tracksuit soaked in sweat. He smiled. Rehana, too, would go jogging every morning. How clearly he could still see Rehana come running down the road just like Ruby, her ponytail flailing in the wind. *Like mother, like daughter.*

Ravinder was going out to talk to her when his phone rang. It was some anal-retentive type from the PMO asking for clarifications about the Summit security plan.

'I will need to get to the office and send them to you,' Ravinder told him.

'All right, Mr Gill, but we need them urgently.'

He hurriedly pushed the laptop into the bag and headed for the car, the water mark and Ruby now forgotten. His mind was whirling with so many conflicting thoughts and worries that, for the first time in years, he did not return the salute of the men standing guard at his bungalow gates.

By the time Ruby came down, Jasmine had left for college. Simran was sitting alone at the dining table.

Ruby nodded hesitantly to greet her good morning.

Simran nodded back as she rose, but it was a cold look. 'Ravinder left early,' Simran said in a monotone. *A weather forecaster would have shown more emotion.* Before Ruby could think of anything to say, Simran added, 'Please sit down. I will tell the servant to serve you breakfast.'

Ruby felt a compelling need to gain her approval.

'I am sorry,' desperate to break the ice, Ruby called out when Simran was at the door. Simran halted and turned to look at her, her face expressionless. 'I know I have disrupted your lives by coming here like this, but...'

'You have.'

'I just wanted to meet my father,' Ruby continued. 'I just wanted to know what he is like. That is all.' Simran did not respond. 'He is a good man, Mrs Gill.'

'I know.'

A distasteful silence stood between them.

'I am glad I came and met him… and all of you.'

There was no response from Simran. Not even an angry look. Even that might have mitigated the wanting churning inside Ruby. She wanted her to say something, anything to break this silence.

'I know how you feel.'

Simran's left eyebrow lifted slightly as though to say, you do?

'I promise I will not disrupt your lives much longer.' Silence. 'I will go away. Soon,' she said finally, her voice breaking.

'Good.' Simran was out of the door.

That parting word echoed painfully in Ruby's head.

Her resentment escalated. Soon the Palestinian avenger was back in control. She felt numb, emotionless. Almost.

Though no longer hungry, Ruby knew she needed energy and ploughed through breakfast before returning to her room. There was work to be done. She started dialling the number of the second financier Pasha had given her.

'Ahmed Siddiqui, please.'

'This is Ahmed.' Though with a distinctly Indian accent, the voice was cultured.

'A mutual friend gave me your number. He asked me to tell you that Sahiba's wedding is on Friday and the arrangements need to be made.'

'Ah!' Ahmed replied, perking up. 'I have been expecting your call for a couple of days now.'

'I was busy.'

'I understand. When would you like to collect the items?'

'Two hours from now. Is that okay?'

'Of course. I have it ready.'

'How big is the package?'

'A small briefcase.' Sensing her concern, he said, 'Barring some for local use, I have kept most of the items in their original form so that…'

'That's perfect.' Ruby felt relieved. Handling large denominations would be so much easier – and also more convenient for her team.

'My man will come to collect it. He will use the same contact procedure.'

'I was told you would come yourself.'

'I would have, but your security sucks.'

'What do you mean?' Ahmed was clearly irritated.

'Do you know Rizwan Khan?'

'Of course, I do. Why?'

'Well, so do the police.'

Ruby heard a sharp intake of breath. 'What are you saying? Are you sure? How do you know?'

'Go visit him if you want to check – if you want the police knocking down your door before the sun sets.' Ruby was reluctant to continue even though she knew chances of the ATTF chief's home phone being bugged were negligible.

After confirming the place and time, she called Mark. Though concerned that exposing him to so much cash was not a good idea, in light of the e-mail she had seen last night, she chose that over the risk of exposing herself.

Her final call was to her driver Kishore to tell him to bring the car. Tomorrow she would change cars, she reminded herself.

Thirty minutes later, Kishore arrived. Ruby knew she'd have to move fast if she did not want to be late for lunch with Ravinder, since she had to collect the cash first. There was no way she would pass up an opportunity to case the target venue.

By the time she met Mark and they arrived at Khan Market, they were already running a couple of minutes late. They lost another fifteen due to the traffic and then while finding the obscure bookstore Ahmed had told them to come to.

Ahmed was waiting outside the shop, holding a big black umbrella to save him from the rain, which was now a drizzle. Ruby saw him from across the parking lot and indicated him to Mark.

'I just go up to him and collect the briefcase?'

'No, you repeat the contact procedure, then take the case and walk away.'

"That's it?'

'Yes.'

'What's in the case?'

'Nothing that explodes,' Ruby chuckled, trying to dissipate the tension. Then she handed him the zippered cloth bag and briefed him.

'Right.' He nodded.

Ruby felt nervous as she watched him walk away. Mark paused near the car he had arrived in and dumped the bag in the rear seat, then continued towards the bookshop.

Ahmed appeared to be behaving strangely, shifting uneasily from one foot to the other, constantly peering at something inside the bookstore. Perhaps Ruby's news that Rizwan's cover had been blown had spooked him. Or perhaps he too had been turned... or blown.

Ruby felt her breathing even out, as though she was going into combat. Her hand instinctively reached for her waist but there was no gun there. Only a horrid, naked feeling. Her fingers clenched in frustration.

Mark stopped near Ahmed. Ruby saw them exchange words. Her tension ratcheted up. If the cops were onto Ahmed, this was when they would make their play.

Apparently they were not.

Ruby felt her adrenaline recede as she saw Mark collect the briefcase and walk away. He was not walking towards her; instead, he angled across the car park. Ruby scanned the area for anyone suspicious. Her eyes swept the area methodically, one sector at a time.

A beggar standing by the dustbin outside a tea stall caught her eye; he seemed to be watching Mark. Then his attention wandered back to the dustbin and he began rooting inside it. *False alarm.*

Her eyes kept sweeping ahead and then looping back, stopping whenever they spotted anything out of sync. She re-checked the beggar. Nothing. She tried to spot people following Mark. Again, nothing. *So far, so good.*

Mark returned to his car and ducked inside. She could not see him, but she knew he would be transferring the contents of the briefcase into the cloth bag. A minute later, he came out of the car, the bag on his shoulder and the empty briefcase in his hand. He walked to a dustbin and dropped the case into it nonchalantly. If a tracking device had been placed in it, it would lead the trackers to that dustbin, or to a rag picker.

Ruby watched as Mark walked to the end of the parking lot and hailed a passing auto-rickshaw. Fifty metres behind him, Ruby followed, keeping a sharp lookout. She stayed behind him as he left the market, went towards India Gate and then skirted around it before returning to Khan Market.

By the time they got back, Ruby was sure there was no tail on him.

'That's a lot of money,' Mark said softly as she walked up to him.

'Yeah.' She scrutinized him, knowing that if greed overcame him he could be dangerous. Ruby wished she was carrying a weapon, but she maintained a calm exterior. 'You said the guys wanted to be paid.'

'That they did.'

'So pay them now.'

He gave her a long, level look. 'I do that?'

'Sure, Mark. You hired them. Besides,' she added casually, 'I trust you. I can, can't I?'

He gazed at her. 'Of course you can.' He laughed softly. 'I know better than to piss off the golden goose.'

'Good.' Ruby smiled back, but her eyes were hard.

When she extended her hand, he held out the bag. Using the cars on either side as cover, Ruby transferred some of the money to her handbag and handed the rest back to him. 'That will take care of the Glocks, the stuff from Chennai and the team. The rest we pay to them only when we finish the job.'

'Got it.' Mark slung the bag back on his shoulder. 'What next?'

'The Glocks.'

'I've chosen the place for our meeting with Nanda. Scouted it out last evening. Want me to show you?'

'Yeah, good idea. We have the time, if we move fast.'

'Let's go.'

When Ahmed reached his office, he headed for the phone and called a New York number.

'I have handed over the items for Sahiba's wedding,' he confirmed.

'Good.' The man on the other end was about to hang up when Ahmed spoke again.

'There is something else. The other party told me that Rizwan bhai is sick... *very* sick. He could go any time.'

There was silence at the other end. 'I will take care of it,' he said brusquely and cut the call. Two minutes later he was on Skype passing on the message to Pasha in Muridke, Pakistan.

Pasha made another Skype call, this one to Aligarh. The man at the other end heard Pasha out carefully. Ten minutes later, he was on his way to Delhi.

It was pushing noon by the time Ruby and Mark checked out the venue for the meeting.

Mark then proceeded to the warehouse to check on the items sent by Chanderan, and Ruby decided to keep the money in her suitcase at the Gill house.

Nobody was home when she reached, except for the security guards who were alert even in the sweltering humidity. She went straight to her room and carefully locked her bag after packing the money inside. She couldn't risk the suspicion that would be raised if anybody found so much money on her.

She was putting away the suitcase when she noticed the maid at the door. The maid seemed to be looking at her strangely. Or perhaps that was only Ruby's guilty conscience. Momentarily she pondered what she should do, and realized there was nothing she could. Giving the maid a vague smile, she left the house in a hurry. She had an important lunch date to keep.

When the man from Aligarh reached the outskirts of Delhi, there was a long line of cars at the security checkpoint. Security had been ramped up for the Commonwealth Games. When his turn came, the man held out a voter's identity card.

The cop took the card. 'What are you going to Delhi for?'

'Going back home, sahib. What else?'

'Where do you live?'

The troubleshooter pointed at the card in the cop's hand. It had a Delhi address. The card was not a forgery so the man was not worried. It would take more than a cursory check to ascertain that the man it had once belonged to was now dead. And it was no coincidence that the dead man resembled the man now using the card.

It had been a fourteen-hour stint for the cop on duty, which was the norm, especially during special events. After all, there were only so many men available for duty. The rain, which seemed to have made Delhi's annual quota of water in a week, was not helping. He handed the card back with a nod. The man from Aligarh waited till the other two cops had checked his car's engine compartment and boot and then drove off. His heartbeat returned to normal as the checkpoint vanished in the rear view. Hardened though he was, such encounters always took a toll.

He now headed for Saket, a residential colony in south Delhi.

Ruby sat back as Kishore navigated through the traffic. The road was covered in large puddles.

Aware that rest was imperative, she used this time to unwind. She was now feeling a bit more relaxed. Things seemed under control and the agent in her had pushed the weak woman with emotional baggage into the background.

Ruby reviewed the situation, ticking off the action points on her checklist. The money had been collected. The strike team would be in Delhi in a few hours. The munitions from Sri Lanka had reached the warehouse. In fact – she checked her watch – Mark should have picked them up by now. He would divide them up between the two Maruti vans they had hired, which the teams would be using, and park them safely. The venue Mark had selected for the Glock pick-up was nice and public – as safe as it could get.

The icy look on Simran's face that morning returned to haunt her. And her anger returned with it. By the time the car pulled up outside the Ashoka hotel, it was simmering inside her, waiting to explode.

The troubleshooter pulled over by the side of a lonely road, retrieved his weapons from the hidden compartment in the back seat and checked them. Both pistols were loaded. He probably wouldn't need them, but out of habit he checked the spare magazines to make sure they were ready.

Parking his car at the entrance of Saket residential complex, he made his way down the road on foot. Due to the rain there were not many people about. He pulled the umbrella low over his face and maintained a steady pace, staying on the side facing Rizwan's house. It took him just one pass to spot the first police vehicle. Parked across the small colony park, opposite the target's house, it was an off-white Tata Safari SUV. He saw three men inside, two in front and one in the back. The one in the back had a headset on and two directional mikes pointing out, facing the house. The mikes were well placed, and would not be visible to a casual observer.

The second cop car, a sky-blue Tata Indigo sedan, was harder to spot. It was sitting in the driveway of the adjacent house. He would not have noticed it if one of the watchers had not stepped out for a smoke.

Still not satisfied, he waited half an hour before making another pass. He needed to be sure there were no more watchers. His life depended on it. Only when he was absolutely certain did he return to his car.

He could have done the job right away, but Pasha's instructions were clear – an example had to be made. He hated such complications, but there was no choice. Pasha's orders had to be obeyed.

He returned to his car, pulled out his mobile and sent a text. Three minutes later, he received the reply. He deleted both the messages and, settling himself behind the wheel, waited.

It would be a long wait, but he was patient. The rain kept him company.

Ravinder was at the fag end of his security review at the Ashoka hotel when his mobile rang.

'Yes, Sanjeev?'

'Sir, it's me... Nanda.'

'Yes, tell me.'

'The guy is collecting the items at four tomorrow.'

'Where?'

'The Garden of Five Senses.'

'Damn!' Ravinder grimaced as he pictured the venue. It would be a pain to put down a team discreetly. 'Why did you have to pick…'

'I didn't. He did.'

A pro, Ravinder reflected. He'd picked a place and time where the crowds would be heavy.

'Okay, we'll be there.'

'Sir,' Nanda asked hesitantly, 'you are going to be there, right? Yourself?'

'Of course I will.'

'Thank you, sir.' Nanda sounded relieved. 'I was worried. Sometimes your people can get trigger happy.'

'Don't worry about it, Sanjeev. I'll be there.'

Ravinder saw Chance and Jennifer coming up to him as he ended the call. 'Is everything okay?' The look on Chance's face made it clear that it wasn't.

'Well, Mr Gill, I don't want to seem overcritical, but we are having a problem with the guards holding onto their posts every time we run an emergency security breach drill.'

'Really?' Ravinder was perplexed; the drill was simple and clear. He had just been through it with Mohite – the minute an alert was sounded, everyone stuck to their posts and ensured nothing moved in or out. 'Why is that? Any specific problem you could identify?'

Chance hesitated, aware he was on shaky ground. But he realized the issue had to be sorted out. If something happened to the British MP *his* arse would be grass. 'I think it is because Mr Mohite keeps countermanding orders from the control room and issuing fresh ones based on what *he* feels the threat is.'

'I see.' Ravinder pursed his lips to contain the curses. 'Let me take care of it.'

Chance saw Ravinder check his watch and realized they should be moving on; he trusted Gill. He thought Ravinder to be a reasonable man and had established a good rapport with him. Jennifer and he exchanged glances and then left.

Ravinder wanted to return to the eighth floor and deal with Mohite immediately, but realizing that Ruby was about to arrive, he headed for the Frontier restaurant instead.

The maitre d' was escorting him to their table when Ruby entered. Ravinder's heart skipped a beat as she spotted him and smiled – so striking was the similarity that he could have sworn it was Rehana.

Ruby was wearing a pale pink dress and had a matching leather clutch in her hand. Her high heels made her look taller and her black hair framed her face in a perfect oval. She looked beautiful and poised;

his heart swelled. Then he noted the aloof expression on her face, it belied her smile, and his heart broke. Though she stood right there, her eyes were far away. As though the closeness they'd achieved just the night before was lost. He sensed an awkwardness hanging heavily between them.

Ravinder could not let it pass. He felt the need to reach out to her.

'What has happened, Ruby? There is something different about you today.'

'Nothing in particular.' Ruby shrugged. 'Just one of those days, I guess.'

'But you're okay?'

'Don't worry about it, dad. I will be fine.'

Ravinder sensed it was more than that, but he did not know how to get through to her.

'The menu, sir.' The maitre d' held one out. Just as he was taking it, Ravinder saw Chance and Jennifer enter the restaurant.

Maybe some company would do both of us some good. Ravinder seized the opportunity.

He stood up and waved to them. 'Come, come. Join us. Meet my daughter.' Ravinder gestured proudly towards Ruby as Chance and Jennifer walked up to them.

Chance's eyes widened. 'So you two *are* related.' He grinned. 'Now isn't it a small world?'

'You know each other?' Ravinder asked, surprised.

Stunned, Ruby struggled to regain her composure.

'I should say we do,' Chance answered before Ruby could. 'We work together.'

'Really?' Ravinder gave Ruby a long look. Why hadn't she mentioned that she worked with the MI6?

Maybe because I never asked… but I did. Now, when he replayed their conversation in his head, he thought she had been evasive. *Oh well, it is not as though MI6 agents would go around advertising it. But I am her father and…*

Chance's voice interrupted his thoughts. 'We have been working together for almost three years now.'

'Fantastic.' That was when Ravinder noticed the resemblance between the two women. And Jennifer's expression – a polite smile plastered on her face, which did not conceal the guarded look she was giving Ruby. He sensed something was afoot.

Are they both vying for this fellow? A mischievous impulse ran through him.

'Why don't the two of you join us for lunch? I would love to hear more about my daughter, since,' he looked at Ruby fondly, 'she does not talk about herself at all.'

The lack of enthusiasm on Jennifer's face was clear. And it was mirrored on Ruby's.

Chance began, 'We don't want to intrude on a family…'

'Nonsense. I absolutely insist. Please…' He rose

and pulled up the chair facing him for Jennifer, so that Chance had to sit opposite Ruby.

'You two look so alike!' He gave Jennifer and Ruby a smile. The fact that neither smiled in return did not escape his attention.

Ruby cursed silently as Chance and Jennifer sat down. She would have to make sure the conversation stayed away from dangerous terrain. All three were already on the lookout for a female British mercenary.

To Ruby's relief, the maitre d' arrived to take their orders just then.

'It is as much fun watching the chefs prepare the dishes as it is eating here.' Ravinder gestured towards the men working the barbeque a few metres away. 'Would you like me to help you with ordering?' he asked.

All three nodded.

'That would be great.' Chance smiled.

'Easy on the spices for me,' Ruby added.

'That's funny,' Ravinder said lovingly. 'Your mother loved spicy food.'

'But I can't handle it.'

'Me neither,' Jennifer chimed in.

Ruby, Jennifer and Chance watched the chefs working expertly with a multitude of barbequed dishes as Ravinder conferred with the maitre d' and ordered.

Soon their table was laden with plates of Peshawari dal, burra kebab, karahi gosht, murgh malai kebab, pulao and raan.

Luckily for Ruby, the conversation remained either on the food or on related trivia. Perhaps, she reasoned, they were reluctant to talk about work in front of her, as it would have to be about the Peace Summit.

It was the murgh malai kebabs that caused a problem. Despite Ravinder's caution, they were too spicy for the ladies. Jennifer started hiccupping as the phirni arrived. Passing on dessert, she excused herself and went to the ladies room. Ruby lasted a moment longer and then she too headed there.

'I am really happy that you two managed to get together,' Chance said as Ruby walked away. 'Ruby had been apprehensive about calling you.'

'Really?'

'Yes, she was. I met her the other day and she...'

'You two seem to know each other well,' Ravinder could not help interrupting.

'Well.' Chance was unsure of how to proceed. 'We have worked together for three years now...'

Ravinder immediately sensed there was more to it.

'I have been worried about Ruby,' Chance continued. 'We all are. You know... considering the horrible way in which her mother was killed. It broke her – so much that the agency psychiatrists recommended she be sent on extended medical leave.' Chance's awkwardness was evident, perhaps because he was saying all this behind Ruby's back. 'There's no way she'll be taken back on duty till the shrinks clear her... it was that bad. I am happy to see her looking so much more relaxed.'

Ravinder could not hide his shock.

'You know about this, don't you?'

'I know that my... that Ruby's mother has passed away, but,' Ravinder shook his head, 'but that's it. Ruby did not say anything else. I guess she does not like to talk about it.'

'That's understandable.'

'What happened?'

'No one knows for sure. Just after the recent terror strikes on Jerusalem, she went to Palestine and was taking part in a peace march. The Israelis say that the Qassam terrorists bombed the march. The Palestinians say that the IDF carried out an artillery attack and shells landed on the marchers.'

Ravinder felt a faint alarm begin to hiss in his head. Something was amiss. Ruby should have told him about this, even if she did not want to talk about her job as an MI6 agent.

The more Chance told him, the louder the alarm sounded. Even as Chance spoke, Ravinder began to relive everything that had transpired since Ruby had moved in. He realized that Ruby *had* been evasive about her life. She had not avoided any questions, but her answers had always been vague and sketchy.

Could Rehana have passed on her obsession for the Palestinian cause to her, he wondered. Could she be the woman Nanda had mentioned? Ravinder couldn't push the thought away.

Could she have been the thirteenth woman that Peled had talked about? Could she be the British mercenary Anwar had mentioned who was expected to meet the LeT financier? And could Chance have some of these answers?

'What do you…' Ravinder leaned forward to question Chance when he spotted the two girls returning. He pulled back, breaking off in mid-sentence.

Chance sensed the sudden shift, looked around and saw Ruby and Jennifer threading their way back. Jennifer looked pale and ill, the spices had hit her hard.

Ruby noticed Ravinder pull away from Chance. She also noted the sudden shift in the conversation. She sensed that they had been talking about her. Perhaps Chance had said something that had put her father on guard.

Instantly she went on red alert. She had to stay focused on her mission. This father–daughter stuff was too much for her to handle.

The troubleshooter from Aligarh watched carefully as the shift changed. A new set of cops came by in ones and twos and relieved the old set. He did nothing, allowing them to settle down.

Then, when he felt things appeared as normal as they could get, he checked his weapons and got ready.

He would do everything to set the example Pasha had ordered. The jihad allowed for no mistakes.

Ravinder had signed the charge slip and was returning his credit card to his wallet when his mobile rang. He grimaced when he saw the number.

'Good afternoon, sir. How are you?'

'I am fine, Gill.' Thakur's unmistakable nasal tone came through loud and clear. 'Where are you?'

'I am at the Ashoka, sir.'

'Good. I am reaching there in a few minutes. I would like to review the security arrangements.'

''There is no need for you to bother, sir. I have just finished doing that.'

'It is no bother, Gill. This is my duty. I am in the neighbourhood so why waste the opportunity?'

'Right, sir.' Ravinder sighed. It was going to be a sheer waste of time, but he was the home minister and had to be pandered to. 'I will meet you in the lobby.' Ending the call, he turned to the others at the table, 'Duty calls. I have to go.'

Chance and Jennifer thanked him for the lunch and left.

'Come, Ruby, let me walk you to the car.' Ravinder wanted to restart the conversation they were having before lunch, but now suspicion had become part of the bag of emotions that hung between them.

They were halfway through the lobby, when Ravinder heard Thakur's voice. 'Ah! There you are, Gill!"

He turned to see Thakur saunter up to them, with his compliment of Black Cat commandos around him. Thakur's modest white kurta and pyjama contrasted sharply with the black combat dress of his PSOs. The thick gold chain around his neck and the gold plated Rolex on his wrist were hardly modest though. And Ravinder was not surprised to see Mohite beside him. What he had been planning to say to Ruby went unsaid.

Thakur spotted Ruby and his politician's smile switched on. 'And who is this lovely young lady with you? Is she the one from the CIA?'

'No, sir. This is Ruby, my daughter. Ruby, this is Mr Thakur, our home minister.'

Thakur was beaming as he shook Ruby's hand. 'How come we have not met earlier?'

'She has just returned from London, sir.' Ravinder kept the explanation brief. 'We were having lunch together. I was just dropping her off to the car.'

'What is this, Gill?' Thakur said with mock enthusiasm. 'If you had told me you were busy with family I would never have bothered you. Anyway, don't let me disrupt anything. Just show me the security arrangements and then you two can carry on.' He turned to Ruby. 'Come, my dear. I shall only take a few minutes of your father's time.'

'I don't think that is a good idea, sir,' Ravinder protested. 'This is a restricted area.'

'Come now, Gill. You must stop being a policeman all the time... she is family, after all. Isn't that right, Govind?'

'Of course, sir.' Mohite did his *Yes Minister* bit.

Ravinder had to struggle to keep his exasperation in check. Before he could respond, Thakur had taken Ruby's arm and was heading for the elevator, talking to her about London. Mohite, fawning over them, led the way.

Ravinder had to follow. They were getting into the elevator when an idea struck him. *If I cannot avoid this... and if Ruby is somehow involved in disrupting the Summit... I could use this opportunity to pass on some disinformation. That would...*

'Let me explain the security plan to you, sir,' Mohite's voice intruded. Ravinder's heart sank. In an attempt to impress Thakur, Mohite was going to spill the entire plan to him, right in front of Ruby.

And Mohite outdid himself by leaving out no detail. 'Every entry point to the secure floors is manned by ATTF personnel, two per post. Similarly, we have a section-sized picket on both the hotel gates and another section at the two roadblocks set up on both sides of the road leading up to the hotel, and three more sections guarding the rear boundary wall. So, as far as the external security is concerned, nothing but a full-scale military attack can get through.'

The elevator doors opened on the seventh floor. Leading the way out, Mohite continued, 'Inside we have two men securing the staircases on either end of the floor. Also, two men at either end of the elevators, so no unauthorized person can enter. This floor will be fully occupied by security and admin staff and the eighth floor is for the delegates... and, of course, for the meetings.'

Turning left from the elevators, Mohite led the way to the first room on the outer side of the corridor.

'This room and the adjacent two have been converted into our security control room. We will be monitoring and supervising the complete operation from here.'

He held open the door for Thakur. The minister sauntered in with his entire party in tow. Men were busy setting up a bank of monitors, there were wires and cables strewn all over.

'They are setting up the CCTV network,' Mohite explained. 'Both gates, most of the hotel periphery, the hotel lobby, the elevators, staircases and all entries and exits to the seventh and eighth floors will be monitored 24x7 from here. The camera feed is also to be beamed to Mr Gill's room, which is just down the corridor on the other side.'

'What are these?' Thakur pointed at an open cardboard carton containing neatly tied bundles of coloured plastic cards.

'Security access cards, sir, for issue to all authorized personnel. No one can enter without these cards. The blue cards are for the seventh floor only and the red for access to the entire secure zone.' He eased out a red card and handed it to Thakur. 'This one is for you, sir. It allows you complete freedom of movement over the secure zone.'

Thakur idly flipped the card around in his hand. He knew he would not need it, but the card had a nice feel. He pocketed it with a smile.

Mohite threw the bundle back in the cardboard box and led them out, once again holding the door open for Thakur.

When he tossed the bundle into the box, some cards slipped out and scattered on the floor. The PSO standing closest to the box bent down to pick them up. Ruby stepped forward and helped him before joining the others in the corridor. No one noticed her palm a red card and slip it into her handbag. Ravinder, on the other side of the minister, saw her bend down, but his attention was on Mohite, he was trying to spot a way to stem his blabbering.

When Ruby joined them in the corridor, Mohite was saying, 'Also on the other side of the elevators are the rooms for the MI6 and CIA agents.' He pointed them out. 'Directly opposite is the room we have kept for you, in case you want to rest.'

Ravinder was disgusted. Did the man have no shame?

Standing at a distance, Ruby watched this interplay with interest. She picked up on the stress between her father and his second-in-command but took care not to show that she was paying close attention.

Mohite continued, 'Next to your room, sir, is mine and beyond that is Mr Gill's. The others are for the security personnel travelling with the delegates.'

'Very good planning, Govind. Your boys have done an excellent job.'

'I am not done yet, sir.'

Thakur glanced at his watch. 'I need to get back to my office now.'

Ruby was dismayed. The opportunity to visit the floor where the delegates would be staying was slipping away. She hoped Mohite would not be dissuaded.

'Certainly, sir, I am sure you have much to do. So I shall just tell you about the rest from here only.' He marshalled his thoughts. 'The eighth floor, which is also the hotel's top floor, has been sealed off. Everything coming into it, including food and drink – even water – is coming from safe, tested sources.' Thakur nodded approvingly. 'It's only for the delegates and, of course, the meetings. We have four conference rooms – one in every corner of the floor.'

'Why four? Will they need more than one?'

'Well, the main one is on that side,' Mohite pointed to the right, 'and three smaller ones in the other three corners, just in case the delegates need to confer in private.'

'Good thinking, Govind.' Thakur turned to Ravinder and beamed. 'You have a good man here, Gill.'

'Most definitely, sir.' Ravinder tried to sound enthusiastic but did not quite succeed.

'Then, of course,' Mohite resumed, eager for the limelight, 'the roof is secured by snipers.'

'Hmm.' Thakur sounded bored now. 'I better get going.' He headed for the elevators.

Mohite raced ahead and pressed the elevator button. While they waited, he persisted with his briefing. 'From day after tomorrow, no one will be able to use these elevators to come up to the two secure floors unless they have the special access cards. Without them the elevators will not go beyond the sixth floor.'

The elevator pinged to a stop at their floor. They trooped in. With the minister's security officers, Mohite, Ravinder and Ruby, it was a tight squeeze. An awkward silence fell as Mohite realized that he had run out of things to say. Suddenly he burst out, 'I forgot to mention that the Air Force is going to enforce a strict no-fly zone around the hotel once the delegates arrive. As a matter of fact, the whole city is a no-fly zone because of the Games. So no chance of an aerial attack.'

'Excellent, excellent. I can see that you guys have looked out for everything.' Thakur now kept glancing at his watch.

'Of course we have, sir.' Mohite became animated again as he remembered something else he had forgotten. 'Just as a precaution—not that we are expecting any trouble—but in case of an emergency we have also secured the top two floors of Samrat hotel and duplicated the same arrangements there.'

'Samrat? The hotel next door?'

'That's the one, sir. It is a logical choice since we have an interconnecting, easy to secure corridor between the two hotels… from the back.'

The doors opened as the elevator reached the ground floor.

'All this seems very good. I am sure everything will go off well,' Thakur announced as they walked through the lobby. One of his PSOs ran forward to summon the car. 'In any case, I shall be here every day.'

'Every day, sir?' Ravinder kept his tone neutral, but the thought of Thakur poking around, adding to their security hassles, was scary. Mohite pandering to him all the time would be a nightmare.

'Yes, of course. I must give the delegates confidence and let them know we are taking our responsibilities very seriously.'

'Of course, sir.' Mohite pre-empted Ravinder. yet again. 'That will be perfect. I will receive you at the gate every morning.'

'I like his enthusiasm,' Thakur declared to Ravinder. 'I will be here half an hour early on the first day so that I can spend some time with the delegates, but from the second day onwards I will come just a few minutes before the Summit starts.' With that he turned to Ruby again. 'Sorry for keeping your father so busy, but this is an important event we are hosting.' Thakur gave her a sickly smile as he shook Ruby's hand. 'I hope to see more of you, my dear.'

'I am sure you will, sir.' Ruby watched him get into his car and drive away. An idea had begun to germinate in her head.

'I am sorry you had to be put through all that,' Ravinder said to her as Thakur drove off. 'You must have been bored stiff.'

Ruby noted the watchful look in his eyes. 'Not at all. Fascinating stuff.'

'Even for you? Don't you see enough of this in your agency?'

So that was what Chance had told him. Ruby kept her face expressionless. She wondered what else he had mentioned.

'Each agency is different. I had no idea you guys were doing such a massive event.'

'Oh, well,' Ravinder broke off as Mohite came back

to them. Before he could say anything, both their mobile phones began to ring. Ruby watched their faces turn serious as they spoke.

'Excuse us for a minute, Ruby.' Ravinder pulled Mohite aside.

Ruby watched them converse intensely. Ravinder seemed angry. Mohite looked defiant. She had a feeling that the calls had something to do with the Summit.

'How the hell did they get past our men?' Ravinder was yelling at Mohite. 'You had assured me that you were looking into this personally.'

'I don't know, sir. I had briefed them thoroughly. They must have done something stupid.'

Ravinder clenched his teeth. This was not the time for this conversation.

'Let's go.' He headed back towards Ruby. 'Ruby, go back home in my car. Something urgent has come up.'

An hour-long hectic drive later, they reached Saket and walked into the carnage that had once been Rizwan Khan's house.

It did not take Ravinder long to realize that the killer must have known about the surveillance. The first surveillance car, a Tata Safari parked nearby, had been bombed into oblivion and the occupants of the second had been gunned down as they ran out to respond.

'It had been detonated remotely,' the man from the

bomb disposal squad told Ravinder. 'Most probably in front of the subject's house. That allowed him to shoot down the men in the second car when they ran onto the road.' Both men lay sprawled in front of the gate. A professional for sure, Ravinder noted. Both had been classically shot, mob-execution style, once in the head and once in the heart. 'Then he ran into the subject's house and took him out.'

The front door had been shot open. Men from the crime team were scouring the house for evidence. One was walking around with a plastic evidence bag, collecting spent cases. '9mm.' He held up the bag for Ravinder.

'Two weapons, both most probably Berettas,' the leader explained as he joined Ravinder. 'He got Rizwan and both his sons.'

The three bodies lay in the living room. The first was a sixteen-year-old boy. His body lay right at the door – *he must have come running in when the firing started*. Rizwan and his second son lay further inside the room. All three of them had been despatched in the same professional manner and chances of survival were nil.

Ravinder felt sick. It had been a while since he'd been at a crime scene, especially one as gory as this. The sickening stench of blood was still billowing through the house. Controlling the urge to hold a handkerchief to his nose, he asked, 'Where is the wife?'

'Luckily she and her daughter had gone to her parent's place in Faridabad. They should be here soon.'

'Any witnesses?'

'Three – two from the house in front and one from the house on the right. They all saw a man in his thirties run out. All three said he was clean-shaven, wearing dark trousers and a dark shirt. A gun in each hand. Beyond that, nothing useful.' After a pause he added, 'But we are still questioning them. I've already called the artist to sit with them and run out an Identikit of the killer.'

'Right. Shoot me a copy ASAP.' Ravinder dismissed him and turned to Mohite. 'I want a detailed report first thing tomorrow. Make no mistake, someone will be held accountable. This is absolutely...' His anger overtook him. 'We may have lost all chance of laying our hands on that woman.'

'I have already had the borders sealed and roadblocks set up all over south Delhi,' Mohite said.

Fat lot of good that would do. By now the killer would be miles away. But Ravinder did not bother to speak. He was fuming as he walked away. Perhaps they'd made a mistake by not arresting Rizwan as soon as they learnt from Peled that he was a Lashkar financier. But then they would have lost any chance of arresting the British mercenary who was expected to collect cash from him. The Mossad Intel on that had also been clear.

His anger continued to stew as he got into Mohite's car and told the driver to take him home. It was only miles later that his anger subsided enough for him to think of the more worrying issue.

How did the killer know about the surveillance on Rizwan? They had just got the lead and mounted the surveillance. Not more than a handful knew about it. There must be a leak… But who?

He was still brooding when he reached home and lay down. But he was so exhausted that sleep came instantly.

Two rooms away, Ruby also lay down to sleep. She ran through the action checklist in her head again – the third time in the last hour.

The launchers and rockets had been collected, and were now safely stowed in the two hired vans, one launcher and two rockets per vehicle. All three heavy hitters whom Mark had engaged had reached Delhi. Tomorrow, as soon as they collected the Glocks, Mark and Ruby would brief them and then give the men time for reconnaissance. Their money was already with Mark. More importantly, after today's visit to the Ashoka and Mohite's briefing, she now knew how to penetrate the secure zone. She even had an access card to enter the secure zone. Now only the Glocks remained.

Tomorrow was going to be crucial – they *had* to

collect the Glocks from Nanda. It was critical that they got this right – the final piece of the puzzle.

But her confrontation with Simran that morning and the afternoon with Ravinder and Chance had left their mark on her. The more she interacted with Ravinder, the more she began to doubt Rehana and everything she had been told in her life so far. Ruby could tell that Ravinder was a straight shooter without a dishonest bone in his body. His relationship with his family and the fact that they knew all about his past spoke volumes about him.

Pangs of uncertainty filtered through her as she tried to sleep. She could no longer shy away from the fact that Rehana had lied to her.

But what else did mom lie to me about? Am I really doing the right thing? Is this my destiny?

She felt a headache building up. If she allowed it to escalate, it would develop into a crippling pain between her eyes. Hauling herself out of bed, she sat on the carpet, turned on her MacBook and began to play Pacman on mute. Playing this mindless game, where only her eyes and fingers moved, usually proved cathartic. But tonight Pacman did not come to her rescue. With an exasperated sigh she ended the game and began to root through her files.

As though working on their own, her fingers flicked through the finder till they settled on the video Pasha had sent her from Dubai.

A moment later the slightly grainy picture, obviously shot on a mobile phone camera, was displayed on the screen. Yusuf's body lay on the hotel bed. There were large gashes on his cheeks... his throat gaped open... Unable to control herself, Ruby vomited on the carpet as the video spooled on. She had seen it earlier – many times. And each time her reaction had been the same.

When she was sure she could vomit no more, she started cleaning up, first herself and then the carpet.

She had reached the end of her tether. She wished she had not thrown away the meds the shrink had given her. *I wish I could put a 'Do Not Disturb' sign on my mind.*

Collapsing on the bed, she passed out. The nightmare assaulted her sleep again.

Yusuf Sharbati, her uncle, had been stripped naked. He was lying flat on the bed. The large slit in his throat was overshadowed by the slashes on his face. Both his hands had been chopped off and were displayed on his chest. The bloody stumps of his outstretched hands gave him a strange, grotesque look. His eyes were still open – wide open. They were staring straight at Ruby. Beseeching her.

Take revenge. You must take revenge, they said to her. *Do not let my death go unpunished.*

Once again, her piteous cries went unheard.

She would have been even more horrified if she had known how meticulously Pasha had stage-managed this video for her. The veteran agent provocateur had known it would keep her on track, it would reinforce her anger, should she begin to falter.

And Ruby *had* begun to falter. But the gory video propelled her forward.

He pulled over to the side of the road. He was miles away now and the deed had been done. Retrieving both pistols from the car, he wiped them clean and dropped them over the side. The murky waters of the sewage drain below swallowed them up. They were good weapons and he was not happy to see them go, but he knew it was the best thing to do. And he knew Pasha would be pleased. Thinking about the fat bonus that Pasha would dish out, the man with many names and no permanent home walked back to his car and drove into the night.

Day Seven

Ravinder knew something was wrong when Mohite rushed into his office the next day.

'What happened?' Ravinder asked.

'SIGINT just intercepted a phone call from Muzaffarabad. They identified the caller as one of the Jaish-e-Mohammed commanders.'

'And?' Ravinder prodded. 'Who was he calling?'

'They're not sure, but it was probably Javed Khan.'

'What was the call about?'

'SIGINT couldn't clarify that.' Mohite looked uneasy. 'They were using some kind of one-time use and discard code. The thing is that they triangulated the mobile on which Javed was talking... It's somewhere in south Delhi, in the Lado Sarai area. The call was very short, so they couldn't get an exact fix.'

'Hmm...' Ravinder understood the implications. Lado Sarai was literally a jungle of alleys and unsurveyed houses. Trying to find a couple of men in it would be like looking for a needle in a haystack – even if Javed was still there. The manpower required was not available but it had to be done. 'Have some more posters of Javed and Aslam plastered at prominent places all over Lado Sarai. And tell the SHO to carry out a cordon and search. Even if they don't find them, at least they will spook them and keep them on the run.'

'Right, sir.' Mohite turned to the door.

'And Govind,' Ravinder called after him. 'Tell…'

There was a loud bang. Both men spun around.

The window had flown open. The latch had come loose. The two men exchanged sheepish glances. Mohite's gun was in his hand and Ravinder's hand was on the butt of his weapon.

Damn! Ravinder realized they were both on edge. *Not good!* The relentless stress was taking a toll on them. *Not good at all!*

Taking a deep breath, Ravinder resumed, 'Tell the duty officer to again take a round and brief the guards at the office and at all three of our residences.'

Mohite nodded unhappily and left. Both knew that till such time as Javed and Aslam were captured, the threat to their lives was acute. Both also knew that their chances of catching the terrorists were slim unless they got lucky… or one of those bastards slipped up.

Ravinder called Gyan to get the window fixed and began to run through the arrangements for Nanda's meeting with the terrorist for the weapons. They needed to get that right. With Rizwan Khan knocked out of the picture, it was now their only hope of catching the buggers and stopping the terrorist strike.

Hopefully it would be the same lot…

The phone rang again. It was Ashish. Before Ravinder could brief him about the latest SIGINT intercept, Ashish told him that Thakur was on his way to the Games Village and wanted to meet both of them there.

Fuck! This was the last thing he needed now. He checked his watch – there was still time for the weapons pick-up. He called Mohite as he walked to the car and asked him to take care of the deployment for Nanda's meeting.

'I will be there as soon as I can,' he assured Mohite. 'Just make sure our teams are deployed carefully, and in time. And ensure that the weapons being carried by Nanda have been dummied. I don't want live weapons in the hands of a terrorist.'

'What's the problem with that, sir? We will take the bastard in as soon as he lays a hand on the weapons.'

'Even so, just make sure you brief Nanda.'

'Don't worry about it, sir,' Mohite perked up, happy at the opportunity to redeem himself after the fiasco at Rizwan Khan's.

But knowing Mohite, Ravinder couldn't help worrying.

Ruby saw Mark cross the road and walk up to the main gate of the Garden of Five Senses. He had seen her and given a discreet nod before heading inside. Ruby continued ahead to the pre-decided spot, at the end of the garden from where she could keep an eye on things without exposing herself.

Located at the Said-ul-Azab village in Mehrauli, the Garden of Five Senses is spread over twenty acres and is one of Delhi's famous tourist attractions. With meandering pathways and beautiful lotus ponds, it is a popular spot and hundreds of people flock to it daily, for exercising, destressing or just plain old-fashioned romancing.

For the next half hour, the deadly duo scoured the ground: one, visually and the other, physically. Between them they raked through every inch, quadrant-by-quadrant, checking for anything out of the ordinary. They spotted nothing.

For once Mohite had used his brains. All three of his teams were couples pretending to use the park for what most couples did: some intimate conversation and a lot of necking. But all three teams had their eyes and ears tuned in – eyes on the garden and ears to the tiny earpieces through which Mohite was controlling them.

None picked up on Ruby, parked at the periphery, but two of them spotted Mark as he entered the park. The third pair was alerted by Mohite. Six pairs of hands instinctively inched closer to their weapons.

Sitting in the car park near the garden's smaller side entrance, Mohite nodded as he watched their target hove into the ambush site. He was sure this massive Caucasian was the man they sought.

'I think our man is here,' Mohite excitedly told Ravinder on the phone. 'Blond firangi… huge… like a bloody tank.'

'Good. That is how Nanda had described him…' Ravinder was running late. As usual, Thakur had kept them hanging till the last minute. 'Make sure everyone is alert. I am almost there…'

'No worries, sir. I have everything under control.'

But that was what worried Ravinder. He cut the call and went back to cursing the traffic. Even with the siren and police light they were not making much headway – a lorry had overturned somewhere ahead, blocking the road for miles. After several agonizing minutes, the car finally passed the upturned lorry and speeded up.

Ravinder parked the conspicuous cop car well away from the garden entrance and walked the rest of the way. He was across the road, facing the garden's main gate, when he saw Nanda drive up in his Mercedes, retrieve a blue carry bag from the car and head into the garden. He halted since he did not want Nanda to see him. The arms dealer appeared nervous and jittery and Ravinder could not risk him acknowledging his presence – that wouldn't do at all since the terrorists would certainly be watching Nanda now.

'The weapons dealer is here,' Mohite said on the phone.

'I know, I see him. Careful now... very careful. Remember, take him down as soon as he hands over the bag.'

'Wilco, sir.' Mohite's voice throbbed with excitement.

Positioned behind a tree trunk, Mark spotted Nanda as soon as he had cleared the main gate. He watched carefully, looking for signs of movement behind Nanda. He saw none. Despite that, he was wracked with unease; something did not seem right. He tightened his scrutiny over the area.

The three surveillance teams stayed immobile, watching, their hands now within reach of their weapons. They needed only a word from Mohite to close in and seize the terrorist.

Though still uneasy, Mark waved at Nanda when he felt certain the man was alone. Nanda changed direction and walked towards him. Mark spotted the beads of sweat on his brow; unusual, considering the chill in the rain-soaked air. Closer observation showed that Nanda was decidedly uneasy. He was trying hard to act casual and kept looking around furtively.

Mark's already tingling internal alarm began to sound louder. He intensified his scrutiny of the people around. The ambush teams stayed still, so he spotted nothing. But he wished to hell he had a weapon.

Well, I will – soon. Mark had spotted the bag Nanda was hefting.

'Are you okay?' Mark asked as Nanda came up.

'Sure.' Mark's scrutiny unnerved Nanda. 'I am not used to doing such stuff myself, but because it is you…'

'Is that the stuff?' Mark ignored him. He was on edge and just wanted to grab the guns and get the hell out. He snatched the bag out of Nanda's hand.

Across the road, Ravinder saw Mark grab the bag and cursed when he saw that none of the teams had moved in.

'*Now!* Take him down now!' he said aloud. The man had clearly identified himself when he'd accosted Nanda and taken the bag. What the hell were they waiting for?

Stupid motherfucker! Ravinder reached for his mobile and dialled Mohite.

Mohite heard his mobile ring, but his attention stayed focused on the two men in the garden.

'Wait! No one move,' Mohite hissed into his radio set. 'I want to see who else is with the firangi.'

The takedown teams stayed still.

'Nobody move. Give him another minute or two.'

Unzipping the bag, Mark saw four Glock 17s in it. They had been unpacked and cleaned, just as he had asked Nanda to ensure. Lying between them were two boxes of ammo. He unslung the cotton bag from his shoulder and tossed it to Nanda. 'Here's your money. Want to count it now?'

'No, no,' Nanda shook his head, too emphatically. He was sweating. The handkerchief in his hand was soaked from his attempts to dry his face. 'I am sure it is all right. I trust you.'

Mark sure as hell did not. Without another word, he turned and began to stride away swiftly. The alarm in his head had begun to clamour loudly. The need for the comforting feel of a weapon overwhelmed him. Dipping both hands into the bag, he expertly broke open a box of ammo and loaded a clip. The magazine slid into the weapon with a satisfying click.

Mohite heard his mobile ring again. This time, seeing Ravinder's number, he took the call.

'What the hell are you waiting for?' Ravinder's fury erupted in his ear.

'I want to see who else is with him. Don't worry, sir, I have it under...'

'Shut the fuck up, Mohite, and tell the teams to take him down. *Now!*'

The last word exploded like a bullet. Dropping the phone, Mohite reached for the radio and screamed into it. 'Move! *Move!* Take him down now!'

Chambering a round, Mark was taking out the pistol to shove it into his waistband when he saw the couple in front of him – about thirty feet away – suddenly spring to their feet. He spotted the weapons in their hands and knew he'd been blown. His mind automatically triggered a response.

Instead of pushing the Glock into his waistband, he brought it up and fired – once, twice, thrice – so rapidly that the sound cascaded into one long roar. Despite the distance, his aim was spot on; both cops dropped. Spinning around, Mark saw Nanda, who had started backing away.

'Son of a bitch!' Two more shots erupted out of the Glock. Nanda took the first in his chest and the second in his neck. He was thrown backwards and hit the ground with a thud.

Mark turned and ran straight towards the cop couple he had hit with his first burst. He knew the surveillance teams in any such operation would be spread out. With the team in front down, this was the safest way out. Clutching the precious bag, he broke into a sprint. He had to make it to the road. With the office hour rush at its peak, that would give him a fighting chance to melt into the crowd. That would also prevent the cops from firing at him.

Mark was moving fast, but not enough to outrun the bullets that now came at him from two sides. The other cop teams had seen what had happened to the first team. As their guns thundered, the Garden of Five Senses erupted in pandemonium. People scattered and ran senselessly in all directions.

From where Ruby was standing, she could see a flurry of movement and Mark going down. Though the gunfire was barely audible, the picture was clear. She felt an acute pain, not just because she had lost her main man, but also because she saw the Glocks fallen in the grass. She needed those. Her mind screamed at her to get clear of the area before the cops spread a dragnet. Reversing swiftly, she pulled out into the traffic, weaving through the cars as fast as she could.

'Motherfucker! Stupid bastard!' Ravinder was unable to contain the string of expletives that exploded out of him as he ran across the road towards the garden. But it was useless. The terrorist had to be dead. No way he could have survived that barrage. Still, hoping for a miracle, Ravinder ran. *Maybe I will get a couple of minutes to question him before he dies.*

I need to know what the target is... and who else is with him... He was racing forward when he almost ran into a cream-coloured Toyota Innova that came barrelling down the road. Angrily waving it to a halt, he skirted around it and headed for the park. He was halfway towards the fallen body when it struck him that the vehicle had seemed familiar. Ravinder knew he had seen it before – recently. His mind began to strain.

'He is dead, sir.' Mohite was feeling the fallen man's neck.

'Damn!' Ravinder slapped a fist into the palm of his hand. 'Why the hell did you wait so long? You should have ordered them to take him down the minute he took the guns from Nanda! And why had those guns not been dummied?'

'I wanted to see who else was with him.' Mohite avoided the second question completely. 'After all, he was not operating alone. Even Thakur sahib agreed that...'

'Fuck Thakur sahib! My orders were *very* clear.' Ravinder checked his urge to slap Mohite. 'And why did you not have the guns dummied?'

'I... forgot...' Mohite muttered sheepishly. 'I didn't think it would matter since we were going to catch him...'

'You didn't think it would matter?' Ravinder was having trouble keeping his anger under control. 'Tell that to the families of those...' He pointed at the bodies of the two cops who had been gunned down by the terrorist. His finger was quivering with fury.

Taking a deep breath, Ravinder calmed himself. It was pointless, the damage was done. Now he had to ferret out the way ahead, to try and salvage whatever they could out of this fiasco.

There have to be some leads here. There are always leads... one just has to look hard enough... and be lucky, of course.

Praying for a break, he brushed Mohite aside and began searching Mark's pockets. He struck gold in the first one, an almost new iPhone. Its memory was blank; no record of calls received or made or any numbers stored on it. Mark was too experienced not to delete the call history after every call. However, there was an unread message. Ravinder clicked it open.

Okay. I will meet you at Machan coffee shop at 7 p.m. RG.

Ravinder checked the time at which it had been received. Only four minutes ago. Around the time Mark was shot.

It was almost five. *The bloody hotel is at least an hour's drive*. He would also need time to deploy the takedown teams. Rapidly making up his mind, he turned to Mohite.

'Get a team ready to leave with me right away.'

'What happened, sir?'

'This bugger was going to meet someone at Machan, the Taj coffee shop, at seven. I'm going to see who it is...'

'Should I come with you?'

'No, just give me four men. You clean up the mess here.'

By now cops of all varieties were all over the garden. They seemed to have dropped down from the trees. Soon the media would land up. 'And Govind,' he called as he walked away, 'I want no impromptu media interviews. Just stay with no comments and the matter is under investigation. Got it?'

Fifteen minutes later he was off with four men from the support party in tow. Ravinder briefed them on the way, making sure he covered all possible contingencies. This time he had to take this man... or woman... this RG – alive.

He wondered if RG would turn out to be the person Nanda had spotted with Mark at Dilli Haat.

The thought of Nanda saddened him. Ravinder knew he had a wife and a couple of kids.

Oh, well... at least he is leaving them with plenty of

dough. Live by the sword, die by it. He should have chosen a safer profession.

Then he began to focus on the task now confronting them. Hopefully there would be no shoot-out.

In the confines of a hotel coffee shop, the damage would be... He shuddered and pushed away the horrifying image.

What could RG stand for? That held his attention briefly. It could be anything. *RG...* There was something about it. Then he remembered Mohite's 'G-string' joke. 'Each of the delegates has a name starting with G... either the first name or the family name... Even we...'

A wry smile creased Ravinder's lips. Even the bloody terrorists attacking Delhi had names starting with G. He marvelled at the coincidence.

RG! Ruby Gill? The shock pulverized him. *Could it be Ruby?*

Ruby's head was still pounding when she reached home. Mark's death, the loss of the Glocks, and then Ravinder suddenly running in front of her car had shaken her badly. It had been too close a call. If he had spotted her the game would be up. As it was, he had been guarded with her ever since that lunch with Chance and Jennifer. She wanted to be home well before he returned, safely tucked away in bed. That ought to preclude any conversation and awkward questions.

With the loss of Mark and the Glocks she would now have to rework the complete battle plan. Her options had narrowed sharply. And they hadn't been great to begin with.

'Would you like me to get your dinner ready, miss?' the maid called out as Ruby was ascending the stairs. Jasmine had told her that Westerners liked to eat early, much earlier than the Indian dinnertime of nine or ten.

'No, thank you,' Ruby replied. 'I have a headache. I think I'll lie down for a bit.' She tore off her clothes and stood under the steaming shower for a good five minutes, finally regaining some semblance of normalcy. Then she lay down to think.

The soft knock on her door caught her by surprise. She was in no mood to chat and hoped it was not Jasmine.

'May I come in, please?' Simran's voice came through.

Ruby sat up, surprised. Pulling herself together, she called out, 'Please come in.'

Simran entered hesitantly. 'The maid told me you have a headache.' She held out a strip of tablets. 'So I thought I would get you some asprin.'

'Thank you.' Ruby took them, trying to get over her surprise. 'Thank you very much.'

For a moment the two women stood looking at each other. Ruby sensed that Simran wanted to say something; she seemed to be groping for words. Then, with a resigned shrug, she turned to leave.

At the door she turned around again. 'It is not you I am angry with,' she whispered. 'Perhaps it is myself. Or Ravinder. I do not know.' She paused. 'I am just human, you know. I have the same fears that we all do – of losing the things we love.'

Ruby could see she was fighting hard to maintain her composure.

'I understand how important you are to Ravinder. He is a good man who will always do the right thing. He is the kind of man who will give his life for his children.' Simran sniffed, trying to regain control. 'He is equally important to me. And to Jasmine.'

Ruby wanted to respond. She felt the angst of the older woman but could not find the words. A gush of emotions rendered her speechless.

'I am sorry about what happened to your mother.'

Now the silence was deafening.

'And I do want you to remember… no matter what happens, he *is* your father… he will always be your father… we will always be there for you. This is your home. You can stay for as long as you want.'

Then Simran was gone. Leaving behind immense pain in Ruby's heart.

It was sixteen minutes to seven when Ravinder finally took up position in the coffee shop. He chose the table in the far corner, from where he could see the whole place.

His team of four cops were spread out – two at tables on either side of the entrance and two in the centre.

He scanned the restaurant – a large rectangular room with about twenty tables – taking it one section at a time. He saw no man or woman seated alone at any of the tables. Not that he could be sure it was just one person.

No Ruby either. He felt relieved.

Six minutes later a tall, athletic looking Caucasian woman wearing a light cotton dress walked in. Ravinder studied her. No, her snug-fitting dress could not hold a concealed weapon… not unless a small pistol was taped to her leg.

She was still a possible. Ravinder took note of her position as she sat down at a table in the centre.

Then two men entered, separately. It only became clear they were together when they sat down at the same table.

Another cluster trooped in. It was hard to tell which of them were together and which on their own. The number of possibles now escalated.

Ravinder maintained a sharp eye on the door, but he also scanned the coffee shop periodically.

A man walked in and caught his attention: broad shoulders and muscled arms under a light green Lacoste T-shirt. Ravinder saw a colourful eagle tattooed on his right arm, only partly visible. He was slouching, as though to camouflage his sense of purpose. But his eyes gave him away. They were moving across the coffee shop swiftly and expertly, too alert to belong to someone not in the game.

Relying on his intuition, Ravinder rose and began to walk casually towards the exit. The money he had left on the table would cover the coffee he had ordered. The four-man team, seeing him get up, got ready to move too.

Willing them all to stay calm, Ravinder withdrew the iPhone he had recovered from Mark's body and dialled the number from which the text had been received. By now he was almost level with his suspect, who was halfway into the coffee shop, his eyes still searching the tables.

Ravinder noted a puzzled expression on the man's face, but no alarm. Yet. The suspect glanced at his watch: it was three minutes past seven. Then his mobile rang.

The shrill trilling was nearly drowned out by the hullabaloo of the coffee shop, but Ravinder, passing right by him, heard it clearly. He thumbed the iPhone, ending the call. The suspect's mobile also stopped ringing.

Ravinder had his man.

Not Ruby! Thank God!

Swivelling around, Ravinder gestured to the nearest cop to move – a sharp and definite nod. He was hauling out his revolver as he did so. Three strides and Ravinder was behind the man.

Perhaps Ravinder had made a sound, or perhaps the man's instincts were acute, but it was already too late.

The suspect had begun to turn when the pistol in Ravinder's hand crashed down on his head, a powerful blow, with as much force as Ravinder dared. He did not want to kill the man. Not yet.

As the man stumbled, two of the cops closed in and pummelled him to the ground. Despite the suddenness of the assault, he fought back hard.

Ravinder felt a surge of satisfaction as they subdued him. One cop slapped a pair of handcuffs on him. The second ran an expert hand over him, checking for weapons – or suicide pills.

Clear!

RG had been taken alive.

Now we will find out what these buggers are up to… satisfaction swept through Ravinder. *At last. At long, bloody last, the break we needed.*

Within half an hour they were interrogating RG at the Chanakyapuri Police Station. Two hours later, they were still no closer to the truth.

'He is a tough bastard.' The SHO, Inspector Jai Ram, a short, powerfully built man with a large belly, came into his office, wiping his hands on a towel. Patches of sweat stained his rumpled uniform. Despite this, he appeared alert. 'Name is Rafael Gerber,' Jai Ram said the unfamiliar name slowly. 'Not a peep out of him. Keeps insisting he's here on holiday and wants us to call his – the German – embassy. Do you want us to give him some third degree, sir?'

Ravinder considered this. It was a sticky wicket he was playing on now. If the man turned out to be innocent, there would be hell to pay. His embassy would raise a furor.

But Ravinder knew he wasn't. *There is no way he can be.* He made up his mind. Whether it was the Games or the Summit, the stakes were too high. *Sometimes one cannot play by the rules. The fucking terrorists never do.*

'Break the bastard,' Ravinder commanded. 'Do whatever it takes, but get him to talk. Fast.'

'Leave it to me, sir. He will talk.' Jai Ram had a cold grin on his face. 'You go home. I will call you.' He was twirling the ends of his moustache. He was quite a contradiction to the godly name his parents had given him.

Ravinder almost felt sorry for the German – Jai Ram was going to give him a taste of hell. Then he thought of the stakes and his heart hardened. What had to be done, had to be done.

'No, I am staying right here.'

'It might be a long wait, sir.'

'No worries.'

The SHO left. This was his chance to score

points with such a senior officer. Opportunities such as this came rarely.

Ravinder continued mulling. Too much was coming together too fast. He could also feel the fatigue wearing him down. He called for another cup of coffee, hoping to caffeine away his exhaustion.

He was on his fifth cup when Jai Ram returned, again wiping his hands on a towel. This one was spotted with blood, as were his hands and the front of his shirt.

'He is talking.' Ravinder saw a satisfied grin on Jai Ram's face. 'In fact, he is more than happy to talk now.'

'Excellent. Who is he and what is he here for?'

'He is German... a freelancer, a mercenary. The dead guy – he says his name was Mark Leahy – had called him down to India for an operation.'

'What operation?'

'He doesn't know. Says he was to be briefed by Mark today and would be shown the target tomorrow.'

'Was it the Commonwealth Games?'

Jai Ram shook his head. 'He has no clue.'

'Damn! Are you sure he is telling the truth?'

'Right now, sir, the motherfu—' Jai Ram checked himself. 'He wouldn't lie if his mother told him to. He doesn't know what the operation is, but he does know that Mark has also called in two more mercenaries for it. He does not know who they are, but he was told they are from South Africa.'

That should give us something to work on. 'Keep the pressure on him, Jai Ram. Set up a relay of interrogators and make sure he does not get to sleep. I want to know everything he knows.'

He was pulling out his mobile as he headed out, when it rang. Prophetically, it was Mohite.

'Govind. Just the man I need.' Ravinder could not resist the pleasure of ensuring that Mohite would now have to be hard at work. It was because of his idiocy that they'd failed to take Mark alive. 'The man we captured at Machan has talked.' He brought Mohite up to speed and told him what had to be done. Then he called Ashish and briefed him as well. As long as they were not sure what the target was, both Ashish and Mohite had to be kept in the loop.

Minutes later an APB went out. The instructions were short. Every available beat constable in Delhi was hauled out.

Every hotel and lodge has to be checked – before sunrise. The two South Africans have to be found. They may be armed. They are dangerous. Exercise precaution and do not approach alone. All sightings are to be reported prior to attempting capture.

Ravinder's car had yet to reach home when hundreds of boots hit the ground. The hunt was on.

Unfortunately neither Rafael nor the interrogator was to be blamed. Rafael Gerber had not lied. Mark *had* told him that the other two men were coming from South Africa. What he had forgotten to mention was that both Shaun Ontong and Gary Boucher were Australians. They'd been operating in South Africa, but held Australian passports.

Ruby did not stop crying for a long time after Simran left. The strip of tablets lay forgotten in her hands, mangled. Not that it mattered, they would have been useless. Her pain was beyond medication. The raging conflict had started fragmenting her, loosening the already tenuous hold of sanity on her mind.

'Why did you lie to me, mom?' she sobbed. 'Why? All these years my life has been a lie.'

'Your life has not been a lie, Ruby.' From the depths of memory, Rehana tugged at her. 'Don't get taken in by all this sweet talk. Ravinder never understood me… us… our cause. For him it had no meaning. He loved the little cocoon he had created for himself. You tell me, can the life of one man be greater than the agony that hundreds of thousands of our people have suffered… continue to suffer? Can it?'

'No! But why did you…'

'You cannot falter now, Ruby. We have sacrificed everything to get you ready for this day. You are our revenge. I could have led a normal life too, but I chose our cause over that. Have you forgotten, Ruby? Have you forgotten what they did to us… to our family… to me?'

The thought pounded her, hammering her down memory lane again.

Ruby found herself back in Palestine. She got out of the car and walked up to her uncle Yusuf. He was tall and gaunt.

Unshaven and red-eyed, he was in jeans and a maroon T-shirt. A cap masked most of his face.

'I can never get over it.' He took her in his arms. 'Do you know how much you look like your mother?'

'Everyone says so.' Her words were a whisper. She began to cry as Yusuf folded her in his arms.

'I told her a million times not to come back,' Ruby heard him as though from far away. 'But she never listened... You know your mother... she would never listen, even as a child.

'Rehana was with the peace marchers, at the front with the leaders... to hand in the petition. It was a peaceful march... even some international participants from peace organizations were part of it. That's when the artillery shell landed, right at the head of the column. Those bloody Israelis! Now they say that one of our people bombed the march... but that's a lie! The bastards... they killed her!' He choked. 'There was nothing much left of any of them...' He couldn't go on. Finally he whispered, 'Come, let us go inside and you can rest for a while. You must be exhausted from the flight.'

'No, not yet. I want to see my mom.'

'I don't think that is a good idea, child. There is not much to see.'

'Whatever is left, Yusuf uncle, I want to see her. She is... was my mother. I want to see her.'

'You are so stubborn, just like her. Okay, if you are sure.'

'I am sure.'

Yusuf called the man who had driven Ruby from the airport. His going to the hospital was out of the question. They would be watching out for him. He had no illusions about what would happen if the Israelis got their hands on him.

An hour later, Ruby was at the hospital morgue, her heart pounding.

'I want to be alone with her,' Ruby said. Her tone did not leave room for discussion. The attendant didn't care; he'd encountered odder behaviour during his decades-long death watch. He flicked on the light.

The ghostly darkness dissipated as white light flooded the room. Puffs of ice-cold air hung in the room, adding to the chill inside her.

The attendant gestured at the long metal tables in the centre. Each one had a body, someone who had once been a person, with a name, a family, friends. 'The third one from the left,' he pointed and left the room.

Never before had Ruby felt so alone.

The silence was more unnerving than the screams reverberating in her head.

How can mom be so small? Ruby's hands were frozen. She willed them to reach out and touch the white sheet which had yellow-red-black stains on it. She pulled the sheet away.

There was so little left of Rehana. The upper body had all but disappeared and even the lower half was charred, tattered bits of flesh and bone. Only her right hand remained untouched, and Rehana's favourite blue sapphire ring shone brightly on it. It beckoned to Ruby. That cemented the reality of her death. Ruby now knew her mother was never coming back.

She retched and her vomit sprayed out all over the floor by Rehana's table. Ruby collapsed. The world around her went black.

When she came to, she was in a bed in an unfamiliar room. The light streaming in told her that she had been out the whole night. Yusuf was sitting by her side.

'I told you not to go, child.'

Ruby did not reply. *How do I explain?* She kept looking at him. After a while she began to sob quietly. Soon he too was crying.

A man entered. He whispered something in Yusuf's ear and left.

'It is time.' Yusuf touched Ruby lightly on the shoulder. 'We... you need to go. They are waiting.'

'You will not come?'

'I cannot, Ruby. They will be looking for me. Say goodbye to her for me.'

'I will.'

It began to rain as they laid the cloth-covered body into the ground. The lifeless bundle now seemed much bigger than what Ruby had seen in the morgue.

The rain strengthened as they began to throw mud over the body. Soon it was as though Rehana had never existed.

It was pouring now. Claps of thunder boomed out. Slashes of lightning tore up the skies. Everything was grey, cold, dark.

Long after it was all over and the handful of mourners had left, Ruby stood in the rain, watching the spot where Rehana's body now lay, six feet under. The torrent of water streaming down her face tasted salty. Ruby was crying. But she felt no sense of finality, no closure. She knew it wasn't over. Something remained unfinished.

Finally she turned and started walking back to the waiting car.

Someone should pay for this.

The thought festered.

Somebody will.

In the Gill house Ruby lay helplessly in the dark guestroom. The darkness outside slowly faded as a new sun rose but the darkness within her stayed.

They should pay for this. Her silent promise now echoed in her head. *I must make them pay.*

'So be it.' Ruby did not realize that she had spoken aloud. 'I will do my duty, but I will not harm any of the Gills... they are family too.'

I am not alone. The thought caught her by surprise. *I never was.*

That was her last thought as she fell asleep, unaware that Gerber had been captured and the noose around her was closing fast.

Ravinder awoke suddenly, his mind crystal clear.

'Sorry, sir,' the dead Nanda was saying to him with a sheepish smile, 'I was too far away to get the number, but the car was a cream-coloured Toyota Innova.'

In his mind's eye, Ravinder again saw the cream-coloured Innova that had almost run him over outside the garden gate today. He saw his hand come up to stop it and a blur of motion inside the vehicle, as though someone had ducked. He ran the scene in his head a dozen times, but he couldn't put a face to the person. It had been too fast, too sudden. His attention had been elsewhere. But Ravinder knew it was a woman. He did not know how, but he knew.

So, she had been there for the weapons pick-up... I should have known... I should have put more teams down to look out for her. Damn!

Ravinder cursed himself for the lost opportunity. As he fell asleep he wondered if he would get lucky again or if that damn woman's luck would continue to hold... *that damn thirteenth woman.*

Day Eight

Ruby wearily opened her eyes as the alarm on her mobile buzzed. She had barely slept an hour. Again she wished she hadn't thrown away the medication the shrink had prescribed.

Things were at a disastrous crossroads. The only saving grace was that Mark had not been taken alive. He was the only one who had known her identity *and* the target.

She was about to fall asleep again when the TV sprang to life; the timer had been set for the morning BBC news.

There was no change in the situation in Israel. The IDF blockade of Gaza was still under way. The turmoil in the Middle East was escalating. The local news came on. Her eyes widened as news of Gerber's arrest played out. The arrest of a foreign terrorist in Delhi on the eve of the Commonwealth Games was hot news and the news channel milked it for all it was worth.

All vestiges of sleep left her. This news devastated her. She hadn't yet figured out how to proceed without Mark and the Glocks, and now this...

Ruby felt another headache begin to build. She forced herself to get up and change into her tracksuit. Perhaps a run would clear her head.

'How is it possible that you have not been able to find those two South African mercenaries? All foreigners have to register,' Ravinder said, annoyed. 'Did you get the list from the foreigners' registration office like I told you? They have to be on it.'

'We did, sir,' said Mohite. 'And we have been tracking everyone on that list.'

'Then someone has slipped up.' Ravinder was furious. 'They have to be somewhere. They cannot check into any hotel without passports.'

'But we have rounded up almost everyone from South Africa who even remotely fits the bill,' Mohite repeated, sounding desperate. 'We have nothing, except some very angry South Africans and a pissed-off embassy official yelling at us.'

'You handle them. And keep the search going. We have to catch those two.' *Well, at least this would keep Mohite busy and out of trouble.* 'There is no time, Mohite. The Summit starts the day after. The delegates start arriving in twenty-four hours.'

Ravinder put down the phone and sat up to think. *What have I missed? There has to be something.*

He was still brooding as he walked into his study and took his laptop out of the bag. There was a whole day of e-mails to be replied to.

The water mark on the table had been wiped clean. Now only a faint ring remained. It bothered Ravinder, irritated him.

He pulled out a paper napkin and scrubbed at it. It grew faint, but would not go away completely. He was about to tell the servant to fetch some wood polish when something tugged at his memory.

Ruby had been carrying a jug of water when I ran into her that night.

He froze. An alarm jangled in his head.

He clicked open his inbox to the date on which he had run into Ruby. It had been late at night. Ravinder began to sift through the mails. The e-mail about the LeT financier caught his eye and the cursor hung over it briefly. The next e-mail too was relevant. It was about the meeting with Nanda.

If Ruby had seen these: Ravinder sat back. *That would account for the elimination of Rizwan Khan. But then why would she still have sent Mark to pick up the guns? Unless she had read the first mail but not the second.*

Ravinder leaned forward and checked the time log. The two had come in almost simultaneously. If she had seen one she would logically have seen the other.

Unless...

He raced out of the study and went looking for Ruby. He had to talk to her and get to the bottom of this. Her room was empty. He checked with the servant who told him that she had left early.

'Did she say where she was going?'

'Not to me, sahib. But she was wearing a tracksuit. It looked like she was going for a run.'

Ravinder returned to his study to think. The stakes were too high. He could not allow anything to happen, to the Games or to the Summit. *Though, knowing the Rehana angle now, if it is Ruby, it would be the Summit she would be targeting.*

His phone buzzed.

'Yes, Ashish?'

'We have found three improvised explosive devices near the Jawaharlal Nehru Stadium.' DIG Ashish sounded grim. 'Big ones, sir. Had they gone off they would have taken out a large chunk of the stadium.'

'Where?'

'Behind the ticketing booth. The bombs seem to have been there a while.'

'An inside job. Round up all personnel who have access to that area.'

'Already started that, sir.'

'Good.' Ravinder was relieved that Ashish was handling it and not Govind. 'Ensure everyone's antecedents are checked. I want that bastard found... whoever he is.'

'Don't worry, sir, I am on it. Whoever it is, we will find him. Or her.'

'Fine,' he said, even though that was not how Ravinder felt when he put the phone down.

Or her.

Ashish's final words ricocheted in his head. There were too many things happening, on too many fronts.

'Slow down the game.'

Ravinder heard the voice of his college basketball coach echo in his memory.

The limited options now available to her churned through her mind as Ruby pounded down the silent road. At this early hour, not many people were around. Puddles littered the road, hangovers of last night's rain. A sense of isolation filled Ruby. She needed help. Or at least someone to talk to.

Should I call Pasha? What will he be able to do from Pakistan? She toyed with the idea. *What other options do I have? Even if he can't help, maybe I can talk it through with him.*

She could think of no one else to talk to and the thought depressed her so much that she felt the urge to scream. She stopped and pulled out her mobile. Her fingers dialled the number of his satellite phone, which was embedded in her memory.

Ravinder broke out of his reverie. The father in him could no longer ignore the fact that his own daughter might be a part of this awful threat.

Could Ruby really be part of this conspiracy? An MI6 agent? Was it not possible that she was just a girl hurting from the loss of her mother, who had turned to him because she needed her father to stand by her at this dark hour? Could the sins of her mother...

The father in him begged him to give her the benefit of doubt. The cop firmly urged him to fill in the gaps in his information, to complete the picture and deal with his suspicions.

Ravinder got dressed and left for office. He would gather more information and size up the threat in its totality. The push-pull between father and cop continued as his car navigated through the traffic.

It was time to slow down the game and seize control... before it spun out of his hands.

Ruby's finger was pressing the final digit of Pasha's number when she paused.

Do I really need him? He will probably send some good-for-nothing footsloggers to my aid.

Do I need poorly-trained zealots breathing down my neck?

Her finger hovered over the button.

And can I trust his security? After all, the cops had known about Rizwan Khan. Who else had been blown?

She made up her mind with a snap.

I can do this without him. Without anyone.

Pushing the phone back into her pocket, she began to run again. She had no idea what molecules sweeping through her caused these abrupt mood and energy shifts. If she had, she might have realized that the medications the shrink had prescribed could have kept her sane.

An hour later, nothing had changed. The reality was stark. She had best acknowledge it and adapt.

I will have to scale down. She saw no other option. *Hell, even if I manage to take down a couple of the delegates it would kill the Summit.*

But then her truant mind started playing games.

And you? You think you will get out of this alive? Without your primary and diversionary attacks?

A wave of sadness overwhelmed her. But, just as abruptly, the double agent took charge, returning to fortify her.

It doesn't matter whether I live or die. But they must pay... She stopped running and hailed the first passing cab.

It was time to get the operation back on track.

Ravinder marshalled all the data. Everything recovered from Mark, along with a photograph of his body, was laid out on one side of his office table. The items found on Gerber and in his hotel room were on the other side, along with a transcript of his interrogation. In the middle, a paper on which he had jotted down all the contra-indicatory facts that he had gleaned about Ruby. He mulled over everything, identified the gaps that he still needed to fill and put together a list. Then he reached for the phone.

The first call was to London, to Sir Edward Kingsley, Director of MI6.

'Does this have anything to do with Sir Tang's visit to Delhi?' Kingsley asked bluntly. The two went a long way back and the director knew he could talk freely with Ravinder.

'Maybe, maybe not,' Ravinder replied. 'That is what I am trying to ascertain.'

'I see. Give me a couple of minutes.' Computers in London whirred into action, but neither Rehana's nor Ruby Gill's names elicited anything useful. However, Sir Edward promised to dig deeper.

Ravinder's second call was to his counterpart in Tel Aviv, the head of their counter-terrorism task force.

'What did you say the names were?'

Ravinder could hear the tapping of a keyboard as he repeated the names. They appeared to get an instant response.

'Would you mind if we call you back?'

'I am in a bit of a rush.'

'It will take only a few minutes. Someone here would like to speak to you.'

Seven minutes later Meir Dagan called him back on a secure line.

'Firstly, I must thank you for all the help with that problem across the border.' Dagan was aware of the risk India had taken. It would have been disastrous if any members of the kidon team were taken alive. 'My government appreciates it.'

'A pleasure, Mr Dagan.' But Ravinder couldn't keep the anxiety out of his voice. Dagan picked up on it and asked him why. Ravinder told him.

'Before I speak further, I want your assurance that this conversation will remain off the books.' Dagan got straight to the point.

'If that is what you want.'

'It is.'

'So be it. Whatever you say will remain with me. Even if I take action, I will not divulge the reasons or the source.'

'Thank you. I must warn you, though, this is going to be unusual. I am not sure if my government would approve of it.'

'These are unusual times, Mr Dagan.'

'They certainly are, Mr Gill. Does the name Yusuf Sharbati mean anything to you?'

'Hmmm... I have heard it... Isn't he the Qassam Brigades commander who was... who met his end at Dubai a few weeks ago?'

'Yes, the very same. Yusuf was the one who engineered the Jerusalem strike with help from the Lashkar-e-Toiba. His death was our payback.'

'I understand.'

'I think you do.'

'I have no issues with Yusuf's death. He got what he deserved. But I am not able to understand what he has to do with my queries.'

'Do you know that Sharbati was not his real name? He took that on as a nom de guerre only when he joined the Qassam Brigades.'

Ravinder felt a sense of something evil coming at him.

'His real name was Yusuf al-Moghrabi. Does *that* name mean anything to you, Mr Gill?'

Ravinder felt sick. 'Moghrabi was my first wife's family name,' he whispered, the shock sinking in.

'Yusuf Sharbati was her brother.'

'But Rehana had said both her brothers had died.'

Dagan did not say anything.

'Does Ruby, my daughter, know about Yusuf? Did she know him?'

'We do not know. We think she does. We have reason to believe that she met him when she came here for her mother's funeral. But to be honest, we are not sure. We picked her up the minute she landed in Tel Aviv. The immigration officer kept her engaged while he informed our office. By the time she left the airport we had a surveillance team on her and a beeper in her suitcase. An hour later she managed to lose both and simply vanished into the West Bank. Why would she have done that if she had nothing to hide?'

Why indeed?

'We picked her up again at her mother's funeral, but once again Ruby lost the surveillance. When she showed up at the airport the next day, we questioned her. Our man specifically asked her if she knew Yusuf... he showed her his picture. She denied meeting him, even denied knowing him. Our man reminded her that as a British government employee, it was her duty to help us track down a known terrorist.'

'What did she say?'

'"I would if I could, officer. I wish I could."'

His words hung between them for a while. 'And since we had no evidence, we could not detain her.'

A brief silence took over, broken by Dagan a few seconds later.

'I must also tell you, almost the same thing happened when Rehana reached Israel after the Jerusalem strike. Our computers picked up her name and we mounted an electronic and physical surveillance. We managed to track her to the house of one Abdul Bari, who had been the neighbour and lab assistant of her late father.

Bari took her to meet Bashshar, the local Hamas man, also a junior Qassam Brigades commander... someone we've had our eye on for some time. A couple of hours later, Rehana managed to lose the bugs and the men watching her. The next we heard of her she had been killed during the Interfaith Freedom March at the main square on Abu Bakr street.

'So, though we have no proof that either Rehana or Ruby met Yusuf, their actions were not beyond suspicion. Why else would they have ditched the bugs or the surveillance? Not something an ordinary person would even notice.'

'Hmmm...'

'So, like I said earlier, no real proof. And yes, there is one more thing. Our people recovered a mobile from Yusuf Sharbati in Dubai. One call was made to it, from a satellite phone, which we traced to Pakistan...'

'Yes. Your man, Ido Peled, told us about that.'

'So we put that satellite phone on our monitoring list and then we picked up a call made to it from London.'

'When was that?'

Dagan told him. Ravinder did the math. It had been made when Ruby was still in London. But what did that prove?

'Was it...' He hesitated, knowing this was the key question. If the caller was Ruby, his duty would be clear.

'We have no idea who it was,' Dagan second-guessed him. 'The caller didn't say a word. The satellite phone was answered by a man, who said his phone was low on battery and he would call back. That was it. So all we know is that the call originated from a public phone in central London.'

Ravinder felt deeply troubled when he put the phone down. He knew he could not stop here. He redialled and minutes later he was on to London again.

'Like I mentioned earlier, Ruby Gill is currently on medical leave.'

'Yes, but I need only to know where she was on these dates.' Ravinder gave out the dates of the fortnight spanning the weeks on either side of the Jerusalem terror strike.

'Well, she was right here... in England. We cannot say where, but she was certainly in the country.'

'I see.' Ravinder didn't know if he should be relieved or disturbed.

Gyan entered right after he had put down the phone. 'Sir, the agent from London is here to see you.'

'Send him in.' Ravinder wondered what Chance wanted, but he was glad to see him. Perhaps he could help.

They had just greeted each other when Chance spotted the photo of Mark's body on Ravinder's table. With the Congo operation fresh in his memory, he recognized it immediately. 'That's Mark Leahy. What's he doing here?'

'You know him?' Ravinder was surprised.

'Yes. He's ex-military, did some work for... our government,' he broke off realizing this was an area he did not wish to go into. 'Ruby knows him too.'

'She does?' Somehow Ravinder was not surprised, but it made his heart slump.

'Better than I do. He was her backup for our last operation. Why?'

Ravinder took a long moment to gather his thoughts and to decide how much to tell Chance. He finally decided to tell Chance everything, except what Dagan had told him in confidence.

'The arms dealer was sure it was a woman?' Chance asked, trying to hide his shock.

'No, but he believed it was.'

'What do you think the target is?'

'If Ruby is involved, it's the Summit.'

'What next then?' he asked, watching Ravinder carefully.

Ravinder flinched inwardly but met Chance's scrutiny head on. 'Then we take Ruby in.'

'Is it that simple, Mr Gill?' Chance leaned back in his chair, running his fingers through his hair.

'What do you mean?'

'With the evidence you have so far, such as it is, our government will blow a gasket if you arrest her. Ruby is a British national – and an MI6 agent. You will not be able to hold her for long – if at all – you can bet on that.'

'It would only be a few days,' Ravinder pointed out. 'The delegates start arriving tomorrow. A week at best and it will all be over.'

'Yes, but I don't see that happening. Not unless you are willing to risk a big international incident.'

Ravinder closed his eyes and pondered. If he arrested her and could not come up with proof, it would be the end of his career. And if he were wrong, it would be the end of a relationship with his first-born.

'Also, if she is involved in any strike,' Chance pointed out, 'how likely is it that she'd be operating alone? How can we be sure that arresting her will stop the strike?'

'From what Gerber has told us, we know she's not alone.'

'Right. And considering the time frame,' Chance said, 'she might already have deployed them and others that we may not even know about, right?'

Ravinder was silent for a while. He knew that taking Ruby in might not actually stop a strike. But he had to be sure he was thinking as a cop and not a father. Finally he nodded. 'Yes, that makes sense.'

'So, then, why don't we leave things the way they are? We allow her to believe that we do not suspect her and maintain status quo. If she continues staying at your house, not only can you keep an eye on her, she may even lead us to the others.'

It took Ravinder time to respond. 'Okay, I agree.'

Even as he said that he felt a nagging doubt tug at him. *Am I doing the right thing? Would it not be simpler to just take her in and...*

Then Mohite rushed in, excited and dishevelled.

'I think we have them, sir.'

'Whom?'

'The two South African mercenaries!'

'Really? Where did you find them?'

'A small guesthouse in Paharganj. One of the whore—' Mohite checked himself. 'One of those disreputable ones.'

'Good!' Ravinder thumped the table, delighted at the break. 'Where are they now?'

'They'll be here any minute.'

'Take them straight for interrogation. We'll be down right away.'

'We?' Mohite threw a pointed glance at Chance.

Chance took the hint. 'I was just leaving.' He got up.

'No, that's all right, Chance. Please stay.' Ravinder turned to Mohite. 'We are batting for the same side, Govind.'

Mohite nodded unhappily. Ravinder sensed he'd soon be hearing more about this from Thakur. But he had bigger fish to fry. If he managed to stop a terrorist strike, even Thakur would leave him alone for some time.

An hour later all the excitement proved futile.

The only thing the two South Africans were guilty of was having picked the wrong day to visit the wrong whorehouse. And they'd compounded their error by trying to fight off the cops – including breaking the nose of a rather vindictive inspector – and trying to make a break for it when the whorehouse was raided. And that both South Africans were solidly built ex-soldiers had convinced the furious cop that these were the two mercenaries wanted by the ATTF.

Unwilling to talk openly with Mohite around, Ravinder waited till he was alone before speaking with Chance again. 'I am going home now. Let me see what Ruby is up to.'

'Do that. Keep her with you as much as possible.'

'Where are you headed?'

'Back to the hotel to check out the deployment again. I am still not happy with how the security guys are responding to the emergency drill.'

He was walking away when an idea struck Ravinder. He was certain it would work, but it required more than a single pair of hands. He also knew Chance was a man he could trust to make it happen.

'Chance, one second.' Ravinder called him back and explained what he had in mind. 'What do you think?'

'Using decoy delegates in case of an attempted strike on the Summit... yes, it could work. This is a brilliant idea!' Chance sounded excited. 'It will keep them safe and also, if we use armed decoys, give us a chance to take down the attackers.'

'But we'll need more people.'

'You can count me in,' Chance assured him. 'Who else do you have in mind? Mr Mohite?'

'No. He already has too much to do.'

Chance had already sensed Ravinder's disconnect with his second-in-command. He didn't say anything, but felt relieved. 'What about Jennifer?'

'She should do, but don't brief her just yet. The fewer who know, the better.' Pause. 'Right now women from the West are not too high on my list of trusted people.'

They both laughed, grim laughs, but desperate for respite, however momentary.

'How about Ido Peled?'

'Peled looks rock-solid. He should be good. I'll speak to him right away.'

'When the time is right, I can speak to Jennifer.'

'Yes. Between the four of us, we can ensure both floors are sealed off and all the delegates guarded. I will detail four of my people, people I can rely on totally, to act as escorts.'

'Sounds good,' Chance concurred. 'What about the decoys?'

Ravinder ran over his options. 'I think our best bet is the NSG – the National Security Guard. Their director general, Kaul, is a good friend. He will give us the thirteen decoys we need.'

The two men ironed out the details of the plan to ensure nothing had been overlooked. The minute an attack was mounted on the Summit, the delegates would be moved to another conference room secured by Ido Peled. Chance would man the eighth floor and Jennifer the seventh, while Ravinder took charge of the control room. The thirteen decoys, who would also be suitably armed, would be moved under armed escort to the alternate venue, the Samrat hotel. The decoys would be used to draw out the attackers who could then be neutralized.

Satisfied that they'd covered the critical points, they went their separate ways. Ravinder first called and briefed the three guards at his house not to allow anyone out without clearing it with him and also tasked a plainclothes team, three men including the driver, to mount surveillance on his house from sunrise to midnight.

'You must not let Ruby out of your sight even for a minute and at the same time ensure she does not know you are watching her.' He noted the puzzled looks on their faces. 'There have been some threats but she refuses to accept protection, so…' He left the rest unsaid.

Ravinder's mind was in turmoil as he started for home.

As the car hit the road he checked his watch. The delegates would be arriving soon. Athletes had already been landing in droves for the Games. There were uniforms and guns everywhere. Delhi, he sensed, was a city under siege.

India was leaving nothing to chance. From Kashmir to the borders in Punjab and Rajasthan, the army had swamped every possible infiltration point into India. The Indian Navy had more ships and boats along the coastline than there were fish in the waters. The air space over Delhi was closed and even scheduled commercial flights were being shepherded by the Indian Air Force. Paramilitary forces had barricaded every road and dirt track into the National Capital Region. The Delhi Police had borrowed every available cop from neighbouring states and had swept the streets clean of criminals. New tenants in every residential colony were being visited by a beat constable and their credentials verified.

As Mohite had succinctly put it to Ravinder, 'The NCR is locked down tight, boss. Tight as a virgin's cunt.'

Ravinder had winced. A city the size and shape of Delhi could *never* be locked down completely. And the fact that the danger may already have penetrated the fort was a possibility he could no longer ignore.

Coupled with this were the unprecedented rains that had not only flooded most roads, slowing traffic to an abysmal crawl, they had also brought about an outbreak of dengue and conjunctivitis, which had laid low many of his cops. Everything that could, had started going wrong.

By the time the surveillance team was deployed outside the Gill house, Ruby was back home. Despite the run of bad luck, her day had been productive. She had not only finalized her attack plan, but also briefed Ontong and Boucher, and mated them up with their vans and rocket launchers.

Both had baulked when she told them what she expected them to do. But their objections faded when she pointed out that with Mark and Gerber out of the running, she would double their payout. Greed gobbled up all their doubts.

With that settled, Ruby returned home, satisfied that things were back on track. Her new, abbreviated plan was as good as it could get in the altered circumstances.

When Ravinder reached home, Ruby was sitting with Jasmine on the lawn. The two were chatting merrily. Jasmine, in the thick of her final semester exams, appeared to be sharing her excitement and stress with her sister. Ravinder could hear Jasmine narrating an incident about the moot court she was in at college. Ruby burst into laughter.

Everything looked so normal. Looking at her, Ravinder found it hard to believe that she could be the one targeting the Summit.

'What are my lovely girls up to?' He concealed his troubled thoughts with a warm smile as he walked up to them.

They both got up and hugged him. If there was anything on Ruby's mind, she hid it well.

Am I being paranoid? Just because Rehana and her brother Yusuf were crusaders for the Palestinian cause, is it fair to tar her with the same brush? Could I be overlooking some other, more real threat?

'I want to take Ruby shopping,' Jasmine's voice intruded. 'She wants to pick up some Indian clothes before she leaves.'

'Leaves?' Ravinder was surprised. 'Where are you going, Ruby?'

'Home.' Ruby's reply was tentative, as though she was not really sure what that word meant any more. 'I can't stay here forever.' She laughed, sounding a little embarrassed.

'Oh!' Ravinder was stunned. Already worried about her possible involvement in the threat to the Summit, this latest news added to his emotional turmoil.

'But before shopping we are planning to catch a

movie,' Jasmine's voice tugged at Ravinder. 'Would you please have your office book the movie tickets?'

'Which movie?' Ravinder was only half-listening. He could feel Ruby's gaze on him. She looked... confused? Expectant? He wasn't sure. He sensed that she was waiting for him to say something to her. But what?

'Would you please?' Jasmine asked again.

'Sure.' Ravinder nodded, glad to be able to focus on something practical. This emotional rollercoaster was getting too much for him to handle. He was exhausted.

'Thanks, daddy! You're a sweetheart! We were thinking of watching *Sex and the City* – the new one. If you could book it at the Select City mall, we can shop there after the movie.'

'I will take care of it, princess. You can use my car too.'

'But we'll be out late. I don't think we'll be back before nine or ten.'

'No problem. I'll tell my office to send another car if I need it, but I don't think I'll be stepping out now. From tomorrow I'll be staying at the hotel for the next few days.'

'You won't be coming home at all?' Jasmine asked.

'No. Not until this event is over. I need to see that things go smoothly.'

'I am also going to be tied up at college for the next three days, moot court in the mornings and then we're all planning to go for the various cultural events that are being held.'

'And you, Ruby? What are your plans?'

'Nothing special.' She looked strangely subdued. 'Just catch up on some more sightseeing... maybe another movie.'

'Why don't you go with Jasmine for the cultural events? A lot of Bollywood stars are here for the Games.'

'Maybe I will. Let's see.'

'That'll be fun.' Jasmine smiled. 'Come, Ruby, let's get ready.' She took Ruby's arm and pulled her away.

'Okay, girls. Have fun.'

He gave them a hug each and watched them walk away. Once they were out of earshot, he called his office and asked his assistant to book two tickets for the girls and two more for the surveillance team a couple of rows behind. Then he briefed the surveillance team.

Ravinder climbed the stairs to his room, feeling confused, as though he had missed something back there, but happy that Ruby would be under close watch till late at night. Abruptly an insidious thought angled in. Would Jasmine be okay? If Ruby had indeed turned rogue she could be dangerous...

Something in his heart refused to believe that Ruby would harm Jasmine. But he could not push away a niggling doubt.

Ruby felt hurt and puzzled. In light of Ravinder's guarded behaviour since that eventful lunch with Chance, she had expected...

Expected what? Is it only my guilty conscience at work?

Willing herself to focus on Jasmine, Ruby got engrossed in their conversation again, but deep inside she was far away, hurting and no longer sure if she was on the right path.

He could have asked me to stay... But he didn't. If he had offered just once... She felt like crying. *Am I being fair?*

As they drove off, Ruby picked up on the surveillance car almost instantly.

So he was having her followed. She started to feel betrayed again. On second thoughts, perhaps this was normal procedure for the ATTF chief's family. Maybe it was just a security team.

These conflicting thoughts thrummed in her ears as she tuned out Jasmine's chatter and leaned deeper into her mind.

He didn't even ask me to stay. The painful thought nagged her again.

Minutes later her resolve was firm again. The hate was back. The avenger knew she could not falter.

Her eyes went to her wristwatch. Barely twenty hours left now. Soon the delegates would be in place.

The time to kill was rushing towards her.

Tuning into what Jasmine was saying, Ruby threw

herself back into the game she was playing – she was being forced to play.

He did not even want to me stay… what kind of father is he? Mom was right all along.

When Ravinder entered the bedroom he could tell that Simran was worried. Several times in the past few days she had tried to talk to him, but he'd pulled away, not knowing how much to share with her. Now he knew his silence was not helping her, or the situation.

He closed the door and sat beside her. Slowly he started sharing his story with her… and his fears.

When he finished, the house was silent. Neither realized that the sun had set and darkness had crept in.

'I know how you must be feeling.' The affection in Simran's voice reached out to him through the darkness. He realized that there were depths to her which he had not yet fathomed, despite their years together.

Have I really given my everything to this marriage? Or have I let Rehana's memories come between us? He was consumed by guilt.

'This must be so difficult for you.' Simran reached out and cupped his face in her hands. Her hands came away wet. 'Don't worry. I know you well, Ravinder. I know you will always do the right thing. Just trust your instincts.'

Ravinder felt an ache in his heart. He realized how deeply he cared for her, despite the bickering and nagging. He reached out and held her close. They kissed, a deep, long kiss as though they had been apart for a long time. Slowly, but with a tingling sense of urgency, they rediscovered each other.

They lay together in an embrace for a long time – content, a shield of love surrounding them.

But suddenly reality dawned on them.

'Do you think it is safe for Jasmine to have gone out with her?'

Ravinder shivered as Simran voiced the same fear he felt. He did not know. Worse, he did not know how to tell Simran that.

They heard the front door open and the sounds of young girls in animated conversation floated up. The clattering of feet followed as Ruby and Jasmine came up the stairs.

'The next time they go out I will also go with them,' Simran said as they heard the girls go into Ruby's room.

'I was thinking of asking Jasmine to take Ruby to the opening ceremony of the Games,' Ravinder mused out loud. He looked at Simran, as if for her approval. 'There is nothing anyone can do to anyone there. It will be safe.'

'But I will still go with them.'

Silence returned. A short while ago it had

been warm and full of love. Now it was cold and forbidding.

By the time Jasmine decided to call it a night, Ruby was exhausted. But no matter how hard she tried, she couldn't sleep. After a while she parked herself in the bay window overlooking the front lawn.

A full moon rode high, playing hide-and-seek between the fluffs of clouds. Ruby saw it all with unseeing eyes.

Her mind was far away, watching a happy little girl playing hide-and-seek with her parents. She could see Rehana and Ravinder walking through the house looking for her.

'Come out, come out, wherever you are...' their singsong chants rang out, making her giggle from the bedroom cupboard.

Then Ravinder was no longer there. Only Rehana, and she did not seem happy. And the little girl was not happy either. They were both quiet and subdued.

Soon Rehana too vanished. The little girl was alone, only not so little now. She was angry. And she felt betrayed.

Across the corridor, Ravinder tossed and turned, dead tired but unable to sleep. It was that nagging feeling of having missed something. Perhaps the feeling that he should have gone with the evidence and taken Ruby into custody. Perhaps that he could not reconcile with the fact that his daughter might be the enemy. Perhaps it was that look in Ruby's eyes when Jasmine had mentioned she was leaving.

He felt an increasing foreboding that something awful was straining to be unleashed.

His uneasiness reached out to Simran. Lying awake beside him, she too was aware of the unhappy young woman who had disrupted their lives.

They lay in silence, almost touching, waiting for the endless night to recede.

Seven miles away as the crow flies, in his room at the Ashoka hotel, Chance also lay awake in bed. Finally, he too gave up, took out a Coke from the minibar and sat near the window, watching the moon outside. The beauty of the calm October night slipped past him, unnoticed.

Like an erratically choreographed movie, bits of the past flowed through him. Ruby loomed large in many of them. Ruby laughing, pensive, morose. He wondered again if she was involved.

And always, hanging like a dark cloud over his thoughts, was the morrow slowly approaching. He hoped the days ahead would pass peacefully and it would all end well.

A few hundred miles to the north, standing on the porch of a LeT safehouse near the Pakistani town of Muridke, Pasha watched the same bright moon. He patrolled the porch restlessly, wondering how his assassin was faring. The shocking assault that had taken out Anwar, and the total absence of communication from Ruby sickened him. The agent provocateur knew that under pressure of the end game, even the best-trained agent could falter. But he also knew that the battle had already slipped out of his hands. As it always did once a mission was launched.

Nothing to do now, but wait.

A neatly dressed man got out of the car and walked up to the main gate of the Gill house. He had a piece of paper in his hand and was referring to it as he approached the gate. Barring the light from an occasional street lamp, the street was dark.

'Excuse me,' he said to the guard standing outside, holding up the paper. 'Can you please tell me where Mr Mahajan stays?'

The sentry shouldered his rifle and held out his hand. 'Show me the house number.'

The man drew closer.

Two other guards heard the exchange and came closer. Now all four men were just a few metres apart.

The sentry was taking the paper from him and failed to see the man's right hand creep up to his waist. There was a soft click, which registered with none of the guards. The bomb wrapped around the man's waist went off with a thunderous roar. Nothing within a seven-metre radius remained standing.

All three guards and a part of the metal gate blew up. The bomber himself disintegrated. Only one of the guards had been standing farther away and he survived, but even he was knocked unconscious.

The roar of the explosion had not yet abated when the door of the car in which the man had arrived flew open and another man leapt out, a Chinese T-56 assault rifle in hand.

Rushing past the body of Aslam, his former cellmate, who had taken out the guards at the cost of his life, Javed Khan headed straight for the front door, his rifle on the ready. The mission given to him by the Jaish-e-Mohammed chief was clear. He had to kill the ATTF chief, or die trying.

Levelling his rifle at the door, he fired a long burst, shattering the lock. He kicked open the remnants of the door and entered the house. He saw no lights on the ground floor. The curtains were drawn and the house was swathed in darkness. Cursing, Javed began to feel his way forward, trying to find a light switch.

To Ravinder the sound was so loud, so close, that he knew the house was under attack. The popping crack of an assault rifle confirmed it. Not pausing to think, he leapt out of bed, grabbed the Browning from the bedside table and, clicking off the safety, headed out.

'Go to Jasmine's room and lock yourselves in,' he yelled at Simran as he ran. 'And call the control room.' In the heat of the moment he forgot about Ruby.

Simran ran for Jasmine's room.

Jasmine too had been jolted awake, but she was befuddled. Then she saw her mother rush in, wild-eyed.

'We're being attacked!' Simran screeched. She reached out and grabbed Jasmine, and began to blubber hysterically.

Simran was still wailing when she reached for the phone and dialled 100, the police control room, managing to get the message across. The two women clutched each other, terrified. In her panic, Simran had forgotten to lock the bedroom door.

Sitting by the guest bedroom's bay window, Ruby saw the blinding flash of the bomb. She froze. The rifle burst galvanized her into action. Instantly, her training took over. She ran for the weapon that should have been by her bedside. But her hand came away empty. Then she realized where she was. The pistol in Jasmine's room flashed in her memory. A dozen quick steps and she burst into Jasmine's room.

Jasmine and Simran screamed when the door flew open.

Ruby took in their condition at a glance. Without breaking her stride, she raced to the jewellery box, snatched out the pistol, her hands instinctively checking if the magazine was loaded. It was. She chambered a round.

A loud metallic clang from the living room spurred her on. She swivelled around and ran out.

—

Cursing the darkness, Javed clawed the walls to find a light switch. He had taken about ten steps when he collided with a large brass lamp. It toppled and hit the ground with a loud clang. *Hell! By now someone would have called the cops and they'd be on the way.* He was still deciding what to do when...

—

Ravinder was at the head of the stairs when the brass lamp hit the floor. The gun steady in his right hand, he smacked the light switch with his left. Fingers of light flashed into the living room. Immediately he saw the intruder. The rifle in the man's hand began to rise. Ravinder's weapon was already levelled. He fired. And missed.

Thirty feet away, the assault rifle roared to life. It was set on automatic. Like pinpricks of light, a volley of bullets flew at him.

Ravinder threw himself down, forgetting that he was standing at the head of the stairs. His head hit the wood, hard. Though the stairs were carpeted, it was enough to knock him unconscious.

Javed saw Ravinder fall. He heard the body hit the stairs and start to slide down. Javed assumed he had hit him. Now he needed to confirm if it was really the ATTF chief or just one of his minions. Javed raced up the stairs.

Racing forward, Ruby was chambering a round when a pistol shot rang out, followed closely by the roar of an assault rifle. Then she heard the thud of a body hitting the floor. She erupted out of the corridor that led to the staircase landing.

The sight before her eyes made her freeze.

Halfway down the stairs Ravinder lay in a heap. On his way up was a man with an assault rifle and a crazed look.

Something inside Ruby broke. She fired. Again. And then again.

The first two bullets, delivered to his chest at close

range, brought Javed to a dead halt. The third blew him backwards. He was almost dead when he hit the foot of the staircase.

But Ruby did not stop. The killing heat was upon her, compounding her rage at the unknown man who had orphaned her. A few feet from him, the intruder still had some life in him. Kneeling next to him she prodded his face with the pistol. Javed's eyes fluttered open.

Ruby leaned closer, right into his ear and whispered, 'You-will-*not*-kill-my-dad. No-one-will-*ever*-kill-my-dad.' Each word hissed out, separately, unforgivingly. Placing the pistol against his forehead, she pulled the trigger. And kept firing till the weapon was empty.

In the distance she heard the wailing of police sirens. She felt empty. Completely hollow. Drained.

Then she heard a moan behind her as Ravinder regained consciousness.

Shocked, she turned and saw Ravinder sitting up, holding his head where it had struck the stairs. He looked dazed but unhurt. Something inside her began to sing again. Something cried. Something snapped.

Dropping the pistol, she ran to Ravinder.

'Are you all right, dad?'

He nodded, still dazed.

Just then Simran appeared at the head of the stairs,

with Jasmine in tow. They saw Ravinder's head cradled in Ruby's lap.

'Ruby saved all of us today,' Ravinder said hoarsely with tears in his eyes.

Both women started to sob as the aftershock struck.

Ruby sat silent and still, stroking Ravinder's hair softly, lovingly. Her eyes were blank and silent. Something inside her head had fragmented. She no longer knew who she was. Where she was. Why she was.

Vehicles came to a screeching halt outside. Cops burst into the house.

Ruby did not see them. She heard nothing. She motioned to Jasmine to come closer and sit beside her. She gently moved Ravinder's head to Jasmine's lap. 'Look after daddy. No one must hurt him.' Then Ruby returned to her bedroom, seemingly oblivious.

Simran, Ravinder and Jasmine watched her go. None of them knew what to say or do.

Ruby collapsed on the bed. For once her mind did not trouble her. It couldn't. Something inside had broken loose. A Rubicon had been crossed.

Unaware of the turmoil awaiting them, thirteen men from seven countries made their way to India.

From Washington, London, Tel Aviv, Cairo,

Damascus and Amman, one by one their aircrafts slid through the skies and swept closer to Delhi.

In their hands lay the fate of millions of people – hope for Palestine and peace for Israel. Their success would mean the return of peace to a land troubled by bloodshed for many years. Each one was keenly aware of it.

Though none of them had any illusions about the gargantuan task that awaited them, they had hope.

Day Nine

A new sun was rising when Senator George Polk's flight touched down at Palam.

Thakur met the silver-coloured US Air Force jet in the VIP area of the Air Force Station. Slightly balding, ruddy-faced, with an aura of power, the senator had a wide smile as he descended from the plane. He seemed a tad disappointed to see the small welcome committee. He had expected some press there to hail America's critical role in this event.

Mohite was hovering around Thakur. Jennifer Poetzcsh was there too, the senator being her responsibility. Suspicious of everything and mistrustful of the security cover provided by the Indians, her hand never strayed from her gun.

Thakur, also eager to make his presence felt, accompanied the senator to the hotel to make sure he was comfortably settled in.

Ravinder joined them there a bit later, still groggy from the events of the previous night. His head hurt less now, dulled by painkillers, but he was still reeling from the emotional jolt. Ruby's actions had left him utterly confused. However, still unable to ignore the evidence against her, he would continue the surveillance until the delegates left India. That seemed to be the safest option.

They had barely settled the senator in when the Saudi delegate, Prince Ghanim Abdul Rahman al-Saud, walked in. Despite his short, stout build and bushy eyebrows, his regal paraphernalia left no doubt that he commanded instant obedience. Two hard-looking, well-built, retired SEALs were flanking him. Ravinder noted that both bore a striking resemblance to Mark Leahy.

And, my God, yes, the two South African mercenaries are still at large. And Ruby. What is she doing? He looked at his watch; it was a quarter to eleven. The surveillance team was to report every hour so the next call would come at eleven, or earlier if Ruby left the house.

That morning Ravinder, then Jasmine, and eventually Simran had gone to check on her. All three had met a locked door. The only response was her voice, telling them she was okay and that they shouldn't worry. But she sounded far from okay. Ravinder was concerned. He hoped it was nothing more than the shock of the previous night's events.

He was still thinking of Ruby when Chance strode in with Sir Geoffrey Tang, the British delegate. Tang was extremely tall and fit, and looked very smart in his tailored grey pinstriped suit. Despite his sixty-plus years, he had a full head of hair, with only touches of white at the temples. With deep-set, coal-black eyes, chiselled features, long sideburns and goatee, Tang looked the epitome of royalty.

'We heard about last night... are you okay?' Chance asked in an undertone. Ravinder nodded. 'And Ruby?'

Ravinder nodded again. But both were keenly aware that the danger was far from over. In fact, it had just become more real with the arrival of the delegates. Whatever had to happen would happen *now*.

When Ruby came down for breakfast she found Simran and Jasmine at the table. Jasmine gave her a big smile and, running up to her, gave her a long hug. Jasmine appeared to have recovered completely. Or perhaps she was in complete denial. At Simran's insistence she was even going to college. It would be better for her to go out than to stay home and mope.

Simran also smiled warmly at her, aware that none of them might be alive today if it had not been for Ruby.

'You are just in time, Ruby.' Jasmine pulled Ruby to the seat beside her. 'Come. Mom is helping me prepare for today's moot court. Would you also like to hear my contentions?'

'Why do you want to bother her?' Simran said before Ruby could respond.

'If that is what you want me to do,' Ruby replied listlessly, ignoring Simran.

'Are you sure?' Jasmine queried. Ruby nodded. 'Great!' Jasmine pulled out a sheaf of papers. 'The case is a real one: Jayant Ganguly versus Mausami Ganguly. I am representing the father and my best friend is representing the mother.' Jasmine began to read, giving details of how she would defend the case in the college moot court.

Ruby was staring at the plate of eggs on the table, and did not appear to be listening. Simran was watching her, a worried look on her face.

'So when the wife, Mausami Ganguly, deserted her husband, she moved to another city.' Jasmine flipped a page and continued, 'From there she managed to obtain an ex-party divorce. She also managed to get legal custody of their four-year-old daughter. The husband, Jayant, contested this in the High Court – the divorce and the custody.'

'Did he win?' Ruby's sudden question, delivered in that same flat monotone, shocked both Jasmine and Simran.

'What?' Jasmine asked.

'So did he get it? The custody, I mean,' Ruby repeated, still staring at her plate.

'The father? Yes, he did get custody, but only later, from the Supreme Court.'

'I see.' Ruby still did not look up.

Jasmine exchanged a glance with Simran, who shrugged her shoulders.

'You can if you want to,' Ruby said as she suddenly got up and began to walk away, heading back to her room. 'You can if you want to... you have to *want* to,' Ruby called without stopping.

Simran and Jasmine heard her go up the stairs, with a heavy, dragging stride. They were stunned.

'Daddy did not want to. If he had, he would have found me,' Ruby's tearful voice rang out. 'Only mom loved me!'

They heard her bedroom door slam shut.

'Mom?' Then more insistently, '*Mom!* Where are you?' Ruby was sitting on the edge of her bed, her face still blank. 'Why is this happening to me? What have I done?'

Nothing.

'Have you also abandoned me? Please. I need you, mom.'

'I am right here, Ruby. I am always here, you know that.' Within the recesses of Ruby's fragmented mind, Rehana reached out and began to stroke Ruby's head.

The shock of the night's assault took over now. Ruby began to cry in deep, shuddering sobs.

'He was going to kill my daddy. I couldn't let

him... even though daddy did not want me. If he had, he would have found me. He does not even want me to stay. If he did he would have asked me to.'

'I know, child, I know,' Rehana said. 'Hush! Don't worry. Everything will be fine soon.'

'What should I do, mom?'

'Do what you have to, Ruby. Do your duty.'

'But...'

'No buts, Ruby. Nothing has changed. Our lives mean nothing if we falter from our duty.'

'But he is my father! I cannot do anything to him, even if he...'

'You don't have to, Ruby. Just finish what you started.' Rehana began to talk, slowly, insistently – first cajoling, then pleading. All the while allowing Ruby to cry, allowing her pent-up feelings to flow.

Even though she was a trained agent fully versed in the art of subversion, she was yet to understand just how strong Rehana's influence on her was. Even now – especially now, when everyone seemed to have closed ranks against her.

Hours later, when the tears stopped, Ruby felt whole again – the avenger was back in control. The embattled, shattered woman had gone underground.

Over the next few hours, one by one, the remaining delegates arrived. Ravinder's team was busy settling them, and Thakur – unwilling to give up the limelight – ensured he spent time with each of them, assuring them that India was delighted to have them.

As soon as the last delegate arrived, Thakur proudly took them all for a grand tour of the secure zone.

Ravinder was half listening to Thakur when he saw Mohite waving at him from across the room. He quietly peeled away and went to him.

'How are you, sir? That was terrible, what happened last night.' Mohite paused. 'I want you to know that we really tried to catch them...'

'That's okay, Govind. Even they get lucky sometimes.'

'Well, we have taken out all three of them now, so maybe they are not so lucky after all. Your daughter did a very brave thing.'

'I know. Thank you. Tell me, why did you...'

'The officer in charge of PM security is here. He wants to speak to you.'

'What about?'

'The idiot says he will only talk to you.'

Ravinder groaned inwardly. Mohite must have done or said something to piss him off.

'Where is he?'

'In the control room.'

'Okay.'

'I will come with you,' Mohite said.

'No, that's okay,' Ravinder replied. Mohite might

just add fuel to the fire… if he was the one responsible, that is.

As it turned out, Ravinder's intuition was spot-on.

'I cannot believe this, Mr Gill! Your deputy actually told me to…' Ravinder allowed him to vent before smoothing things over. It cost him the better part of an hour. And a blinding headache.

He then went back to the eighth floor and buttonholed Mohite. 'How can you tell anyone from the PM's security to bugger off, Govind?'

'You are always in a hurry to judge me and condemn me, sir. He was being such a nuisance and interfering with everything. I—'

'Come on, Govind! He was only doing his job. The PM will be here tomorrow morning. And they need to do what they need to do. That's their regular drill.'

'How are you, Gill?' Thakur interrupted. Having finished networking with the delegates, he was calling it a day. 'I heard about the incident last night. Glad to see you are okay.'

'Thank you, sir.'

'I believe your daughter did a fabulous job. Brave girl. You must be proud of her.'

'I am, sir.'

'Excellent. Give her my best.' Thakur threw a pointed look at his watch; he seemed to be in a hurry. 'Do you mind if I have Govind for a bit?' Without waiting for a reply, Thakur gestured and Mohite sauntered off behind him like an eager puppy.

Ravinder returned to his room on the seventh floor. He needed to lie down. The painkillers were making him groggy. The headache made it worse. A bank of monitors displayed the feed from all the cameras set up to maintain a 24x7 watch on all entry and exit points and, more specifically, the seventh and eighth floors. The master feed was beamed into the control room to the left of the elevator bank, which was manned by four ATTF men per shift.

Ravinder lay on the bed and began to watch the live feed. He saw Chance and Jennifer emerge from the elevator. They said something to the guard. It must have been a joke because all three laughed. Leaving the guard still grinning, the two headed for their rooms – Chance to the one directly opposite Ravinder's and Jennifer to the one next to it.

I wonder if they will use the interconnecting door later. Ravinder smiled at the thought.

He remembered when he had been that age. Rehana flashed into his memory. Hard on her heels came Ruby. Stress returned. He fretted about her and wondered how Ruby was doing now. Simran's call about her behaviour at the breakfast table had alarmed him. He would have gone to her if he could. His eyes flicked at his watch. The last call from the surveillance team had come in twenty minutes ago; Ruby had not left the house all day.

There was a knock at the door. He looked up at the monitor scanning the corridor. It was Mohite. He let him in reluctantly, hoping he had not created some new problem.

'I want your permission to have the city hotels checked again tonight, sir. Maybe we can get hold of the South African mercenaries now.'

'Won't it take away too much manpower? We need every man we have to secure the Games Village, the stadiums and this hotel…'

'I think it is worth the attempt.'

'Let me check how Ashish feels.'

'He is okay if you say it is. I already checked with him.'

'I will appreciate if you go via me in future.' Ravinder did not hide his displeasure.

Mohite nodded. 'I wouldn't have done it, but Thakur sahib agreed that we need to keep looking for the terrorists.'

'You discussed this with him?' Ravinder confronted him. 'How many times have I told you…'

'I didn't, sir. We were just talking and he asked me so I gave him my opinion.'

Realizing it was futile, Ravinder ignored him and considered the situation. 'Okay, go ahead, but use only personnel on non-critical duties.'

Mohite left and Ravinder went back to watching the monitors. He could see the delegates moving around on the eighth floor. Several of their PSOs were also mingling on the seventh floor. The guards on the stairwells and elevators were alert and in position. Everything seemed normal.

But would it last? His instinct warned him that a storm was about to break.

Unable to sleep, and despite the pain and grogginess, he decided to check on the guards in the lobby and at the hotel gates. Everyone was alert and in position. Then he walked down the street to the roadblock five hundred metres away. To his surprise, he met Mohite and one of the control room officers walking back.

'What are you two doing here?'

'Checking the guards, sir,' Mohite said, looking like he was hard at work.

'And him? What's he doing here? I made it clear that no one is to leave his post.'

'He is just keeping me company, sir.' Mohite's expression was sheepish, but his voice was defiant.

'Get back to your post.' Ravinder waved the control room officer away. 'You have to stop doing this, Govind. No one... I repeat, *no one* is to leave his post even for a second. I shouldn't have to tell *you* that.'

They walked back, a sulky silence between them. They were parting at the elevator when Ravinder realized that now only one man was guarding it instead of two.

'Where is the second man?' he asked the guard.

Before he could reply, Mohite jumped in, 'I have reduced all non-essential posts by one man each and am using them to beef up the hunt for the two terrorists. I spoke to you about it, sir.'

Ravinder could not believe his ears.

'Only from the non-essential posts, sir,' Mohite repeated, almost smugly.

'You consider the main access points non-essential?' Ravinder was seized by an urge to hit him. 'How long will it take you to call them back?'

'Call them back? Why?'

'Mohite, which part of my question didn't you understand?' Ravinder was on the verge of losing it. If he did not rein himself in, Mohite would be missing a few teeth. Taking a deep breath, he forced himself to calm down. 'Call them back. *Now!* I want every damn post in the hotel at full strength. Clear?'

'Right, sir,' Mohite recoiled. 'I will have them back in one hour.' He scooted towards the control room.

One bloody hour! Pulling himself together, Ravinder called Chance and asked him to keep an eye on the eighth floor. He himself began to patrol the seventh, hand never too far from his weapon.

When the security posts had been restored he retired to his room and, taking another pill, he lay down. He finally dozed off, but the unease stayed with him and he did not sleep much that night.

Day Ten

The morning light on the day of the Summit was but a pale streak on the horizon when Ruby exited the Gill's gate. Dressed in a maroon jogging suit with Nike emblazoned across it, her ponytail jutting out of a matching maroon baseball cap, she started running.

The events of the last thirty-six hours had faded. Having stayed cooped up inside her room since the attack, Ruby was now raring to go. There was no trace of the stunned zombie of yesterday. Today her mind was at rest, allowing only operational matters to be dwelt upon. Rehana's magic had worked – her weapon of vengeance was primed and ready for action once again.

Her pace increased slowly and her strong, muscular legs began to chew up the distance. Eager for exercise, her lungs sucked in the chilly early morning air. Soon she got her second wind and settled into a steady, loping run.

Ruby's mind was clear. It went over the list of actions that she needed to take.

The shrill ring of his mobile startled Ravinder awake.

'She is doing what? Jogging?'

'Yes, sir,' the surveillance commander replied, 'the guards tell me she is following the same route that she follows every day.'

'Stay with her.' Ravinder pushed his sleep away. 'And keep me informed.' In a way he was glad that Ruby had finally come out of her room. Perhaps she was getting over the shock.

He headed for the bathroom. It took several splashes of cold water before he was fully awake.

Today is the first day of the Summit... the thirteenth of October. Damn that fucking number!

He got ready and headed out. There were a million things to check, to secure. Whatever was coming at them, it had to be stopped. And Ravinder knew that something... *someone* was.

The surveillance team was crawling along in fits and starts to make sure Ruby did not stray from their sight, yet not getting close enough to be spotted.

Not once did Ruby turn to look over her shoulder. She had heard the car start and knew she was being followed. Slowly, imperceptibly, she began to pick up her pace, but stayed on the road, where it would be easy for them to keep an eye on her. The car speeded up commensurately, as though tied to her with an invisible umbilical cord.

Barring the occasional vehicle and a handful of other morning walkers and joggers, the four-laned road – a green, waist-high, metallic barrier in the middle – was almost empty. Ruby swerved around an elderly couple, chancing a quick glance over her shoulder. Sure enough, the cop car was there. She stayed the course for another two hundred metres. Now there was no break in the metallic divider for maybe a mile on either side. She slowed down and began to bide her time. A minute later the opportunity presented itself.

She could see that the auto-rickshaw coming on the other side was empty. She waited till it was almost abreast with her and with a burst of speed, she headed straight for the barrier. By the time she hit it she was sprinting. Her left hand reached out, landed on the top rail and leveraged her body across in a neat vault. Ruby landed almost in front of the rickshaw. Grabbing a five-hundred-rupee note from her pocket, she thrust it in the startled driver's hand.

'Hyatt Regency. Fast. *Very* fast.'

The money did wonders to the rickshaw driver's driving skills. Like Schumacher hitting home stretch, the vehicle shot away as fast as its rickety engine would allow.

By the time the surveillance car accelerated and made a U-turn at the next traffic island, her auto was long gone.

The surveillance team took two swift passes on both sides of the Ring Road, even stopped several auto-rickshaws, but to little avail.

Ruby had vanished.

Once in the hotel, Ruby headed for the sky-blue Maruti van left by Mark in the basement parking lot. Three minutes later she drove out. This was a part of Delhi she had familiarized herself with, and knew that to get to the Ashoka hotel she had to take a U-turn, go down the road till the next traffic signal and then turn left. At this time of morning, it would be a ten- or fifteen-minute drive at best. Handling the manual gearshift a trifle gingerly, she drove at a sedate pace, ensuring she drew no attention.

The 84mm Carl Gustaf rocket launcher and ammunition box kept under a tarp in the luggage section made dull, thudding sounds as the van crossed a rough patch just short off the Chanakya Complex.

Ashoka hotel lay dead ahead.

'What do you mean you lost her? How the hell can you lose a person jogging on the road at this time of the morning?' Ravinder drew a deep breath, struggling to regain his composure. 'Do everything you can to find her and call me back.' Then he dialled Chance's room. 'Ruby is on the loose. They lost her.' He could sense the man's muttered curses though he couldn't really hear them.

'I'll ensure the top floor is secure with Ido.' Chance was now fully alert. 'I'll tell Jennifer to man the seventh.'

'All right,' Ravinder replied. 'I'll join her in a minute. I want to first go down and check that the lobby and gates are secure.' He stopped at the control room to order a Code Red alert. 'It is a drill,' he replied when the duty officer asked him why. 'I want to check things before the PM gets here. *Move it!*'

Satisfied that nothing could get through the inner cordon, Ravinder raced down. He had an urge to call Ruby and ask her where she was. Not unusual for a father to do.

At this hour of the morning? Why not?

Then deciding to give it a little more time, he headed for the security posts at the gates. Both were alert.

Everything seemed normal – so far.

The next hour passed slowly. Code Red was on. Guns were at the ready. Fingers hovered close to triggers.

Across the road, driving slowly past the hotel, Ruby caught a glimpse of Ravinder pacing between the two gates. The security men at both gates looked alert, weapons at the ready. They had adopted an all-round defence, ensuring anything coming in could be covered and, if required, cut down immediately. A couple of handlers with sniffer dogs prowled in front of the porch.

So they were all alert. She had expected this.

She watched Ravinder with mixed feelings till her van had moved past. Before any ambivalence could set in, she pushed away all thought and focused.

Rehana has to be avenged. And Yusuf uncle... and thousands of others. I will not let these bastards sell us down the road.

Her hardness returned, bringing with it the clarity she needed.

How long will these buggers stay alert?

She knew that nothing could be guarded in totality. *Especially if the attacker no longer cares for her life.*

The last thought caught her by surprise. She let it turn in her head as the van headed back the way it had come, with Nehru Park on her right. By the time she had taken a U-turn and brought it to a halt in the parking lot near the park gates, the thought had crystallized. She was not afraid to die. If that was the price to be paid for the conference to be ruined, she would pay it.

I will make my mother proud.

She locked the van and made her way back on foot towards the hotel, stopping when the main gate came into view. Confirming that none of the security cameras on the hotel's walls were pointed at her, she settled down under a tree. To wait and to watch.

Now that her mind was not acting up, she could sit there the whole day.

Soon she saw things at the hotel gates settle down and return to normal. Body postures became less aggressive. Rifles were slung back on shoulders. Even the dogs stopped patrolling.

Code Reds cannot last forever.

Ruby knew this. She had planned on it.

Ravinder was pacing between the gates when Mohite came out, looking sharp in a new, perfectly fitted and ironed uniform.

'You called a Code Red, sir? What is the problem?'

'That was almost thirty minutes ago, Govind.'

'I know, sir. The control room officer called me, but he said it was only a drill.' There was no hint of contriteness on his face. 'I was getting ready to receive the minister, sir.'

'Just a drill, Govind?' Ravinder gave a soft sigh. Did he need to be reminded that a drill meant everyone responded? Especially at his level? *Oh, fuck it!* 'Yeah, just a drill,' Ravinder repeated.

'Oh!' Mohite pouted, then shrugged. 'Would you like me to call it off now?'

'No. The PM is due shortly.' He checked his watch. It was almost eight.

'Actually, that is a good idea. Thakur sahib is about to arrive... I just spoke to his aide. It is good if he sees everything on high alert.'

Ravinder was about to unleash a scathing retort when Thakur's mini-cavalcade drove up – a security vehicle in front and two behind Thakur's Toyota Camry. Except for the driver, Ravinder did not see any security personnel in the last vehicle, but this did not surprise him. He had learnt early on that the home minister was superstitious. He did not consider the number three auspicious, hence the fourth car.

People and their eccentricities. Ravinder bit back a smile. Then he remembered his own phobia of the number thirteen. Forcing a smile, he went forward to meet the minister.

Mohite was already four steps ahead.

Ravinder's smile had faded well before the minister entered the elevator to the eighth floor. Ruby's absence worried him. He pulled out his phone and dialled her mobile.

Sitting in the park, camouflaged by the tree she was backed up against, Ruby watched the home minister's convoy zoom down the road and enter the hotel. It was just a few minutes past eight.

A little later she felt the phone vibrate in her pocket. She gave a quick glance at the calling number. It was Ravinder. She returned the phone to her pocket. The next time it rang, she ignored it.

She was observing the patterns of movement at and between the gate security posts and the roadblocks on either side.

Sirens rent the air again. A longer cavalcade swept in, led by two motorcycle outriders. A dozen-odd cars swept past the gates and came to a sharp stop at the porch. Security men leaped out. Hard, alert eyes raked the area. When it became certain there was no threat, one of the PSOs opened the rear door of the Mercedes 500 SEL at the centre of the convoy and the Indian PM emerged, a bespectacled, slightly built Sikh, clad in white, with a light blue turban. Ruby caught a brief glimpse of him before a ring of Kevlar-clad bodies closed in around him. They vanished into the hotel.

Both the gate security posts, now reinforced by the PM's men, looked alert and keyed-up, their stance aggressive and weapons ready. Any move towards them now would be met with a fiery response.

But she was in no hurry. Rocking back on her heels, she settled down to wait, her yoga-hard body ensuring she was at rest. Her eyes stayed on her target.

An hour later the PM emerged, once again surrounded by armed men. He stepped into his Mercedes and the cavalcade disappeared. Within minutes she noted a change in the security men at the gates. They did not all sit down, but a softening was apparent. Here and there a cup of tea emerged. Even the occasional cigarette.

Ruby smiled. It was the same the world over.

An hour later, she took out her mobile phone, inserted a new SIM card and called the police control room. Her whispered bomb threat provoked an instant response. The change in stance of the security details was instantaneous. A beehive of activity erupted. Teams of security men armed with metal detectors and sniffer dogs began to sweep the hotel.

Ruby knew it would be a while before the alert was called off. They would have to scan and clear the hotel. She would do all that she could to tire them out. To make the red alerts common so they'd get used to them. *That* would be when lapses would occur.

Satisfied, she returned to the van, dropped it off in the parking lot of the Hyatt, walked across to the crowded passport office, and caught a cab back to the house.

'She is back? When?' Ravinder said on the phone. 'How did she get back? Did you speak to the cab driver then? Where did he pick her up? I see.'

With the bomb threat having proved to be a hoax, and the Summit now safely underway, Ravinder was returning to the control room when the surveillance leader called. Having given up trying to find her, the team had fallen back to the house to wait for her to resurface.

He mulled over this for a minute and decided it was time to change tactics. He again dialled Ruby's mobile. Where the hell had she gone and what had she been up to?

A grim smile crossed Ruby's face as her mobile rang. She had been expecting the call.

'Where did you go, Ruby? I was so worried. I have been trying to call you for some hours now.'

'I went out for a run, father. Sorry, I left my phone behind. I just got back.'

'Why did you ditch the security car? We were so worried about you.'

'I didn't realize there was one with me.'

'Come on, Ruby. After that night's fiasco... do I need to spell it out? You can't take such risks. We never know who else is out there.'

'I am sorry, father. It will not happen again.'

'But where did you run off like that?'

'Well, I got tired of jogging and did not want to return... too much on my mind, I guess. Then I remembered Jasmine mentioning that the Red Fort is worth a visit early in the morning, so I caught an auto-rickshaw and went off to see it.'

'But...' Ravinder broke off, realizing he could not let her know that the driver of her cab had told them that she had hailed him from near the passport office in Bhikaji Cama Place, nowhere close to the Red Fort. 'Anyway, I'm glad you're safe. From now on, whenever you wish to go anywhere, just tell the team and travel with them in their car. That will make it easy for everyone.'

'Not a problem, dad. I will do that. Thanks.'

The distaste of deceit lay heavy with both when the call ended.

Ruby wondered how much he knew. He had to know something, else why the surveillance? But if he had been able to confirm whatever Chance may have told him, he would not have allowed her to run free. *Would he?*

Is he just concerned about me – like a father would be?

Ravinder too wondered what she had been up to.

Am I just tarring her with the same brush because of Rehana? Maybe she does not really know the reality of Rehana... and Yusuf.

With the Summit in progress, Ravinder returned to his room and went to work. The next few hours passed quickly as he coordinated between Ashish and Mohite, ensuring that things at both ends proceeded smoothly.

The spate of false alarms, sightings, unidentified

bags and suspicious people was keeping the cops terribly busy. For several months now, the Delhi Police had been conducting awareness training for waiters, cab drivers, private security guards and shopkeepers. They had all been told to keep their eyes and ears open and report such things, and it seemed a lot of them had taken the briefings seriously.

Each call had to be investigated. But so far, none had resulted in anything meaningful. Nothing, however, could be ignored.

Although he tried not to think of it, he could not forget that it was thirteenth October.

Bad things happen on the thirteenth.

Ruby spent the rest of the day in her room, waiting.

'The wait is always a bitch.' Mark's words came back to her. She grinned and then remembered Mark was dead and gone. The grin evaporated.

The Summit had made no real progress on day one, but the ice was broken. Both sides had at least acknowledged that the killing would only end if they talked. As the day progressed, a rapport was established and hope brightened.

Ravinder's tension escalated as the day wound down. Though he tried hard, he was unable to forget that today was the thirteenth. The hourly calls from the surveillance team which confirmed that Ruby had not moved should have helped, but didn't.

Have I been so wrapped up in Ruby that I missed some other, more real, threat?

With every passing hour new questions cropped up to plague him. As darkness closed in, his anxiety increased.

In Muridke, Pakistan, his eyes and ears riveted to the news channels, Pasha eagerly awaited word of his assassin's strike. Anticipation turned to disappointment and then to fury as the curtain came down on the first day of the Summit. He was unable to sit still any longer.

Day Eleven

The new dawn brought with it an overcast sky. The first sign of the heavy fog that paralyses most parts of north India during winters appeared.

Ravinder again awoke early. Some primal cop instinct was gnawing at him. He dialled his home phone, a direct line to his bedroom and study. Simran was the only one who answered it when he was not home. She picked up on the first ring, as though she had been waiting for him to call.

'Are you all right?' she asked.

'I am fine, love.'

'I was worried. I wanted to call, but I did not want to disturb you. I know how busy you must be right now.'

For a moment they shared the comfort of silence.

'Simran, I wanted to check on Ruby. How is she?'

'I think she is okay, but other than her morning run, she has not left her room. I had to send all her meals to her room. Not that she ate much.'

'I see. Is she still there?'

'I think so. I didn't hear her go down. You want me to check?'

'Could you, please? But quietly. I don't want her to know you are checking on her.'

'Hang on.'

He heard Simran put down the phone and walk to the door. Then silence. He was starting to worry when he heard a crackling sound as she picked up the receiver.

'She is there. I peeped in and she is still sleeping.'

'Hmm... okay.' Something was tugging at his mind but he was not sure what. 'Right, then. I will call again when I can.'

'And take care of yourself.'

'I will.'

'Have you eaten?'

'I will now.'

'Don't forget. You get a headache when you skip meals.'

'I won't forget.'

'Ravinder, if you want I can check on Ruby again.'

'No, don't fret about it. The surveillance car is at the gate. They'll let me know if she steps out.'

He sensed that Simran wanted to say more. He did too, but somehow this did not seem like the right time. It was only later that he remembered there is never a bad time to tell someone you love them.

Still uneasy, Ravinder put down the phone and

went out to run a check on the security set-up. And he did forget to eat. And he did get a headache.

Ruby counted to thirty after the door had closed before she threw off the bedcover and left her bed.

She had heard someone walking up to her door, the footsteps muted, as though the person was trying not to be heard.

Someone up to no good.

She had pulled the bedcover over her body, right up to her neck, leaving her face uncovered

She glimpsed the door crack open silently and saw Simran peep in. Ruby pretended to be asleep. Then Simran's face vanished.

Ruby ghost-footed to the door and listened. She heard only silence outside. She carefully slid the door open and peered out. An empty corridor met her eyes. Six quick steps and she was at the door of Ravinder's bedroom. She could hear Simran's voice and placed her ear against the door to listen carefully.

'Ravinder, if you want I can check on Ruby again,' she heard Simran say. Moments later she heard the phone being put down. Ruby returned silently to her bedroom, filled with anger.

So, they are checking on me. They suspect... But maybe daddy is just worried... But then he would have called me, not Simran!

Reaching for her mobile, she sent a short text to Ontong and Boucher. Delivery confirmation arrived seconds later. Ruby deleted the messages and started to dress.

Within minutes she was in her usual baggy black jeans and a loose, full-sleeved, blue cotton shirt. Her hair was tied back in a neat ponytail. She looked just like she had that day in Congo, but without the bulletproof vest and without her weapons. She missed them but knew that even if she had them with her, she would not have carried them. Not today. Not where she was going. Today everything would be improvised, on the fly. She had a plan, not as foolproof as she would have liked, but it was the best she could do, given the constraints and the loss of her key props.

Deep in thought, Ruby missed the sound of someone approaching her room and only became aware of it when the door began to open. Jasmine's head peeped in. Ruby started. There was no time to make it back to her bed.

'Ah! You are awake.' Jasmine smiled. 'Good. I wanted you to wish me luck. Today is...' She noticed Ruby's outfit. 'Wow! You are dressed so differently. You look so... so cool... Where are you off to so early?'

It seemed to be an innocent question. *Was it?* Her instincts told her it was, but could she take a chance? *What difference did it make? I cannot – will not harm her.*

'Nothing much.' Ruby held her gaze. 'Thought I'd step out for some exercise.'

'Hmm…' Jasmine's mouth puckered up. 'You look so different… so deadly… like a spy!' She laughed. 'Anyway, I must be off. I'm late for college. Have to rush. We are winding up early today,' she pattered on. 'Are you sure you don't want to come for the Games? I still have all three passes… just in case you've changed your mind.'

'I'm sure, Jasmine. Thanks anyway.' Aware of the ops clock ticking away, Ruby was aching for Jasmine to leave. 'And all the best for your moot court. I'm sure you'll blow them away.'

'Thanks a lot. Have fun!' Jasmine started to leave the room with a grin on her face. She turned around and said, 'And you blow them away too!'

I will, babe. That's the general idea.

Despite the nonchalant thought, it took a moment for Ruby's breathing to return to normal.

Now time to eat and get moving. In the distance she heard the gates swing open and Jasmine accelerate out of the drive. Silence returned to the Gill house. Then she heard the dull clang of a bucket, perhaps from the kitchen. Moments later the distant hum of a lawn mower could be heard.

Ruby turned to her ops checklist.

Eat and move.

But she felt no hunger. Generally she wolfed down

a healthy breakfast, no matter what lay ahead. Today she forced herself to eat. She had to be on top of her faculties. She finished the cold chicken sandwich Simran had sent up last night and washed it down with a glass of orange juice. By the time she was done, it was time. She checked her watch to reconfirm. Ontong and Boucher would start out in a while.

Grabbing the black tote bag she had packed, Ruby silently went down to the security... *or surveillance...* car at the gate. She had to time this part perfectly or there was no way in hell she would succeed.

No one heard her leave the house. She confidently approached the surveillance car.

'I need to go to the hotel,' she told the driver. 'Father needs some stuff.' Ruby held out the tote bag.

Ruby saw the driver exchange glances with the cop beside him, obviously the surveillance team commander. He thought it over, and then nodded. What harm could there be if she was with them?

'Fine, miss.' He held the door open for her. Minutes later they were off. The commander decided it would be awkward to call Ravinder and report on Ruby in front of her.

Ravinder ran into Mohite when he emerged from his room. Once again, Mohite was dressed in his Sunday best.

'Are you going down to meet the minister?' Ravinder asked, though he already knew.

'Yes, sir. He is on his way.'

Ravinder checked his watch; twenty past eight. The delegates would be finishing their breakfast soon and going to the conference hall.

'Fine. Have a look at the lobby security, Govind,' Ravinder instructed, 'and both the gates and roadblocks. I'm going up for a round on the eighth floor.'

He was heading for the elevator when he realized he had left his digital radio behind in the room. He went back to his room and found the radio next to the bank of monitors in the corner. The monitors were still on; he'd forgotten to switch them off. He surveyed them for a moment as he slipped the radio into his belt.

On one of the monitors he saw Mohite emerge from the elevator and head across the lobby. The men on the other monitors looked alert. Nothing unusual. Satisfied, Ravinder turned them off and went to the eighth floor.

On the camera set up at the hotel porch, he failed to see Mohite walk out of the hotel gates and head towards the security barrier down the road as the surveillance car Ravinder had deployed at his house drove up.

Despite her best effort to time her arrival, Ruby had reached a little too early. The problem was that she could only say so much to the driver. And asking him to halt outside the hotel might have aroused suspicion.

When she saw Mohite walk out of the hotel and head towards the security barrier, she spotted an opportunity. She told the driver to slow down beside him and powered down the car window.

Mohite turned and spotted her.

'Good morning, Miss Ruby. How are you?' Mohite was all smiles. 'That was such a brave thing you did the other night... We were all so glad that everyone was safe, thanks to you.'

'Thank you.' She gave him a bright smile as she got out of the car. 'It all happened so fast that...' She shrugged.

'So, how come you are here today?'

She pointed at the tote bag on her shoulder. 'I just brought some stuff along for dad. He has not been home since yesterday so I thought...'

'Ah, the dutiful daughter.' Mohite gave a big smile, the one that appeared when he needed to impress someone. The boss's daughter was definitely someone to impress. After all the fuck-ups, just bad luck as far as he was concerned, Mohite was eager for a helping hand. 'Come, Miss Ruby, let me take you to him.'

Ruby turned to the surveillance team commander. 'Could you please wait for me to come back?'

'You can park there,' Mohite chipped in helpfully, pointing at a vacant slot beside the gate.

'I should be back soon,' Ruby added with a smile.

Together, Mohite and Ruby began to walk past the hotel gates. With the men from the PM's security gone, the detail seemed thinner. Ruby did a rapid head count. *Ten armed men entrenched behind sandbag fortifications. Enough to stop even a well-organized assault. At least till reinforcements clocked in.*

The guard commander saluted as Mohite walked past. 'Excuse me, madam,' he called out to Ruby, 'that bag needs to go through the scanner.' He pointed at the tote on her shoulder.

'Of course.' Ruby placed it on the rollers of the X-ray machine. Similar machines had been installed at all major hotels since the 26/11 Mumbai attack. She wasn't worried as the bag disappeared inside the machine. It contained nothing except some snacks. It was simply her excuse to get in. Even if Ravinder was called and questioned her, Ruby had an answer ready – she needed to see him since she had decided to return to London.

The surveillance team leader had been explicitly ordered to call Ravinder, but lulled by Ruby and also Mohite's presence, he did not do so. There was also the fact that while tasking him, Ravinder had ordered him to keep Ruby safe and he knew she was safe inside the hotel. The car pulled into the slot Mohite had indicated and the surveillance team settled down to wait.

Mohite and Ruby had passed the X-ray machine when the whooping sound of a siren became audible. The sound grew louder. Ruby knew what it signified – Thakur was arriving. *Just on time.*

As Mohite sprang forward to receive him, Ruby checked her watch: ten minutes short of nine.

Perfect. Ruby permitted herself a small smile. *By the time they reached the eighth floor, the delegates would be settling down to their talks.*

Thakur's oily face broke into his politician's smile the minute he got out of his car and set eyes on Ruby.

'Ah! So we meet again, young lady,' he said. 'How have you been? What you did the other night was very brave! The whole police force is talking about it. Good, good... So, what brings you here today?... Really? Off already? Why?... Come, come, let's get you to your father...'

Engaged in conversation, Thakur, his two PSOs, Mohite and Ruby headed for the elevators. Seeing the home minister *and* their DIG, the elevator guard did not question Ruby's presence.

The mistakes were accumulating.

The avenger had broken past the barrier into the secure zone. Hunting season was open.

Ruby strode forward. She could feel her body gird itself for the coming battle.

Just a few minutes more...

Someone else had been watching for Thakur's arrival.

Dressed in faded jeans and a full-sleeved blue sweatshirt, the burly, nearly-bald Shaun Ontong stood at the same spot in the park where Ruby had taken position the previous morning. He wasn't feeling too good; something did not feel right.

Ontong saw the minister's cavalcade pull up at the porch. He immediately called the only number stored in his mobile. It was a new phone with an unused SIM card purchased specifically for this operation. He'd drop it in some convenient gutter on his way to the airport.

The call was answered by Gary Boucher, who was seated in a van parked one click away from the roadblock outside the hotel, the one further away from Ontong. He was taller than Ontong, whiplash-thin, deeply tanned and had close-cropped hair. Like Ontong, Boucher too was in jeans and a dark green sweatshirt.

'Five minutes,' Ontong said tautly. 'We are on.'

'Roger. I'm rolling in five.' Boucher dropped the phone on the seat. He was tense, but far more confident than Ontong. Perhaps because Boucher did not worry too much.

Ontong and Boucher collected their thoughts and rapidly replayed Ruby's instructions in their heads. They knew they had a small yet decisive role to play today. And both hoped whatever lay ahead of them would be painless.

Adrenaline was pumping through Ontong's body as he left the park and walked back to the Maruti van. He had already checked the rockets and the launcher. Both were ready to go.

Ontong kept his pace slow and easy. He knew he still had a few moments in hand. Boucher was going into action first.

Boucher was moving by the time Ontong reached his van. He drove at a steady pace. He wasn't in a hurry and did not have to go far. The shooting position he had selected was just ahead.

The 84mm Carl Gustaf produced by Saab has an effective range of approximately 1,100 metres against troops in the open and can also take on an armoured target 700 metres away. Unlike other such weapons, it uses a rifled barrel to spin stabilize its projectile. Both Boucher and Ontong were comfortable with it, though, like most Aussies, they preferred to call it the Charlie Gusto.

Boucher knew that a rocket launcher team normally comprised two men and could launch four to five rockets in a minute. But with just one man firing and reloading, the rate of fire would drop to less than half, since the user had to bring down the launcher, crack open the rear, slide in a new rocket, close the breech and hoist it back onto his shoulder. But this did not bother him. He needed only to fire twice before he dropped the weapon and melted away. With the element of surprise on his side, it would be a cakewalk. Ontong, coming into action minutes later, might not have that same advantage, but he would be able to exploit the shock of the opening assault. Also a potent advantage.

Taking a deep breath, Boucher pulled over at the spot he had reconnoitred; it was on a curve, a blind spot from the security post in front. Not the optimal position, but keeping in view the security deployment, it was the best possible one.

Boucher quickly moved to the rear of the van and reached for the already loaded weapon and the second rocket, ready for an instant reload.

Taking position off the road, clear of the vehicle, he placed the second rocket near his feet and raised the launcher to his shoulder. The play was out in the open now, no time to dick around.

Mohite halted the elevator on the seventh floor and held the door open for Ruby. 'Please go to Mr Gill's room... that one,' he pointed, forgetting that Ruby had been on the security tour a couple of days ago. 'I will let him know you are here.'

Ruby walked past the elevator security guards and headed for Ravinder's room. The ping of the elevator door behind her let her know it had closed. She threw a quick backward glance.

Both the elevator guards had turned to see off the minister and had their backs to her.

Altering direction, she swiftly crossed to the other side of the corridor and headed for Chance's room. Using the red access card she had purloined earlier, she eased open the door and entered.

Jennifer was returning from her hourly check of the stairwell guard at the end of the corridor when she saw Ruby enter Chance's room. She noticed that Ruby did not pause at the door, which to her implied that someone had opened the door for her or...

Chance? Wasn't he supposed to be on the eighth floor? Or did Ruby have an access card to his room? Neither thought felt good. Her relationship with Chance was still too new; she had yet to understand him or feel secure about him.

Also, Ruby's presence in the secure area alarmed her even though she was not privy to Ravinder's and Chance's suspicions. Frowning, she headed down the corridor.

If Chance is two-timing me... Jennifer felt a surge of anger.

Caught up in an admixture of alarm and jealousy, Jennifer forgot to radio her sighting to the control room or call the reserve guard to back her up.

Both were big mistakes.

Ruby halted in the centre of Chance's room. The curtains were pulled back and light filtered in.

A black, hard-shell suitcase lay on the wooden rack beside the TV. It had been with Chance for as long as she could remember. Having lived with him, she knew his habits. The suitcase was locked. Ruby rotated the numbers of the combination lock. The case clicked open. He was forgetful and always used his birth date as the combination for the suitcase. She sighed with relief. Chance hadn't changed.

Hasn't he? She pushed that thought away. *Not now, damn it! Focus!*

The pistols were exactly where she had known they would be – at the base, wrapped in a piece of thick, soft cloth. She quickly unfolded it and found a pair of classic Browning Hi-Power pistols.

His choice of weapon hasn't changed either.

Chance always carried a spare pair. Ruby had banked on it. Picking them up, she tested their heft. Perfect. They fit with the comfort of an old sweater.

A silencer and two spare magazines were also wrapped in the same cloth. The magazines, each with a capacity of thirteen rounds, were full.

Ruby did the math. A total of fifty-two rounds in the four magazines.

If that was not enough, nothing was…

Swiftly loading one weapon, she chambered a round, clicked on the safety and slid it into her waistband. Thrusting the spare magazines into the pocket of her baggy jeans, she loaded the second pistol, again chambered a round and began to screw on the silencer. Her fingers were confirming that the silencer was fitted on securely when she heard the door behind her open. Ruby swung around, holding the pistol behind her.

Jennifer entered the room, spotted Ruby and ground to a halt. Behind Jennifer, the solid wood door slowly swung shut. Its click masked the snick of the safety catch being pushed off by Ruby.

'What are you doing here? Where is Chance?'

Before Ruby could reply, a thunderclap rang out. The windowpanes rattled as the 84mm HEAT rocket fired by Boucher boomed out.

'What the hell was that?' Jennifer instinctively turned towards the sound, alarm on her face. There was another boom as the rocket struck and exploded. This one was closer, much louder. Jennifer ran to the window.

Ruby stood still. In her mind's eye she could see Boucher bring the launcher down from his shoulder, crack open the loading port and shove in the second round, then raise it to his shoulder and place his eye to the sights. Her body tensed.

Jennifer saw the expression on Ruby's face. That Ruby had shown no surprise at the explosions registered with her. Jennifer halted in midstride and reached for the gun in her belt. Her hand moved like a blur of lightning.

Equally fast, Ruby's hand came out from behind her back.

The sight of the silenced weapon almost froze Jennifer, but the point of no return had been crossed. She clawed out her weapon, knowing it was futile, yet hoping.

Jennifer's weapon started to come level, aligning on Ruby. Her finger had already completed half the trigger squeeze.

Boucher's first rocket slammed into the roadblock on the road to Ashoka hotel. Fired from 400 metres away, the FFV551 HEAT round decimated the waist-high wall of sandbags and rampaged through the men behind. There were no screams. None of the four men survived long enough to scream.

The six guards at the other end of the road were alive, but overwhelmed by the shock and by the debris that billowed out and now lay like a dark cloud over the roadblock. They were trying to figure out where the attack had come from when there was another massive flare of sound and light.

Boucher had fired again.

The second shot, an FFV441B HE rocket, was aimed at the hotel's eighth floor. It slammed explosively into the wall of the hotel, missing a window by inches. The thick stone walls stopped the HE round, but Boucher's job was not to cause damage. It was to create a diversion.

The explosion echoed harshly through the eighth floor, rattling the windows, shattering some. Bits of plaster broke free from the ceiling.

The second explosion masked the plop of the silenced pistol in Ruby's hand. The 9mm round caught Jennifer in her face, just above the upper lip. The impact threw her backwards. The pistol in her hand fired reflexively and the bullet thudded into the ceiling, sending out gouts of plaster.

Jennifer's body hit the ground with a thud. Life had already deserted her.

The smell of blood rose, mingling with the smoke curling out of the Browning in Ruby's hand. For a second she froze, but then her training took over.

Time was short. Ruby ran for the door.

Ravinder was pacing the corridor on the eighth floor when Boucher's first rocket decimated the roadblock. Galvanized into action, he ran for the elevator to get to the control room. He was halfway there when the second rocket struck, just a few windows away from the conference hall.

Silence returned. But he knew the attack had just begun and that rockets fired from a distance could only be a diversion.

From the other end of the hallway he saw Chance and Peled racing towards him. They all had only one thought: the delegates needed to be secured.

'Code Red.' Grabbing the radio from his belt, Ravinder snapped into it. 'I say again, *Code Red*. Lock down the floors.'

Boucher dropped the rocket launcher and raced towards the taxi stand 200 metres down the road. He would commandeer a car from there. In his head he had already begun to race towards the airport.

What Boucher had not factored in were the snipers on all sides of the hotel roof. Ruby had known of them, but had conveniently forgotten to mention them when the two Aussies showed some reluctance during her briefing. Their lives meant little to her, considering she was putting her own on the line.

Despite the confusion below, the Indian Army

sniper manning the side from which Boucher had fired was watching his area with eagle eyes. He spotted Boucher when he started running. Though he had seen the flares of the launcher's back blast, he had not seen Boucher due to the overhang of a tree. But the minute Boucher ran for the taxi stand, the cover had been removed.

The sniper did not hesitate. Rocket launchers going off and a man running away from the place they'd been fired. The picture was clear. The weapon in his hands steadied. His cross hairs sought out the running man and homed in. He took a lead to compensate for the target's motion. His finger curled around the trigger of his Snayperskaya Vintovka Dragunova Sniping Rifle and began to squeeze. A soft click.

A 7.62x54mm rimless round snapped out of the barrel and raced forward at a velocity of 830 metres per second. It covered the distance before Boucher had managed to take one more stride. The bullet smashed into Boucher's back, tearing out his heart.

No second shot was required.

After dropping Thakur off to the conference hall, Mohite was returning to the control room. He was in the elevator when the rockets exploded. The canned music playing kept him from hearing either of the blasts. Unaware that the Summit was under attack, he was entering the control room when Ravinder's voice erupted out of the radio.

'Code Red!' Ravinder's voice was strident with urgency. 'I say again, Code Red. Lock down the floors!'

'What the hell is happening?' Mohite asked the men at the monitors.

The minute Ontong heard the first rocket fired by Boucher explode, he grabbed hold of the rocket launcher in his van. He knew the second blast would soon be on its way.

He had already loaded the launcher. His second rocket was also ready to go. Double-checking everything, Ontong shouldered the weapon and stepped out of the bushes, as the second rocket fired by Boucher slammed against the walls of the top floor.

Starting the count, Ontong steadied the launcher on his shoulder and took careful aim.

Ten, nine, eight... Ontong fired.

Ontong's HEAT round smashed into the security post at the hotel's entry gate. Its boom, much closer now, echoed dully through the control room.

Mohite ran to the monitor for the main gate. It had suddenly gone dark.

Unaware that the rocket had killed the camera,

Mohite thumped the monitor, trying to bring it back to life.

'What the fuck happened?'

Ontong reloaded swiftly, now in a rush to get it over with and get clear. He had no idea what had happened to Boucher but didn't wish to tarry a second longer than he had to.

Moving quickly to his left, he brought the security post at the hotel exit gate into his gun sight. He steadied himself and fired again. But in his hurry to finish and get away, he forgot that the Maruti van behind him had been on his left when he had fired the first time. When he had moved left to acquire the second target, he had strayed too far. The van was now directly behind him, just metres away.

He'd made a small mistake, but a fatal one.

The furiously flaming back blast of the rocket launcher caught the van head-on. Ontong had reversed the van before he'd parked it so he could take the weapon out of the luggage compartment and bring it into use instantly. The back blast caused the fuel tank to explode, decimating the van. Flaming shards of metal sliced out in every direction, scything through everything in their way. Including Ontong.

Ontong's second rocket destroyed the security post at the hotel's exit gate. Another monitor in front of Mohite went blank as its camera too succumbed. However, a peripheral view of the carnage at both gates was visible from the feed of the cameras mounted in the porch. He could see that both posts were in serious trouble.

Jolted, Mohite grabbed his radio and screamed, 'We are under attack. Both gates are down. All seventh-floor security personnel and reserve guards, move down and reinforce the lobby!' His voice was shrill. 'They must not get through. Seal everything off!'

He kept shouting instructions into the radio as he ran. Accompanied by the three men held in reserve in the control room, he ran for the elevator and pressed the button to the lobby. As the elevator doors opened, he grabbed both the elevator guards and hauled them inside.

In response to his orders, the guards at the stairwells on both ends of the floor also grabbed their weapons and headed down.

Silence fell upon the now unguarded seventh floor.

Yet another mistake had been made. *This* was a cardinal one.

In Chance's room, Ruby was hurrying past Jennifer's body when an idea struck her. She grabbed the baseball cap Jennifer had been wearing. Her fingers immediately felt its sticky wetness. The touch of blood sickened her. She fought off the nausea, but could not keep her eyes away from Jennifer's face. She saw blood all over it.

Then Ontong's first rocket exploded. She stiffened and began to pull off Jennifer's flak jacket. Some blood had seeped into its collar. But this time Ruby's face stayed expressionless as she quickly wiped it clean on Jennifer's shirt.

She was wrong. I am right. Wasn't that reason enough for me to have pulled the trigger? Of course it was. That is all there is to it… nothing to fret about.

The sound of the second rocket explosion goaded her into action.

Slipping on Jennifer's jacket, Ruby raced to the door. The ping of the elevator closing greeted her. She peered out.

The floor was empty. Even the elevator guards had vanished. Not believing her luck, she ran out, the red master access card in one hand and a pistol in the other. She'd have to move fast if she wanted to exploit the opportunity Boucher and Ontong had provided.

'Just as a precaution… not that we are expecting any trouble… but just in case of some emergency we have also secured the top two floors of Samrat hotel and duplicated all the same arrangements there.' Mohite's briefing to the home minister echoed in her head as she used the access card to open Ravinder's room and slipped inside.

The bank of monitors was what she needed so that she would know as soon as they began to evacuate and which route they would take. It had to be either of the two staircases or the elevator, though that was less likely – one elevator would not hold all the delegates and the security team would be reluctant to split them.

So far, things were working out... better than she had hoped.

They are wrong. I am right... the words now played like a litany in her head. One by one, she began to switch on the monitors.

Waiting impatiently for the elevator to reach the eighth floor, Ravinder, Chance and Peled caught Mohite's transmission loud and clear.

Anger exploded through Ravinder.

That fucking idiot! He's done it again. Instead of waiting for the attackers to come to them, he had started reacting to a still unclear threat. *How could he even dream of abandoning the control room? That fucking...*

Cursing under his breath, Ravinder reached for his radio set and began to speak when he realized that Mohite was still talking. Realizing that he would not be able to transmit until Mohite released the transmit button, and itching to get to the control room, Ravinder decided to take the stairs. The floors needed to be resecured, no matter the cost. And he needed to keep an eye on the top two floors of the hotel, which was why the control room needed to be manned by a senior officer at all times. His every instinct was screaming at him that the security breach had already taken place, that the rocket attacks on the gates were not the real threat.

They have to be diversions. So where is the real attack coming from?

He suddenly wished he could check on Ruby's whereabouts, but now was not the time.

We need to draw out the attackers.

'Activate Plan Bravo!' he yelled at Chance and Peled.

Chance and Peled ran to the conference hall and herded the delegates to a conference room at the other end of the corridor. Peled took position outside the door. Chance ran down the corridor to activate the second part of the plan. The decoys were ready and waiting.

The first set of monitors that Ruby switched on showed the confusion in the hotel lobby. The second set remained black. Ruby did not know it, but these were the ones that had been connected to the cameras installed at the hotel gates.

Next, the monitors connected to the cameras on the seventh floor flickered to life.

Ruby was surprised to find both stairwells empty.

Where are the guards? Is this some trick?

Her mind ferreted forward to spot a trap. She was activating the next monitor when she saw Ravinder rush out from the stairwell on the left and charge towards the control room.

Then the eighth floor monitors came alive, flickering a bit before the picture stabilized. Chance hove into view. Weapon in hand, he was in the lead. Behind him was a ragged line of men in a variety of outfits. Bringing up the rear was one of the Palestinian PSOs. Ruby saw the two ex-SEALs travelling with the Saudi Arabian prince running up to join them. They took position at the head and tail of the column and headed for the staircase closest to the conference hall.

Bingo!

She began to study the deployment of the security personnel and to freeze them in her head. She also took note of their firepower, a formidable array of Uzis, Glocks, Magnums and Brownings. She evaluated her options and made her decision.

From the rear, that's where I'll attack. I just need to take out the guards and two or three of the delegates.

She stopped to study the stairs, especially the landings. She needed a place to hide, for just one moment.

In the control room, Ravinder too was studying the secure zone. His attention, however, was not on the party moving behind Chance. He was searching for some other movement. *Any* other movement.

'Come out, come out... wherever you are...' he muttered aloud. 'Whoever you are...'

That reminded him. He needed to find out where Ruby was. His eyes continued to track the monitors as he reached for his mobile. 'Where is Ruby?' he asked when the surveillance team leader answered.

'In the hotel, sir. Haven't you met her yet? She went up with Mr Thakur and Mohite sir.'

Ravinder went still. He couldn't breathe. Suspecting was one thing. Having it confirmed was another. All this while, he had hoped that Ruby would not be involved in something so heinous. Now there was no doubt.

Why, Ruby? Why?

His head began to spin.

Not now. Right now you have a duty to perform. A quote from the *Bhagavad Gita* echoed in his mind:

And do thy duty, even if it be humble,
Rather than another's, even if it be great.
To die in one's duty is life.
To live in another's is death.

'I know you well, Ravinder. I know you will always do the right thing. Just trust your instincts. It will all work out in the end,' Simran's words returned to him.

He no longer knew how this could end well, but he was determined to take charge.

On the monitors he began to scour the seventh floor. It lay still and silent. But he knew she was out there somewhere, waiting for the right moment to strike.

'Ruby, come out, come out...' He barely noticed his lips move. 'Come out, come out... wherever you are...'

His ears did not hear his words.

His eyes remained riveted to the monitors.

His hands held a gun.

Their childhood game of hide-and-seek had turned deadly.

Satisfied with her plan, Ruby withdrew both weapons from her belt and calmed herself. Her eyes were still focused on the monitor, watching for any change in the deployment of the men she meant to ambush.

Chance's party had reached the stairwell between the two floors.

Perfect. Ruby took a deep breath, willing her metabolism to slow down, but her adrenaline had peaked. By now her body was craving to catapult forward.

She knew the next few minutes would be her last. But it was okay.

Mom's waiting. She – they – are banking on me. I will not let them down.

Drawing a long breath, she stilled her nerves once again and started to turn.

That was when the third man behind Chance looked up, an inadvertent glance, not aware that the camera overhead could capture him so clearly.

He was dressed like Sir Geoffrey Tang and made up like him, right down to the slightly greying, long sideburns and pointed goatee. But Ruby knew he was not Sir Tang. She had travelled with Tang for a week and knew the British MP well enough to know that this man was an imposter.

Ruby held back. One by one, she began to closely examine all thirteen men behind Chance. The subterfuge was obvious. Despite their clever make-up, she could tell they were not the delegates; they were all imposters, decoys. As she intensified her scrutiny, she noticed that they were carrying concealed weapons.

Ruby's mind changed gears.

Where are the real delegates?

The answer arrived with a snap.

In one of the other conference rooms on the eighth floor.

It was logical.

Her mind began generating a new plan.

If that guy had not looked up I would have walked right into their trap.

A new feeling of respect for Ravinder swept through her. He was one hell of an adversary.

Like father, like daughter? But he did not want me… Stop! Think!

The minute they launched the decoys, hadn't they also given her an open playing field?

Every tactic has a weakness: the more daring it is, the more crucial the weakness. That was the nature of the beast.

Ruby could not see any security personnel on the eighth floor. She knew they would be there, but not too many. A lot of guards on a supposedly abandoned floor would have been a dead giveaway.

Adapt!

Ruby re-evaluated. *If the decoys had been deployed, it meant that they knew she had penetrated the secure zone.*

By now the decoys had crossed the seventh floor and were continuing down. Ruby watched Chance peel away at the landing and head for the control room. She waited till he pushed open the door and entered. The door began to swing shut behind him. The corridor was clear.

Now!

Strike!

Ruby raced out, headed for the stairwell on the far side, away from the control room. She was moving silently, as fast as her feet could carry her, straight for the eighth floor.

Going for the kill.

The control room door was swinging shut behind Chance when Ravinder saw Ruby on the monitor, charging out of his room. Pistols in both hands, she was sprinting down the corridor. He knew her destination. That she was moving *away* from the decoys showed that she had seen through their plan and spurned the bait.

He ran out of the control room, shouting at Chance to follow him. As they ran, he explained. A few words were enough. The two put on a burst of speed, knowing that the delegates were in mortal danger.

They were passing the elevator when the door pinged open and a harried Mohite stepped out. He was about to say something, but Ravinder pulled him out of the way and dove into the elevator with Chance behind him. Chance stabbed at the eighth floor button, frantically willing the doors to close, but they took forever. The elevator began to rise, slowly and sedately as always. The two men inside strained to be unleashed.

The doors pinged open and they dashed out on the eighth floor.

There wasn't a soul in sight.

Ruby raced up the stairs two steps at a time. Though she was in peak condition, her breath burned through her lungs in short ragged bursts. Her mind stayed sharp and focused. Her fingers were curled around the triggers of the Hi-Power Brownings, itching for the delegates to appear. Nothing else mattered.

She reached the eighth floor a split second after Ravinder and Chance. She heard the ping of the elevator doors before she saw them. Swivelling, she changed direction, heading for the two smaller conference halls across the floor.

It has to be one of those two rooms.

Chance saw her, a blur of movement, and shouted. The two turned and chased after her. Despite the hours in the gym, Ravinder was not moving as fast as he wanted to. The younger, fitter Chance began to pull ahead but he too wasn't moving fast enough. Summoning up his reserves, Chance ramped up the pace.

Suddenly Ruby spun around and fired – twice. Then she was off again.

Both shots went wide, but forced Chance to drop. Coming up from behind, too fast to stop, Ravinder blundered into him. By the time they got up, the distance between them and Ruby had increased.

Ruby was flying, her feet skimming over the carpeted corridor in long flashing strides. As she skidded around a corner, she spotted Ido Peled standing at the door of the conference room on the right, and knew the delegates had to be behind it. Like a linebacker, the tall, fair Peled stood with his back to the door, weapon in hand. He tensed as she charged around the corner and came at him full tilt.

The body armour and baseball cap must have confused Peled. He'd seen Jennifer wearing those just a while ago. So he hesitated a second before bringing up his gun. That fraction of time cost him his life.

Ruby fired the unsilenced gun in her right hand for its longer range and accuracy. The shot boomed and reverberated, spurring on Chance and Ravinder.

Peled was dead before his body hit the floor.

Chance, now within range, raised his weapon and fired twice. The first bullet buzzed past Ruby's head and thwacked into the thick wooden door of the conference room. The second hammered into Ruby. Jennifer's jacket limited the damage, but the high velocity shock made her stagger. Still, she managed to throw open the door and charge into the conference room. She hit the door hard with her heel as she raced inside. It slammed shut behind her with a bang.

That was followed by more bangs, sharper, louder and so close together that Ravinder could not tell how many shots had been fired.

Then he saw Chance reach the door. Without checking his stride, Chance shouldered it in and raced inside.

Ravinder burst in hard on his heels.

Chance ground to a halt, the pistol in his hand still half-raised. He froze; the slightest move and Ruby would put a bullet in his head. Her weapons were up and smoking. Ravinder ran in behind him.

The pistol in Ruby's left hand was pointed straight at Chance's head. Her face was alabaster. Frozen. Immobile. Emotionless. Only her eyes hinted at the turmoil inside her – tiny seething dots, tense with concentration.

She was about eight feet away, her breath heavy, but the Brownings in her hands were rock steady. The weapon in her right hand was placed against Senator George Polk's head – now no charm or smile on his face, just sheer panic. A low, almost inaudible, keening sound emanated from of him.

Raj Thakur, Ghazi Baraguti and Prince Ghanim Abdul Rahman al-Saud lay in grotesque poses around the conference table. They had been the closest when Ruby stormed in and opened fire. It did not matter to her. Every delegate was fair game. And she had gone for the headshot with all three.

Thakur's body had slipped to the floor. The top half of his pristine white kurta was bright red. Baraguti was half in his chair and half sprawled across the table, about to stand when he stopped a bullet. Thick blood seeped from his head and onto the teak tabletop. With his face blown away, there was nothing regal about the Saudi prince any more. Bits of blood, brain and bone were sprayed across the other delegates, all frozen in horror. Gun smoke furled in the stark room.

For one tiny but endless second, everything came to a standstill.

'Ruby, don't do it. *Please,*' Ravinder's voice broke the frozen tableau. He was having trouble speaking. He could have sworn it was Rehana standing in front of him. 'Don't! It's over. No one else needs to die.'

'No, father, it's not.' Ruby's voice was high-pitched and tightly drawn. Her face was a grim mask. 'It will never be over till our people are allowed to live in peace and with dignity. The killing has to stop.'

"That is why they are here. To stop the killing!' Despite her fiery posture, Ravinder could sense an uncertainty within her. Somehow he had to keep her talking. *As long as she is talking, her guns will stay silent.* His mind lanced out, seeking the right words.

'No,' she intoned, 'they are not here for justice. They will sell us out, the way they have always done. This Summit cannot go on,' she continued in that same high-pitched Rehana-like tone flushed with emotion. 'Our people cannot be sold out any longer.'

'But there is no need now for more killing, Ruby,' Ravinder's voice had taken on a softer, neutral but firm, negotiator's tone. As he spoke, he inched slowly to his right, trying to ensure Chance was no longer in his line of fire.

'Stop that, father!' Ruby gestured with her weapon. 'Don't move.'

'Fine, I won't.' Ravinder slowly raised his left hand, palm forward, in a placating gesture. His right was at his side, still holding his revolver. 'Don't you see how pointless all this is? The dust will never settle... neither for the Palestinians nor the Jews... not until they sit down and talk. Drop your weapons,' Ravinder pleaded, 'Please. I promise I will do everything possible to defend you in court.'

'No, father, I will not be taken alive.' He heard the sorrow in her voice. And even though her tone was firm, he sensed flecks of indecision.

He might be able to talk her down.

'Ruby...'

Without warning, the door flew open and Mohite burst in with a gun in his hand. His eyes widened as he took in the scene. His gun hand began to rise.

Ruby's eyes narrowed into sharp slits.

'No!' Ravinder yelled.

But it was too late. Ravinder's cries were drowned out by gunfire.

Both of Ruby's weapons blazed into action, the soft plop of the silenced one submerged by the booming roar of the other.

The gun in her right hand fired and the senator's head disintegrated, spraying the table with chunks of bone and blood. Some of it sprayed onto the faces of

Yossi Gerstmann and Ghafar Al-Issa, the Jordanian, across the table. Both recoiled. Someone else screamed. But the continuing roar of gunfire drowned it out.

The gun in Ruby's left hand missed its mark. Instead of shooting out Chance's throat, it caught him high on the collarbone, just above the upper lip of his body armour, and spun him to the left. Ruby's gun had meanwhile moved onto Mohite. The bullet slammed into his face and made the back of his head a bloody fresco all over the door he had just raced through.

Simultaneously, Chance jerked his gun hand and fired. He got one shot off before he was hit. As his body took the hit and spun to the left, he fired again. Both bullets took Ruby in the middle of her body and once again, the body armour shielded her. But the double blows delivered at such close range threw her backwards. Chance kept firing till his clip ran out.

As Chance spun to his left, Ravinder's field of fire cleared. His hand came up like a flash and his gun thudded to life. Once. Twice. Thrice.

In the confines of the conference room, the boom of gunshots was endless thunder.

The terrorist was down.

Ravinder watched Ruby being thrown back as bullets pounded into her. She hit the wall behind her. Then slowly her body slid to the ground. For a moment she lay still, and then painfully curled up in a foetal ball.

The Rehana-like harpy who had terrified them had vanished. All Ravinder could see was the little girl who had once loved pink frocks and lick lollies.

The pistol in Ravinder's hand felt like a block of ice, but heavier... much heavier. He barely knew when he let go and it hit the carpeted floor with a thud.

Then someone moaned and reality struck like a sledgehammer.

Ravinder the cop stepped forward and kicked the guns away from Ruby. And Ravinder the father knelt beside her.

The door blew open and a horde of security personnel rushed inside.

Kneeling beside Ruby, Ravinder was oblivious to the hullabaloo around him. He had zoned out. The cop had done his duty. He had been made to walk the hardest path that his karma could have called for, and he had not flinched.

But the cop was no longer there. Only the father.

Ravinder wished he were dead. He wished he had

not fired. He wished *he* had been the target of Ruby's guns, not the delegates, not Chance, not Mohite. Just him. He would have paid the price eagerly.

Ravinder cradled Ruby in his arms. As he did so, her eyes flickered open. She was alive, but barely. Ravinder sensed that time was abysmally short and he wanted to be with his little girl one last time.

Ruby opened her mouth. She seemed to be trying to say something, but only frothy bubbles of blood emerged.

With her eyes she beckoned him closer. His ear was against her mouth. The low whisper, when it emerged finally, was drawn out, barely audible.

'Jasmine told me... that whenever... she was hurt... you would... hold her... and put her to sleep.'

He nodded, unable to say a word.

'I am... hurting... daddy.' The words emerged in broken gasps. 'Will you... put... me to sleep... please?'

'Yes, princess.' Ravinder managed to speak, a bare whisper. 'Of course I will.'

Ravinder could feel her slipping away. Never had he felt so helpless. He held her close. He could feel her breath mingle with his; cold, like her blood which soaked his shirt. Her lips touched his cheek. For a moment they were one again – father and daughter.

The pressure on his cheek tightened. And then Ruby lay still in his arms, cold and lifeless. As empty and cold as the void inside him.

By the time they managed to get Ravinder to release her, the light had faded from Ruby's eyes.

His precious princess was gone – again. And this time she would not be back.

The Days After

With five delegates dead, there was no hope that the Peace Summit would proceed. The surviving few, still shocked delegates left for their homelands just hours after the attack.

People, those in the know and those who would take decisions and could influence change, knew that the dust would never settle, at least not anytime in the near future.

Not until sense and compassion took hold. *If* it ever did.

Safely ensconced in Muridke, Pasha was thrilled to hear of the carnage. And the fact that the British had trained Ruby made his victory all the sweeter. How gratifying, after all, to kill an enemy with his own sword. Poetic justice, since Pasha believed that it was the British who had destroyed the Ottoman Caliphate and were primarily responsible for the plight of the

Palestinians. It was on their watch that Israel had crushed the Palestinians.

Pasha was jubilant when he shared the news with Saeed Ahmed, the LeT supremo.

'We must extract maximum mileage from this,' Ahmed asserted.

'True,' Pasha agreed. 'Operations with such massive propaganda value rarely happen.'

'Use this opportunity to strengthen our ties with Hamas. There is much we can do for the jihad if we work together.'

'What do you have in mind?'

'Why not go down to Damascus and see what *they* have in mind?'

Pasha agreed that it was worth pursuing.

Miles away in Tel Aviv, a Mossad duty operator put down her headset and reached for the phone.

Two days later, when Pasha left Muridke, a select group of men and women from various cities in Europe moved. Several of them had travelled to Dubai a few weeks ago.

The kidon team was in place when Pasha's flight landed in Damascus. The deadly ring closed around him as he exited the airport and headed for the safehouse his hosts had arranged.

'This one is for you, Ean Gellner,' the lean, hard-faced kidon who had once painted *Born to Kill* on his army helmet muttered as he cleaned the blade of his knife on Pasha's headless body.

As Pasha's body slumped to the floor, a few thousand miles away, in the holy city of Haridwar, a gleaming black BMW 750 Li came to a halt.

Retired Inspector General of Police, Ravinder Singh Gill, emerged draped in white. He had lost weight, acquired a decade of wrinkles and had a gaunt look. It was as though everything he had ever had, had been lost.

Jasmine, in a pristine white salwar-kameez, alighted and followed as they made their way to the edge of the water. She walked near him, watching him closely; she knew he needed her.

Simran did not leave the car. She could not forgive Ruby. But she had travelled this distance with Ravinder, because him she did care for.

There were thousands of people clustered on both sides of the holy river. An endless sound rumbled on both banks. But none of this impacted Ravinder and Jasmine. They felt alone.

They strode into the water, stopping when it was ankle high. It was icy cold but neither felt it.

Ravinder's hands trembled as he tried to untie the string holding the red cloth covering the small earthen urn. Jasmine came to his aid. In the past week he had retreated into a cold, silent zone, and his silence frightened her. She could feel his pain as their hands met at the urn.

The red cloth finally came free.

Together they tipped over the urn and a swirl of grey ashes tumbled out and fell into the water. Some were carried away by the wind. Soon no trace remained. Neither in the air nor in the water.

But they didn't look away from the spot where the ashes had first hit the water. They kept looking, unable to let go. Both believed that in this release lay salvation for the soul that the ashes represented.

The chill from the water began to seep into their bodies, merging with the chill in their hearts. After a long time, both bid a silent farewell to the lovely young woman who had come into their lives, so recently... so briefly... so sadly. A woman who had torn them apart, yet brought them together.

Ravinder and his second-born turned as one and slowly made their way back to the waiting vehicle.

Just before he got into the car, Ravinder looked back at the grey waters of the swiftly flowing Ganges. But it was not the river he saw. Nor did he notice the sky above it.

All he saw was a three-year-old girl in a pretty pink frock. She seemed to be waving at him.

That brought a small smile to his lips. That was how he always wanted to remember Ruby.

Acknowledgements

This book would never have been possible if it had not been for certain people who came into my life at the right time. Al Zuckerman of Writers House, who was invaluable in giving the story shape and holding my hand from start to finish. Fran, Avital, Idit, Gabriella, Jawad, Lilach, Ido, Karim, Amatullah and Lynette, to name a few more, who shared priceless insights to their wonderful countries and various other aspects that flummoxed me. They made me feel emotionally connected to the characters in a special way. To each one of you, I offer my humble and heartfelt thanks.

To my wonderful family for giving me the time and space to indulge in the (almost) solitary love of my life: writing.

To P.M. Sukumar, Karthika V.K., Neelini Sarkar, Natasha Puri, N.S. Krishna and Amit Sharma at HarperCollins India – as always for the support and encouragement they have provided me over the past five years.

To my comrades-in-arms in the Indian Armed Forces who were kind enough to ensure that I did not make any major blunders while writing about tactics, weapons and weapon systems. However, I must stress that all technical data used in this book has not been provided by anyone, it is already in the public domain and available on the Internet and in libraries.

To the National Arts Council of Singapore for providing me the wonderful opportunity to finish this book in double-quick time. Singapore has been a fantastic breeding ground for me, freed me from so many worries and enabled me to focus single-mindedly on writing.

And, of course, last but not the least, to each one of you, dear readers, who have egged me on with praise and criticism by writing to me, by blogging about my books and, of course, buying them...☺

Any errors, factual or technical, that still exist in this book are solely my fault or have been deliberately left in there by me to prevent any misuse of a technology or an idea.